# Worse Than Death

A HENRY HOLT MYSTERY

A HENRY HOLT MYSTERY

# Worse ≪≪≪≪≪≪≪≪≪≪≪≪
# Than Death

## Thomas
## Bunn ≪≪

HENRY HOLT AND COMPANY · NEW YORK

Published by Henry Holt and Company, Inc.,
115 West 18th Street, New York, New York 10011.
Published in Canada by Fitzhenry & Whiteside Limited,
195 Allstate Parkway, Markham, Ontario L3R 4T8.

Library of Congress Cataloging-in-Publication Data
Bunn, Thomas, 1944-
Worse than death/Thomas Bunn.—1st ed.
    p.   cm.
ISBN 0-8050-1072-6
I. Title.
PS3552.U472W67    1989
813'.54—dc 19                           89-30652
                                             CIP

Henry Holt books are available at special discounts
for bulk purchases for sales promotions, premiums,
fund-raising, or educational use. Special editions
or book excerpts can also be created to specification.

*For details contact:*

Special Sales Director
Henry Holt and Company, Inc.
115 West 18th Street
New York, New York 10011

First Edition

*Designed by Paula R. Szafranski*

Printed in the United States of America
10  9  8  7  6  5  4  3  2  1

*For my wife, Mary Kennedy*

# Worse Than Death

A HENRY HOLT MYSTERY

# 1 ◀◀◀◀

Joyce paused just inside the door of the coffee shop and shrugged off her coat. She was looking for me, scanning faces, standing tall in her tailored suit and leather boots, a touch of gold at her ears and throat. I waited a second before catching her eye, watching her tug her long black gloves off her long white fingers. A couple of construction workers were watching her, too.

Joyce had a woman with her, the one she'd called me about. The woman was in her mid to late thirties, attractive, with glossy black hair cut in a longish pageboy. She had on a gray wool coat and looked as if she'd been crying.

Joyce caught sight of me and spoke to the woman and the two of them started toward me, Joyce walking the way she always does, proud and purposeful, as if she'd just scored a second sixty-thousand-dollar-a-year job.

The construction guys liked the way she walked, too. One of them complimented her on her rhythm and Joyce turned, stepped up to him, and asked if his mouth was under warranty. He gave her a weak grin, but didn't say anything. His warranty must have expired.

Joyce turned her back on him and headed for my booth. She dumped her handbag on the bench and sat down next to me, settling her coat on her shoulders. Her face was flushed, but not from what the guy at the counter had said. The wind was fierce today, and there were flurries, hard-driven pellets of snow that stung like bird shot. It was April in Michigan.

I leaned toward Joyce. "Want me to beat him up?"

Joyce shook her head. "You've got your good clothes on."

I was taking down storm windows when she called to ask me to drop everything and meet her at our favorite coffee shop by the capitol. At that point I'd already dropped a window and wasn't in any mood to make things worse by putting on a coat and tie, so I was still wearing a jacket, sweatshirt, and jeans. I was dressed just like the boys at the counter, who were plainly wondering what I had that they didn't. It was a mystery to me, too, but one I never wanted to solve.

Joyce introduced the woman with the red-rimmed eyes as her "colleague," Nora Toland.

I held out my hand. "I'm Jack Bodine, Joyce's husband."

"I've heard a lot about you," said Nora Toland huskily, sitting down opposite us.

"Joyce keeps calling those press conferences."

Nora Toland smiled, but it was obviously an effort. I was her first private eye, after all, and her boss's husband in the bargain.

Joyce made a stab at small talk as we settled into the booth, but Nora Toland's troubles had her tied pretty tight, so I decided to get down to business. "Joyce told me over the phone what happened," I said. "What I'm wondering is, why didn't you call the police?"

My question hung in the air. I knew the answer from my conversation with Joyce, but I wanted to ask it while staring into Nora Toland's face. She had deep blue eyes, and they looked away from mine, down to her lap, where she began fingering the tortoiseshell handles of her leather purse.

Joyce started to speak, but I held up my hand and waited for Nora.

2

"It's so . . . difficult to tell," Nora said shyly.

"You mean embarrassing?"

Joyce glanced at me as if I were treading too heavily for a woman in Nora's condition.

Nora Toland reached out toward Joyce and took a deep breath. "It's all right, Joyce. I *am* embarrassed. And ashamed. I've got nobody to blame but myself, and if Jack can help me out of this, I'll be forever grateful." As she spoke, her voice got steadier. If I hadn't remembered Joyce mentioning Nora in happier times, talking about the "competence" and "maturity" of her new assistant, I might have been bothered by the suddenness of the change in her mood. Nora Toland said, "I just never thought something like this could happen to me."

I nodded. "You're a professional who's got herself in a jam. It happens. I'm a professional who gets people out of jams. All you've got to do now is tell me about the jam without holding back. This is a privileged conversation, by the way, like with a lawyer."

"Think of him as a lawyer with knuckles," Joyce said.

Nora smiled.

"Start from the beginning," I said.

Nora began to speak, but the waitress came up to the booth, clattered cups and saucers onto the table, and asked Joyce if she wanted coffee. Joyce asked for hot tea, no sugar, no lemon, no milk. Nora Toland held out her cup and the waitress poured coffee from a carafe. I had a refill. Neither of the women wanted anything to eat, so I went along with that, my stomach having words with me while I listened to Nora Toland start from the beginning.

"For many years now," she said, "I've had to live with a digestive disorder known as regional ileitis. It was much harder on me in the early days, but in the last five or ten years a number of new medications have been developed that have helped me a great deal, and I've felt really very good. I've got a fine doctor, and a husband who's been great through it all. And I don't mean

3

just holding my hand and saying 'There, there.' He's known for a long time now that we shouldn't have children, and he's never complained or held it against me."

"This is because of the ileitis?"

"Yes, for reasons the doctors don't understand, it can be aggravated by a pregnancy. My doctor warned me it might even be fatal, and Dirk has never wanted me to risk it."

A point in Dirk's favor. From the few things Joyce had said over the phone, however, Nora's hubby was a long way from breaking even. "Go on," I said.

"Over the years Dirk and I have devoted ourselves to our careers," Nora continued, "always telling ourselves that when the time was right we would adopt a child. Well, about two years ago we suddenly realized it was now or never, and we tried very hard to adopt a baby, but we were turned down by all the adoption agencies in Michigan, even those that handle foreign adoptions."

"Why?"

"Not all of them," Nora corrected herself. "Several of the mainstream agencies were willing to put us on their lists, but they had waiting periods of up to seven years. Others would have let us take in children on a foster-care basis, and almost all of them had retarded or handicapped children available, but Dirk and I felt we wouldn't be up to that kind of a challenge. If we'd had such a child on our own, that would be one thing. We would have coped. But to adopt one, it just seemed like there'd be too much stress, which is something else my doctor has warned me against."

I thought of my son, Eddie. Eddie was eight, and as normal as a hot dog with mustard. But if I ever wrote a book it was going to be called *Stress, Thy Name Is Parenthood*.

"So, aside from those few agencies," Nora continued, "we had no luck adopting an infant. We were turned down because we were too old, or because we weren't churchgoers, or on account of my being a professional who intended to keep working after we adopted. Things like that. But the main difficulty was this crazy

4

condition of mine. In all honesty, I'm not sure I would have mentioned the ileitis to them, but there was always this pressure to produce medical documentation stating I'm infertile, which I'm not. One way or another it would always come out that I had a problem, and they would write us off on the grounds that, as a mother, I'm a health risk. The thing is, my problem's been under control for a long time now. And my doctor has assured me I have every chance of living to a ripe old age. As long as I don't get pregnant."

"Catch-22," said Joyce.

"That's it exactly," Nora said. "Dirk and I became so frustrated we started looking beyond Michigan. But we ran into all sorts of complications outside, too, usually the same ones we'd encountered here at home. I don't know, perhaps eventually if we had relocated we would have found a child to adopt, but we couldn't help feeling that time was running out. We were getting older and not getting anywhere with adoption agencies, and, well, that's how we got involved with a man named Agnew. Did Joyce mention him to you?"

I said, "The guy who runs the surrogate-mother outfit?"

"Yes."

"I thought that kind of thing had been declared illegal in Michigan."

"No," Nora said, "the court ruling is vague. People can still enter into surrogate arrangements where there is no contract and no compensation paid to the mother other than actual medical expenses and reasonable legal fees."

"What's this Agnew's full name?"

"Sam. Sam Agnew."

I pulled out my pad and pen. "How did Mr. Agnew explain the setup to you?"

"He assured us that except for hospital costs and attorney's fees no money would change hands. He said the women he sponsored participated voluntarily because they were committed to his efforts to help people like Dirk and me. He has a book full of

5

pictures of women who are willing to become surrogate mothers." Nora looked down at her hands again.

I did, too. They were nice hands to look at. So was her wedding ring. I glanced at Joyce's plain gold band and said, "Go on, Nora."

"I wasn't entirely comfortable with what we were doing," Nora said, "but Dirk and I had reached a point by then where we wanted a baby so much we weren't thinking clearly. So we chose one of the women in Agnew's picture book, and he arranged for us to interview her at her apartment, just Dirk and myself and the surrogate. She seemed superficial in a flashy sort of way, but pleasant and basically reassuring. By the end of the session Dirk was eager to go ahead with it. That's when she told us she expected to be paid on the sly for her services. She figured she had us hooked."

"How much?"

"Twenty thousand dollars. We said we'd try another surrogate, but she insisted that all the women charged huge fees. She said Agnew was unaware of it, that the fees were something discussed only by the surrogates and the prospective parents. I didn't really believe that, though. How could Agnew not know? So I insisted we leave. Afterwards I told Dirk I didn't want to buy a child, but I think, looking back on it, that I just wasn't keen on the whole idea of having another woman carry Dirk's baby. Needless to say, Dirk and I were even more depressed about our chances of having a child." Nora was gazing out the window at the streaks of shot snow as if they were her lousy odds made visible. "Will spring ever come?" she said softly.

I glanced out the window at the pinched faces of state bureaucrats hurrying down the streets of Lansing, the snow peppering them as they headed for lunch. It had hit sixty yesterday, but today the only thing hitting sixty was the wind. "But you finally got a baby," I said.

Nora set her cup down. "It was through a woman who works for Dirk. She'd left the man she'd been living with. Or maybe he

6

kicked her out, I don't remember. I think he'd been abusive. The point is she was pregnant when she left him, although she didn't realize it till several months later. She told him then, but he accused her of being pregnant by another man and wouldn't have anything to do with her. She's Catholic, so she decided against having an abortion. But as an immigrant, without any English and no skills other than those she'd acquired at Dirk's shop, she knew she was in trouble. Eventually she'd have to quit work and go on welfare or ADC, and she didn't want to do that."

"She emigrate from the moon?"

"Vietnam. She got out of there last year on something called the Orderly Departure Program. Anyway, she was living with her daughter, who'd come to the States with her. Dirk had got her daughter a job working for us as a housekeeper, and it was through the daughter that he learned that the woman was pregnant and depressed, without any idea of how she was going to manage after her child was born. She was having a problem with morning sickness, too, and had already missed quite a few days at the shop. So Dirk went to see her. He learned to speak Vietnamese in the war and was able to have a direct conversation with her. He sensed that even though she was determined to have the baby, she wasn't looking forward to being tied down by it. She mentioned giving it up for adoption and on impulse Dirk said we'd be glad to take it. The woman agreed, and after all those fruitless months, we suddenly had a real chance at a baby. Dirk and I were overjoyed."

I tried to imagine Nora Toland looking overjoyed, eyes glittering, teeth flashing, cheeks rosy, no circles beneath her eyes. It took an effort. "It's my impression the Department of Social Services frowns on that kind of thing," I said.

"That's true. The State of Michigan won't permit direct-consent adoptions unless it's within a family, an aunt adopting a niece, for instance. Lawyers and doctors aren't allowed to arrange adoptions either. Those are called independent, or black-market, adoptions, and they're strictly forbidden. Adoptable children must be placed through state-approved agencies, no exceptions. But Dirk and I wanted that baby, and we saw no reason why we couldn't offer it a good home. That's how we got mixed up with Mr. Agnew again."

The waitress brought Joyce's tea, and refilled my cup with coffee.

When the waitress went away Nora said, "You see, it occurred to Dirk that if the Vietnamese woman claimed she was a surrogate mother and named Dirk as the biological father, then all she'd have to do is enter Dirk's name on the birth certificate and sign over custody of the baby to him. But since I wasn't biologically related to the baby I would have to file for adoption. That's why we needed someone who knew the ins and outs of the surrogate procedure, and who could give this . . . scheme of ours an air of legitimacy."

"And?"

"Mr. Agnew was happy to help us . . . for a price."

"Let me guess. Twenty thousand?"

Nora nodded. It wasn't shame or embarrassment she was feeling now. It was disgust. And anger. She said, "I knew then, and in no uncertain terms, that Agnew was a crook. But Dirk and I felt like it was our last chance. So we agreed to Agnew's terms, and when Mai was born Dirk paid him at the hospital. That was in late January. We brought her home and I took a leave of absence. Then, several weeks ago, I returned to work on a part-time basis. Xuan, our housekeeper, watched Mai while I was at the office." Nora paused and sought my gaze. "Jack, I can't tell you how much I've come to love my baby."

I waited for her to tell me, but she didn't, and it took me a moment to realize that, just as she claimed, her love for baby Mai was ineffable. "And then?"

"I didn't come into the office yesterday because Mai was fussy . . . I think she's already beginning to teethe. It was so unexpectedly warm I took her out into the backyard for a little sun. The doorbell rang and Xuan answered. It was Sam Agnew. I went in to talk to him while Xuan watched Mai. Agnew was in a foul mood. He said he wanted his money. As far as I knew, Dirk had paid him in full that night at the hospital, but Agnew insisted we still owed him thirteen thousand dollars. He claimed Dirk had promised him the balance of the money the week following Mai's birth, and that he'd been waiting ever since. This came as a complete surprise to me. I told him he should get in touch with Dirk. Agnew said he'd been trying to do that for the past two months, but that Dirk hadn't returned his calls. I told him I was certain we could work something out, but Agnew turned nasty and insinuated that he wasn't going to go away empty-handed. At that point I insisted that he leave. He did, but there was a smug look in his eye, almost as if he'd got what he'd come for. I ran out into the backyard and there was Xuan, standing next to an empty basket. Mai was gone. She'd been kidnapped."

# 2 ◄◄◄

"My first thought was to call the police," Nora Toland continued, "but I realized they would find out we'd got Mai illegally. So I called Dirk instead."

"And what did Dirk do?"

"He went to see Agnew."

"You didn't go with him?"

"No. Xuan was shaken up. Dirk wanted me to stay with her." Nora paused and frowned, as if something about the time she'd spent with the baby-sitter bothered her.

"Did this Sue Ann describe the person who actually carried out the kidnapping?" I asked.

"She said it was a white man with a gun."

"Your tone suggests you doubt that."

"It's just that the girl was behaving strangely."

"She'd just witnessed a kidnapping."

"Yes. But there was something furtive in her manner."

"As if?"

"As if she knew this white man with a gun."

"Did you ask her about it?"

"I tried to, but she doesn't speak English well at all and I don't speak any Vietnamese. It's a tonal language, very difficult."

"So what did Agnew say to Dirk?"

"Just that we'd get Mai back when we cleared our debt. But the problem is we're broke."

"Did Dirk explain why he didn't pay Agnew the full amount at the hospital?"

"Yes. Last summer he closed out our mutual funds and invested the money as venture capital in a software firm that was starting up in Okemos. It later failed. He lost everything. He said he was ashamed to tell me."

"Where'd he get the seven thousand he gave Agnew at the hospital?"

"It was Dirk's IRA money. He paid a stiff penalty to get it and never mentioned that to me either. I guess I should have been taking more of an interest in our finances. I asked Dirk about applying for a cash advance on our cards, but he reminded me that we borrowed against them to come up with a down payment for the redecoration of the nursery."

I said, "How about a second mortgage?"

Nora sighed and shook her head with a kind of weary dismay. "When we got Mai we decided it was finally time to buy a house, but we only had enough to put down the minimum, so there's no equity for us to borrow against."

"How about friends? Relatives?"

"My parents. I mentioned them to Dirk, but he wouldn't hear of borrowing from them."

"Why not?"

Nora was staring out the window again. The snow flurry had petered out, and now there was just the wind. Newspapers soared into the air like birds flushed from cover. "Dirk and my father don't get along," Nora said. "Whenever they're together they argue. It all goes back to the fact that my father was West Point, whereas Dirk was in the marines. It's so childish, this animosity of theirs, but that's the root of it. I was naïve enough to think that maybe it was all over when my father asked my mother to knit a nightgown for our baby. That was when we first started trying to adopt through local agencies. It was a gesture of optimism, my father's way of saying he was sure we'd succeed in having a child someday. He even asked my mother to knit the West Point motto into the gown along with the Marine Corps motto. It was the most he'd ever attempted in the way of rapprochement between Dirk and himself. My father was trying to tell Dirk it was all right if our child, our son, ended up a marine or a cadet at West Point. Either way. Of course, when he found out later that we were adopting a Vietnamese girl, well, there were hard words between Dirk and my father. Things were said that can never be taken back. That's why Dirk isn't about to ask my parents for money, not even if it means losing Mai."

"Marines have a lot of pride," I said.

Nora Toland took a moment to study me. "Are you saying you're sympathetic to Dirk's point of view?"

"No. Nor do I look favorably on Mr. Agnew's method of dunning his clients. But you did make a deal with him, crook or not. If Dirk won't take your parents' money, can't you try somewhere else for a loan? Pawn something, perhaps?" I said this without looking at her wedding ring.

Nora Toland sat back and tucked a wave of dark hair behind her shapely ear. "I paid off Mr. Agnew this morning. I borrowed the money from my mother. Agnew took it, locked it in his safe, and demanded ten thousand more because of the trouble we'd given him. He called it a penalty, an interest penalty."

"Does Dirk know about this?"

Nora shook her head, and her hair slipped out from behind her ear. "My father doesn't know, either. But if he finds out, he will never let Dirk forget what I've done." Nora bit her lip, envisioning the perpetual reminders. "I mean, it would be one thing if I'd got Mai away from Agnew. But to have borrowed the money from my mother without Dirk or my father knowing, and to have left Agnew's without my baby, I just feel terrible. He said he'll sell Mai to someone else if I don't come up with the extra ten thousand. And my mother doesn't have any more money."

12

Joyce patted Nora's hand and glanced at me, an eyebrow raised expectantly. She said, "Kidnapping? Extortion?"

Joyce continued to stare at me, letting the words sink in. It wasn't as if she were asking me whether I thought Nora's problems warranted action. She was asking whether I thought I was up to tackling them, as if, like Nora Toland, I had a condition that might be aggravated were I to take on a case involving anything so demanding as kidnapping and extortion.

I wasn't about to explain Joyce's look to Nora, but the truth was I hadn't taken a major case since my father's death. My partner, Ed Quinn, had brought Dad into the business after Dad's retirement from the force, and in those several years before he died, we became more than partners, more than father and son: we became friends. And then he was gone, and I regretted not only his loss but the sad fact that we hadn't been friends when I'd really needed him. His passing made plain the importance of doing right by my own son, of making sure that I was there when he came home from school, for instance, instead of having a baby-sitter waiting for him the way we'd done in the past. Joyce figured I was crawling into a shell, but it seemed to me I was rediscovering the importance of having one, and of enjoying the little guy who shared it with me. Eddie wasn't a special kid, but he was mine, which meant he was everything to me. So I knew what Nora Toland was going through. It was bad enough losing a parent, but I didn't have to lose my child to know it was the worst thing that could ever happen to you, worse than anything. I said, "I'll get your baby back, Nora."

Joyce squeezed Nora's hand as if the cavalry—no matter that its ranks were thinned—had just bugled its steeds into action.

Nora gave a guarded smile. "Please understand," she said, "that we won't be able to pay you for quite a while. Dirk and I are truly broke."

"Good thing Joyce got that promotion."

"You have no idea how much this means to me," Nora said, "just to have someone to talk to."

"You've got more than that," I said. "Now, do you have any idea where Agnew's holding your baby?"

"All I know is that she's with one of his interim sitters."

"His what?" ·

"You see, before any of Agnew's surrogates sign a baby over to its father, Agnew insists on placing the child for a week's waiting period with a woman who baby-sits it. This is in case the surrogate changes her mind about letting the baby go. They don't sign contracts with the fathers, so, according to Agnew, it's a way of separating the baby from its biological mother while at the same time preventing the adoptive parents from becoming prematurely attached to the child. I don't know why a crook would care about such things, but he does."

"All right," I said, "let's start by paying a visit to the sitter Agnew used for your baby."

Nora shook her head. "In our case he didn't use a sitter."

"Why not?"

"Because the night Mai was born her real father, this Vietnamese man with a terrible scar on his face, showed up at the hospital. He'd been drinking. Dirk had words with him and got him to leave, but Agnew was suddenly worried that there might be trouble. Or that if there was trouble, he wouldn't get his money. So he had the birth mother sign over custody to us right then, rather than make us go through the one-week waiting period, which was fine with Dirk and me."

"Okay, then let's pay a visit to a couple who's been through this with Agnew and get the names of his sitters from them."

Nora kept shaking her head. "Agnew keeps the identities of these women secret so there's no temptation for the prospective parents to try to see their baby before the week is up."

"Wait. How do you know your baby's with one of Agnew's sitters?"

"I told him I was worried sick about Mai and he said to take it easy, that she was safe with one of his 'people.'" Nora said this

14

while staring down into her empty coffee cup as if it were the basket from which her baby had disappeared.

I thought for a minute. "Okay, I've got a way of doing this."

Nora looked up, her face tinged with apprehension. "You won't . . . talk to Dirk about this, will you?"

"Not if you don't want me to. But are you sure it's wise to keep him out of the picture?"

"Yes. At least until I get Mai back."

"All right, I'll stay out of his way. I'll also handle Agnew so he won't realize what's going on till it's too late." I clicked my Bic. "Where do I find him?"

Nora gave me his address, and I wrote it down.

"And this Vietnamese baby-sitter, Sue Ann? How do you spell her name?"

"It's pronounced 'Sue Ann,' but it's spelled X-u-a-n. Xuan Nguyen, N-g-u-y-e-n. Are you going to talk to her, too?"

"Yes, if things don't work out with Agnew." I had Nora give me the spelling of the baby's name, as well as the name of the biological mother: Thanh Chi. Nora didn't know the name of the Vietnamese father, the man with the "terrible scar." I said, "Is Xuan at your place now?"

"I'm not sure," Nora said. "She usually comes in by seven fifteen, but when I left the house this morning at quarter to eight she hadn't arrived."

"Have you tried calling her again?"

"I tried her apartment, but there wasn't any answer. I'm worried about her. I'm sure I just imagined that she knew something she wasn't telling us yesterday after the kidnapping."

"Have you tried calling your place to see if she arrived late?"

"No. She has a key, but if she was there she wouldn't pick up the phone."

"Why not?"

"As I said, her English isn't very good, so we have an answering machine that takes our calls during the day."

15

"I see. Do you have any idea where she might be if she's not at her apartment or at your place?"

Nora shook her head. "I'm sure she wouldn't have gone to her father. It was my impression she didn't get along with him any better than her mother did."

"Her father's the guy with the scar?"

"That's my impression, but I'm not certain. All I know for sure is that Mai's biological mother wasn't actually married to the man with the scar. Agnew made a point of having Dirk find out about that. For some reason it was legally important to the surrogate proceedings."

"Where does this man with the scar live?"

"I'm sorry, I don't know. There's something called the Asian Refugee Community Center on North Walnut, however. Maybe they could be of help."

"Where's Xuan's apartment?"

"She lives on Beal Street." Nora recited the girl's address and phone number. "I'd be glad to go with you. Xuan would feel more comfortable if I was there."

"No. She might mention me to your husband. I'll tell her I'm from the INS. What's your address?"

"We're in East Lansing off Harrison and Grand River Avenue." Nora gave me the street and number.

"And where's your husband this morning?"

"At his office."

"What kind of work does he do, by the way?"

"He runs a micrographics operation, microfiche, that sort of thing."

I closed my notebook. "Okay, Nora, you head back to the office. I'll call as soon as I have a chance to run my ruse on Agnew. Then you and I will get your baby."

Nora stared at me as if she didn't believe it would be that easy.

"The coffee's on me," I said. "Just go on back to the office, and don't worry."

Nora made an effort to appear unworried, but now that her

problem was out of her hands she seemed reluctant to let it go. "All right. Thank you, Jack. I—"

"No problem. With Joyce on the case, it'll be a snap."

Joyce stopped tugging her gloves onto her hands. "With *me* on the case?"

"In order to pull this off, Red, I'll need forty-five minutes of your time." I winked.

Joyce gazed at me. "Just like *The Thin Man?*"

"Just like Jack Bodine and Joyce O'Connell."

Joyce said, "Eat your heart out, Nora Charles." She looked over at Nora Toland. "I'll walk you to the door, tell you who to shuffle and what to shake when you get back to the office."

Nora stood, pulled on her coat, and picked up her handbag. She seemed concerned about what she'd got Joyce into, but I told her once again to take it easy, that everything would be fine.

Joyce went to the door with her and gave her a few quick instructions. Nora gave Joyce a hug and stepped out into the wind. I watched her climb into a silver-gray Honda Accord. Along with the construction workers, I watched Joyce climb back into my booth.

"You know," she said, "I've never been with you on a case."

She looked even more flushed than she had when she'd come in out of the wind. I said, "The thought of it seems to agree with you."

"So far it's better than a budget meeting." Her knee touched mine.

I said, "I'd like to touch Agnew's knee with a baseball bat, but as you heard, my client doesn't want her hubby to know I'm involved, and Agnew might call him to complain. Therefore, I'll have to get Agnew to tell me where the baby is by being ever so subtle. And if you're with me when I talk to him, you can make me seem that way."

"Mission impossible."

"You're up to it. Have you got twenty cents for the phone, by the way?"

Joyce searched her purse. "Who are you going to call?"

"Agnew."

I got up and headed for the phone at the rear of the coffee shop. Joyce followed me, watching me slide the dimes into the phone, listening to me tell Agnew's secretary my name was Jack Lackason, and that the missus and I wanted very much to talk to Mr. Agnew about procuring the services of a surrogate mother. I smiled at Joyce.

The secretary told me Mr. Agnew was booked solid till May tenth.

I told the secretary I couldn't possibly wait that long to see him.

The secretary told me she couldn't possibly do anything to alleviate my impatience.

We went around and around and eventually Agnew's moll cut me off.

I hung up.

"What's the matter?" Joyce said.

"Another instance of blatant feminine intransigence."

Joyce glanced at Agnew's number in my notepad, tucked the receiver under a curtain of red hair, and called Agnew again.

"Yes," she said, brightening as she spoke, "my name is Dr. Joyce O'Connell. I've been thinking for some time now of volunteering to be one of Mr. Agnew's surrogate mothers? Could you . . . O'Connell. Yes, Doctor O'Connell. Um-hm. All right, fine. Yes, I will." Joyce hung up.

I said, "Yes you will what?"

She said, "Be there in twenty minutes."

# 3 ◄◄◄◄

Joyce and I stopped by the house on the way to Agnew's office so I could slick a tie under the collar of a clean white shirt, pull on a three-piece suit, and jam my square feet into a pair of round-toed dress shoes. I intended to pose as Joyce's attorney, but I felt more like her pimp.

We hit the road again refining our strategy for dealing with Mr. Agnew, and arrived at his office with a few minutes to spare. His place was north of East Lansing in a new complex that looked more like a cruise ship than an office building: lots of tubular metal railings and cantilevered, prowlike balconies that jutted starkly into the gale-force wind. There was a painted iron pole out front, and at the top of it Old Glory was snapping and popping in the wind like the Fourth of July.

Joyce and I went in and took a stainless-steel elevator up to five, perfecting our personas on the way. We were ready when the elevator hummed to a halt. It sighed open and the two of us headed in silence down a carpeted catwalk. Off to starboard, through a plate-glass wall, we had a distant view of the Lansing skyline. Off to port, over the tubular railing, we had a straight drop to the flagstone floor of the lobby.

Agnew had the first office at the end of the catwalk. I opened the door for Joyce and followed her in. I expected deck chairs and life preservers in Agnew's reception room, but the man wasn't into nautical. Antiques were his thing, but not the kinds of "pieces" that had once supported the posteriors of powdered-wigged Frenchmen. Agnew, or his decorator, was odd for the sort of refuse you could find at the bottom of the hill behind my grandparents' outhouse: paint-flaked tables, and chairs with straight backs and bone-hard seats that might have seemed inviting if you'd just driven up from Ohio on a buckboard. I'm not talking early American, either, but stuff that looked minimally awful in the company of old milk cans, horse collars, and hay rakes. Country.

Anyway, it was lunchtime and Agnew's reception room was empty, not even a secretary. I walked over to the inner door and listened. I could hear someone in there, a deep male voice murmuring intimately. If your business is babies, I guess that's how you talk. I knocked and leaned into his office.

He was on the phone, a big guy with the receiver clamped between a fleshy ear and a meaty shoulder. He had a sloppy sandwich in one hand, a Styrofoam cup of coffee in the other. His size-twelves were propped on a table desk that looked as though it had once been covered with a sheet of enameled steel so you could hose off the chicken blood or whatever it was that had warped and stained the surface underneath. Or maybe Agnew kept spilling his coffee, which he almost did when I swung the door open so he could get a good look at Joyce. I said, "This is Dr. O'Connell."

Joyce swept into the office with her head held high and her hand extended. Agnew hauled his Florsheims off the table and said into the phone that he'd call back. He dumped his sandwich onto a wrinkled square of waxed paper as he rounded the table, reaching for Joyce's hand with his ring-spangled mitts, telling her how glad he was to meet her, his smile radiating a training-table appetite. An ex-jock, Agnew, and not yet running to fat. Even his teeth looked athletic.

Joyce introduced me as her legal beagle and Agnew grabbed my hand, giving me a friendly if faintly wary smile. He pulled back a chair for Joyce that looked as though it had once been used to dunk possessed women. Joyce sat down on it and crossed her legs, showing perhaps a bit more knee than was necessary. I declined to sit, and stood behind her and off to one side, projecting an air of unobtrusive attentiveness.

Agnew settled in behind his rickety table desk, leaned forward, and gazed at Joyce as if they had a lot in common. "I'm sorry Trish wasn't on hand to show you in, Dr. O'Connell, but she took your call just as she was on her way out to lunch."

Joyce said, "That's quite all right. I had several cancellations and decided to give you a call on the spur. I appreciate your taking time to see me."

Agnew waved away the implication that Joyce had somehow inconvenienced him, his voice modulating into chat mode. "So, tell me about yourself, Dr. O'Connell. I've never had the pleasure of working with a physician before. What's your area of specialization?"

Joyce had a Ph.D. in ed psych, not a medical degree, but we both agreed on the way over that we'd have a better chance of gulling Agnew if she posed as an M.D.

Without missing a beat, she smiled at him and said, "I'm an obstetrician."

Agnew looked at Joyce as if her reply had been a squirt in the eye with a lemon. "Dr. O'Connell, I sure hope you aren't here on behalf of someone else."

"Someone else?"

"I sympathize with girls in trouble who don't want to abort. But I don't do black-market adoptions."

"No," said Joyce, "it's nothing like that. I'm here in my own behalf. Although, in a way, I'm doing this as much for my patients as for myself."

Agnew acknowledged this with a shrug that seemed to say he

21

was willing to hear out any woman as attractive as Joyce. "I'm all ears."

He was, indeed, but Joyce didn't say so. She said, "I deal with pregnant women ten hours a day, sometimes, if I have back-to-back deliveries, twenty-four hours a day. I encourage them, cajole them, console them. They look to me as an authority on all things having to do with the having of babies. But I myself have never had a baby. I've decided therefore that I have a professional responsibility to experience pregnancy. However, I simply don't have the time to raise a child."

Agnew glanced at the ring on Joyce's hand. "You're married?"

We hadn't thought of that one, but Joyce was as cool as a con with an airtight alibi. "No," she said, "I'm divorced. I wear the ring for professional reasons only."

Agnew, who'd begun making notes on a yellow legal pad, underlined something twice, then looked up at Joyce and gave her a nod of approval. "That's good."

"Oh? Why?"

"Well, you see, under Michigan law a woman's spouse is considered to be the father of her children even if they've been sired by another man. Now, this legality hasn't seemed to present much of a problem for other surrogate operations in the state, but my partner and I take pains to avoid any situation that could result in a conflict down the road. Ben, by the way, handles the legal details and normally I'd have him explain all this to you, but he's out of town." Agnew sat back and raised his hands as if to slow things down. "I don't want you to feel as though I'm rushing you, Dr. O'Connell, but the fact that you've had your attorney accompany you means to me that you're serious about this."

"I am, indeed."

Agnew gave her a "good gal" wink and checked his watch. "I'm scheduled to meet with a couple in a few minutes, so I'll dispense with my usual screening procedures and let you screen me." He said this with another toothy smile and a degree of modest charm that was intriguing in a guy who looked like a onetime tight end. Not charm, exactly, but a kind of boyish vulnerability.

Joyce responded with a smile of her own, one that looked all too genuine to suit me. She said, "Well, Mr. Agnew, I guess I'm curious to know what your usual screening procedures entail."

"Please, call me Sam."

"Thank you, I will."

Agnew gestured at several framed diplomas on the wall behind him. "I have a background in psychology and I make it a point to put my prospective surrogates through an intensive, two-hour preliminary interview. I do this because many of the women who want to become surrogate mothers have got some rather skewed motivations. Mostly they're figuring on making some easy money, bringing a child to term. That kind of thing's been outlawed in Michigan, however, including surrogate contracts. The ACLU's been working against the ruling, and five years down the road, who knows how things will stand? But none of that bothers me either way because I've never had a woman sign a surrogate contract, nor have I had a surrogate bear a child for a couple on a remunerative basis. Ever."

I said, "Then how do you get the women to do it?"

"I don't 'get' them to do anything, Mr. Bodine. They come to me out of their own desire to help others less fortunate than themselves. The good ones do. The others I don't take into the program because it's more them wanting to have a baby out of some kind of compulsion or other. That's what I try to discover during my preliminary interviews with new surrogates. I'm willing to dispense with that in your case, Dr. O'Connell, because in my opinion your reason for wanting to become a surrogate mother is as sensible as any I've heard since I committed myself to this cause. I see in you a woman who knows her own mind." Agnew winked again.

Joyce smiled.

Agnew was right, of course. Joyce did know her own mind. It didn't take a genius to figure that out, though, while this mesomorph with a vocabulary seemed to think he was some kind of Sigmund Freud. I said, "So, how does Dr. O'Connell proceed from here?"

Agnew gestured toward a low table across the room. There was a fat photo album on it. He said to Joyce, "First we set up an appointment for you to have your picture taken. I post it in my book so prospective parents can get some idea of your physical attributes, which, if you don't mind my saying so, are considerable." Agnew gave Joyce another Big Ten smile. Joyce beamed back and recrossed her legs, basking in Agnew's admiration of her attributes.

The guys who'd ogled Joyce at the coffee shop hadn't irked me half as much as Sam Agnew. I told myself I was willing to give men who did an honest day's work a little leeway, but this anger toward Agnew, it was something I wasn't sure I wanted to figure out, like the mystery of my marriage to Joyce. Through clenched teeth, I said, "Exactly what's in it for you, Mr. Agnew?"

Agnew arched his eyebrows. "You mean financially?"

"I mean financially."

Agnew shrugged. "Ben and I receive a onetime fee of five thousand dollars from the prospective parents. This covers legal work, adoption papers, counseling, and so on. It's far below the going rate, believe me."

"So you must be in it for something more than the money?"

"Absolutely. I have seven children myself. I love children and I feel terrible whenever I meet people who can't have kids. One in six couples can't, by the way. I have so many inquiries I have to turn folks down. It breaks my heart, too, and not because of lost fees. When I hand over a baby to a couple who've been through the heartbreak of being disappointed by adoption agencies and all the rest of it, well, when I put a baby into the arms of a woman who's been through all that, I feel like a rich man." Agnew turned to Joyce. "Perhaps you'd like to meet the people I'm about to see? The husband's a general agent for an insurance firm and his wife's a high-school guidance counselor."

24

"That would be nice," Joyce said, "but I've got a huge patient load this afternoon."

"I understand. Well, we can meet later in the week if you like. Ben will be back then and Mr. Bodine can talk with him, discuss the legal end of things. We can have Trish take your photograph at that time, too. I assume as a doctor you're more or less familiar with artificial insemination techniques?"

"Certainly."

"Great. We do that at a local clinic, by the way. We can get into the details of your cycles and so forth at our next meeting." Agnew sat back and tapped his hands on his desk with a small flourish. "I really do look forward to working with you, Dr. O'Connell. Is there anything else I can answer for you at this time?"

"Call me Joyce."

"Well, thank you, Joyce."

"And yes, there is one point I'd like to settle before I go. Everything else pretty much depends on it."

"Oh?"

"Please understand that having a baby isn't a casual decision on my part."

"Of course it isn't."

"I've thought about this now for months, and while I'm doing it primarily for the benefit of my patients, I also feel a responsibility toward the child."

"Naturally. But I'm sure, as an obstetrician, you're well aware of a pregnant woman's nutritional needs, and so forth?"

"My sense of obligation extends a good deal further than that."

"Yes?"

"Yes, Sam. I'd very much like to be allowed to choose the couple who will receive the child."

Agnew shrugged. "I have no problem with that."

"You'll permit me to interview them?"

"Of course. Most couples are eager to meet the birth mother."

"Good. One other thing. Studies have shown that the bonding

process between infant and mother begins at once, as soon as the child is born. I'll want the adoptive mother not only to assist during labor, but to take over the care and feeding of the baby from the moment of birth."

Agnew was taking notes again, his pen looking no larger than a woman's eyebrow pencil in his huge hand, which suddenly ceased its scribbling. He sat back, looking vaguely troubled. "I'm sure that's sound practice in a normal birth situation, Joyce, but what we're dealing with here is something pretty different."

"How do you mean?"

"Well, I've found that it's best to place the baby in, well, let's call it a 'neutral' setting for a week or so immediately following its birth."

"A neutral setting?"

"Yes, with a woman who's trained to care for newborns."

Joyce frowned. "But why?"

"Because you may change your mind about wanting to give the baby up."

"But as I told you—"

Agnew said gently, "I know what you told me, and as I said, I believe you know your own mind. But now I'm talking about your heart, and the baby may capture yours. If you go for a week without wanting it back, then the chances are good you're free of it. But if you change your mind, it's most likely going to happen in that first week, and if the father and his wife haven't got it, I won't have to break their hearts by taking it away from them. They won't have got 'bonded' to it, to use your phrase. And, hopefully, having been separated from the child, neither will you. I'm sure if you give this some thought you'll see why we've determined that this is best for all concerned." Agnew had suddenly switched to the first person plural as if to suggest he'd instituted these measures after consulting not only his partner, Ben, but a panel of experts as well.

"Who are these women who care for the baby during that week?" said Joyce.

"Why, they're mothers themselves. They—" The intercom buzzed and Agnew leaned over and pushed a button. "Yes, Trish?"

A little voice said, "The Deckers are here to see you, Mr. Agnew."

"I'll just be a minute, dear."

"Yes, sir."

Agnew folded his hands on top of the legal pad. "The Deckers are good people, Joyce. Are you sure you wouldn't like to meet them?"

Joyce shook her head. "There's no sense in meeting anyone if the baby has to spend a week with a . . . a sitter."

Agnew looked wounded. "These women are much more than baby-sitters, Joyce. If you knew them as I do . . . why, they're like the difference between hospital food and home cooking, ha ha."

Joyce shifted uncomfortably in her chair, pulling her skirt down over her knees.

Agnew's expression clouded. "Please believe me, Joyce, my home-care ladies are two of the finest women you'll ever want to meet."

I cleared my throat and said to Joyce, "Maybe that's the solution. If you had a chance to interview Mr. Agnew's home-care women, you might feel better about letting the baby stay with one of them."

Joyce glanced at me, then fingered her hair while staring down at the rag rug beneath Sam's desk. "Well, I don't know."

For a woman who knew her own mind, it was a moment of Oscar-winning indecision. I was holding my breath.

Joyce said to Agnew, "You know, Sam, maybe Mr. Bodine's right. If I could see these women in the same setting in which they'd be caring for the baby, it might set my mind at ease."

Agnew rubbed his jaw, thinking. Behind us, as if trying to warn him off, the wind walloped the expanse of glass that formed the west wall of his office. But Agnew didn't pay it any mind.

My wife was a prime heifer and Agnew wasn't about to let her get away. He said, "Well, I'll tell you what, Joyce, I'll see what I can do."

"When could I expect to hear from you, Sam? I'd like to get going on this as soon as possible."

"Sure. How about tomorrow?"

"I'll have to check my schedule and get back to you."

"Just give Trish a call."

Joyce said, "Perhaps, if I have any additional cancellations, I could meet with your home-care women this afternoon?"

Agnew raised his eyebrows thoughtfully and exhaled through pursed lips. "Tell you what, when I get a free minute later on I'll call my ladies and explain the situation and get back to you or Mr. Bodine later this afternoon. How's that?"

I said helpfully, "You could give me their addresses and phone numbers and I'd be happy to make the calls and set up the appointments with them. Save you the time."

Agnew said doubtfully, "I don't know. Neither of them has had to have an interview before. No, I think it'd be best if I talked to them."

I said, "Okay. Call me when you make the arrangements." I gave Agnew the number of my answering machine.

Outside Agnew's office Joyce gave me a look of apology. "You think he saw through me?"

"All he saw through was your panty hose."

"It's hard to believe he's an extortionist. He was surprisingly professional. And likable, too."

I didn't disagree. My wife knew her own mind, after all. What my own mind knew was that I'd probably be knocking Sam Agnew down before the day was done . . . all that "professional" talk of attributes and insemination.

"Jack, I really am going to be busy this afternoon. The department's having a whole string of budget meetings with the education committee—"

"No problem. When Agnew comes through with the sitters' names the only person I'll need with me is Nora, just so I don't snatch the wrong kid." I glanced at my watch. "Meantime, I'll have a talk with the Vietnamese baby-sitter."

"Speaking of sitters, should I call one for Eddie?"

Our boy would be getting out of school at three fifteen. "No," I said. "I'll be there when he gets home, and if I have to go out again, I'll take him along with me." As we stepped into the parking lot the wind howled as if I'd said something silly.

# 4 ◄◄◄◄

After dropping Joyce at her office downtown, I found a pay phone and called the Vietnamese baby-sitter's apartment, but no one answered. Didn't mean she wasn't there.

I tried Nora Toland's home number, but all I got was the recorded voice of her husband telling me to leave a message, he'd get back to me. Didn't mean the Vietnamese baby-sitter wasn't there, either.

I drove out Michigan Avenue toward East Lansing. If there was anything to Nora Toland's misgivings about the Vietnamese girl, I might be able to save myself a lot of time and toil by talking to her, find out if she did in fact know the guy who'd snatched Nora's baby, pay him a visit, find out which of Agnew's sitters he took it to. Coercion might be called for, but that would be the snatcher's problem, not mine.

I hit the Toland neighborhood first. They lived in an area where the trees and the homes were what the realtors call "established." It wasn't far from the Michigan State University campus and had an appropriately tweedy, professorial air that suggested elbow patches, briar pipes, and tenure. But not students. Like the utility poles, the students were out of sight.

The house itself was a thirties-vintage, all-brick Tudor with an ivy-covered chimney capped by a trio of two-foot-high cylindrical flue tiles—a Mary Poppins chimney, except that the center tile was blue, which meant the builder had been a Dutchman, which had nothing to do with the fact that the driveway was empty and the door of the built-in garage was down.

I concentrated on this, idling at the curb, pondering the home's original steel-framed casement windows, two of which were set into the exterior wall of the garage. It occurred to me that I could take a peek through the partially open venetian blind of the foremost window. An empty garage would suggest an empty house, unless the Vietnamese baby-sitter had walked to work. A car in the garage might mean that the girl had driven to work, or that she was not at home alone, that perhaps the prideful Dirk Toland was inside, too, whose path I'd promised Nora Toland I would not cross.

I got out of my car and leaned into the wind, thumbed the Tolands' doorbell and waited, gazing out over their yard at the twigs and small branches strewn across it, the work of the wind. If Toland answered I decided I'd swing into a spiel, tell him I just happened to be in the area speaking to his fellow homeowners, several of whom had encouraged me to see old Dirk because his place still had those ancient steel-frame windows and if anybody needed a free estimate on the cost of installing True-Tight, triple-glazed, aluminum-reinforced vinyl replacement windows, he did. I pushed the bell again and listened, but I couldn't tell if chimes were bonging inside the house because of the wind groaning in the attic louver high above. I hammered the heavy, wrought-iron knocker, but no one answered that either, so I returned to my car with the wind at my back, shoving me like an impatient cop.

I checked the address of the baby-sitter's apartment and drove across Grand River to Beal Street. Beal was only a block from campus, a short street with maybe twenty-five homes and four smallish apartment buildings, a student neighborhood. Signs in the driveways of the apartment buildings said things like DON'T

31

EVEN THINK ABOUT PARKING HERE. WE TOW. The street was jammed with parked cars. Come June the jam would thin considerably and the street would be lined instead with grease-encrusted ranges, corroded, foul-smelling refrigerators, burned-out sofas, and gutted mattresses. The students would have departed on summer break by then, leaving the absentee landlords and the sanitation department to deal with the aftermath.

According to the address Nora Toland had given me, the Vietnamese baby-sitter lived in an old rooming house. It was white and looked to be a gable shy of seven. Its roof was layered with shingles of MSU green. A few of the shingles were flapping in the breeze, but otherwise the place was in fair shape compared to the rest of the block, which was suffering from an acute case of student rentalitis.

I pulled into the driveway and noticed a small, shabbily dressed old woman out back of the house where a number of cars were parked. She was crouching down beside the front end of a sleek black Camaro Z-28. I pulled a little closer, watching as the woman drew from under her baggy cardigan a survival knife with a serrated ten-inch nonreflective blade. Still watching, but not quite believing what I was seeing, I saw her plunge the knife into the bulge of the Z's right front radial, dropping the big black car like a bull that had just taken a knife in the neck.

The job done, the woman tugged the knife free of the flattened tire, saw me, got to her feet, and stood as straight as the blade in her hand, brandishing it boldly, an honors graduate of the Rambo School for Surgeons. I had no idea what Rambo would do in a situation like this, but I'd given up the idea of a citizen's arrest.

"Students got a right to park here that pay me rent," the old woman shouted.

I could hear what she was saying because I'd made the questionable move of climbing out of my car. I hadn't closed the door, though, nor had I cut the engine. I said, "Maybe we could work out a short-term arrangement?"

"You ain't no student."

"Not in any course that gives credits." I followed this up with a smile.

"You ain't no merce, neither, dressed like that, so you got no business with me." She pointed the way out with the knife. Being more than a little walleyed, she did this while looking at me and the way out simultaneously.

I hesitated, thinking this was like a medieval quest: the Vietnamese princess was somewhere inside the harridan's castle, but my garb was inferior and my vocabulary deficient. I said, "What's a merce dress like, ma'am?"

"Fatigues. Combat boots. A while back one of them snuck into my bedroom in a Ninja outfit." A thought occurred to her and she cocked her head knowingly. "I bet you're here from the government 'bout the ad I ran in *Soldier of Fortune*."

I guessed she was pushing seventy, but she was facing into the wind with unflinching steadfastness, not at all intimidated by the weather, me, or the recollection of the Ninja who'd snuck into her bedroom. I said, "Did the ad mention a Vietnamese girl by any chance?"

"Wasn't advertising for no girl, and you know it."

I manufactured another smile and made an effort to relax the language of my body, but I couldn't seem to unhunch my shoulders. I said, "I really don't know anything about the ad, ma'am. I'm looking for a Vietnamese girl by the name of Xuan. I'm told she lives here."

The woman reappraised me and my three-piece suit. "Who're you?"

"Jack Bodine. I'm a private investigator. The suit's a disguise."

"What you want with the Viet girl?"

I shrugged. "Talk to her."

"Sure you're not from the government?"

I shook my head and edged close enough to her to show her my license. "I just want to talk to the girl. If I could park my car here, I wouldn't be a minute."

The woman looked me over again. "You got a good build. You work out?"

"Heaviest thing I lift is my backside out of bed."

She glanced down and leaned her head to one side. "Don't look so heavy. You run?"

"Not unless I'm chasing someone."

The woman thought about this. "You want some coffee?"

"I want the Vietnamese girl."

"Tell you what. Park over there, and come on inside for a coffee." She marched to the house and went in.

I parked in one of the two places her divergent gaze had indicated and walked over to the rear door of the house and knocked on the aluminum storm.

She let me in and sat me down at an old table that had been antiqued an avocado green and had a squat vase in the center of it containing several sprigs of spent forsythia. She moved the vase aside and said she'd be right back. There was a Pyrex pitcher of water inside a big microwave on the kitchen counter. The microwave was on, its digital timer flashing a count-down. She came back into the kitchen four seconds before the beeper sounded, a book beneath her arm. She made instant coffee, one cup, and placed it in front of me. The book she laid facedown on the table. She said, "People hire you, right?"

"Right."

"To find people?"

"That and more."

"You good at it?"

"I'm so good at it I have coffee with total strangers just to ward off the boredom."

She stared approximately at me. "My name's Celia Gore."

I held out my hand. "As I said, I'm Jack Bodine."

She shook my hand with a firm grasp. "What's the farthest you gone, Jack?"

"Well, all the way, I guess."

"I mean looking for somebody."

"Been all over the country, Mrs. Gore."

"Think you'd go farther than that?"

"If I had to. I happen to be on a case at the moment, though. The Vietnamese girl?"

"I can wait. I been waiting twenty-one years already." She slid the book toward me, saying, "Got my other kids raised. My husband's gone. There's only this to do and I'll be done." She opened the book and pointed to a pencil portrait of an army private, a handsome young man with a faint mustache and a wide face like Celia Gore's. On the facing page there was a short paragraph that said Tommy Gore was a boy who was always bringing home injured animals. It said, too, that he'd been reported missing in action in Quang Ngai Province, August 20, 1968. The book was entitled *Unforgettable Faces* and it was filled with drawings of missing soldiers, sailors, and airmen, each portrait accompanied by a half-page of biographical data. I closed the book and shook my head, not looking at Celia Gore.

She said, "All right. You don't have to go all the way to Vietnam. Might not be a good idea, anyway. You'd stand out too much. That's why I started advertising for Viets instead of Americans. Americans that show up are all crazy or sick-minded, anyhow. I just need someone like you, a pro, to come to Texas to back me up while I talk to this bunch of Viets that answered my ad."

"What are they doing in Texas?"

"Shrimpers. They know boats. I got money."

"You've got guts, too, Mrs. Gore, but I don't think it's a good idea."

"I'm not as old as I look. I run ever other day. I took ever survivalist course I could get into. I know karate, you name it."

I kept shaking my head, not naming it.

Her odd eyes searched my evasive ones. "You won't help me?"

"What I won't do is say yes just to get you to tell me where I'll find the girl named Xuan."

"Okay. But you'll think about it?"

"I'll think about it. You can count on me thinking about it."

"All right. I converted the attic couple years ago. Girl lives up there with her mother. Been there since last summer."

I stood up. "Thank you."

"But she ain't there now."

"Mind if I check?"

Celia Gore shrugged. "The steps're out back by the garage. Her mother ain't up there, neither. They left their stuff, few clothes and things, but I don't think they're coming back. Guess I've been taking advantage of you."

"If she's not there, have you got any idea where I might find her?"

"There's two people might know."

I waited.

"There's the man helps pay their rent. Name's Toland."

"And the other?"

"Ain't you going to write it down?"

I pulled out my pad. "Who's the other person to check with?"

"He's a Viet. Don't know his name. Got back from my run yesterday evening and he was pulling the girl down the stairs, yanking on her arm. She wasn't fighting him, but she didn't look happy, neither. He hauled her down the street that way, down toward Michigan Avenue. She ain't been back since. He looks like one of those Viet gangsters you read about, making life miserable for their own kind here in America. You heard about them?"

I said I hadn't.

"He's got a scar across his cheek and most of an ear missing."

"I don't suppose you know where he lives?"

She shook her head. "Know where he works, though. Seen him at that Viet restaurant down by the campus. Ate there once to see if I could stomach the food. He's a waiter. With that scar of his and that ear—just a little puckered thing—he's somebody you don't forget. This was maybe six months back, though. Might not work there anymore."

"What's the name of the place?"

"Don't recall. It's on that street next to the Arab market. Sure got a lot of foreigners around here anymore."

I gave her a grin and a look of friendly speculation. "Even got folks from Texas."

She looked up at me. "Tommy was born in Houston, but mainly he was raised up here. Then he enlisted."

Seemed to me she'd made an odd mental jump, but then I hadn't been living with Tommy Gore's loss the last twenty years. Probably most of her thoughts made that jump. She'd said it worriedly, too, as if maybe her son's Michigan upbringing hadn't prepared him for the rigors of life wherever it was she was sure he was at. Vietnam. Or Laos. Or the fearsome jungles of her imagination. I didn't know what more to say to her, so I patted her hand the way Joyce had patted Nora Toland's hand in the coffee shop.

On the way out I paused, but I still hadn't thought of anything to say, so I closed the door behind me, walked around to the exterior staircase, and climbed to the third floor of her house. The wind tore at me as if I were scaling the mast of a clipper rounding Cape Horn. I held on to the banister with one hand and pounded on the door with the other. No one answered. I tried the door, but it was locked. I thought about forcing it, but I believed Mrs. Gore when she said she was sure there wasn't anyone inside. I turned to leave. I didn't look down until I was down, then I backed out of Celia Gore's drive, found a phone booth, and fanned though the yellow pages. There was a place called Nguyen's Nook on Ann Street in East Lansing. It didn't sound like the kind of place you'd find a scarfaced, one-eared waiter, but East Lansing was quirky enough I thought I'd give it a try.

# 5 ◀◀◀

Nguyen's Nook was a block from campus, sandwiched between
Farah & Sons and the Aardvark pet shop. Its main competition in
the restaurant business—just a couple doors either way—looked
to be Bilbo's Pizza and the Small Planet. Of course there was
America's Cup over on MAC Avenue, Olde World Bread and
Ale, El Azteco, and a half dozen other eateries and swilleries
within a thousand-foot radius of Ann and Albert, possibly the
funkiest corner in East Lansing. I'm not talking major-league
funk, Times Square, or even Harvard Square; just your pink-
haired punks, horny frat boys, hornier professors, suicidal
skateboarders, bag ladies, and miscellaneous de-institutionals.
The first really warm spring night they'd sprout like mushrooms.
But this afternoon, with the wind whipping out of Siberia, Ann
Street was safe for married guys in three-piece suits. I found a
parking space in one of the metered slots across from Nguyen's
Nook and went in.

The place was long and narrow. There were plants up front by
the window with booths along the walls, tables in the middle,
fans overhead, sawdust on the floor, and a bar at the back,
mirrored booze on display. Decorwise you had faded travel
posters of Vietnam, framed glossies of the Spartans' champion-

ship hockey team and the Rose Bowl football squad, Budweiser beer backboards with Nerf ball hoops, Oriental sconces, and papier-mâché dragons. There were war sounds coming from a pair of video games off the kitchen, the electronic explosions counterpointing the reggae on the radio. The owner of Nguyen's Nook knew how to survive in a college town.

I didn't see any scarfaced Vietnamese waiters, though. I didn't see how there could be two Vietnamese men with vicious scars in town, either, so it was my guess that the waiter Mrs. Gore had seen here was the biological father of Nora Toland's baby, the man with the "terrible scar" who'd shown up at the hospital the night of the baby's birth. What interested me was the fact that he'd disappeared Xuan the very day Nora Toland's baby had been kidnapped. That was definitely something worth looking into, and I had a couple hours yet before I expected to hear from Agnew.

I was shown to a booth near the window by a coed doubling as a hostess, a strapping young woman with a flood of blond hair. I asked her for a Vernor's, got a smile, a menu, and a promise that she'd return.

The menu, like the decor, was eclectic. Ga cari (curried chicken cooked with carrots and potatoes Saigon style) took equal billing with the Nook club sandwich (shaved turkey, tomatoes, and bacon on rye). You had the bun bo xao (beef sautéed in onions, served with rice noodles, lettuce, and Saigon sauce) right opposite the Spartan burger deluxe. I decided the nam xao hat dieu (Oriental vegetables sautéed with cashew nuts) looked intriguing. So did the deep-dish pizza with three cheeses. That or the Saigon sub.

The hostess came back with the ginger ale. I said, "Have you got any Vietnamese waiters working here today?"

The hostess gave me a blank look. "There's Tony."

"Is Tony Vietnamese?"

"Gee, I don't know. I think he's Italian."

"I was told a Vietnamese waiter works here, a guy with a scar?"

"You mean Hung?"

"Hung?"

The hostess blushed. "It's not his nickname or anything. He's a busboy. He's out in the kitchen. You want me to call him, or what?"

"Or what. I'll order first." The nachos had caught my eye.

"Your waitress will be with you in a moment."

The hostess returned to the counter by the door, greeted a smartly dressed Asian couple, and escorted them to the rear of the restaurant. Craning a bit, I observed that most of the dozen or so patrons in the rear of the place were Asian. Several of them were seated around a large circular table and appeared to be immensely charmed by a distinguished, silver-haired gentleman of the Orient who was wearing a silver-gray suit, tassel loafers, and a pair of stylish wire-framed glasses with rectangular lenses. He looked like a successful salesman with Hong Kong Mutual. As he spoke to his luncheon companions he snapped his fingers as if to attract the attention of an idle garçon.

A young woman with long dark hair went up to his table. She wore a bright blue, snugly fitted sheathlike dress that reached almost to the floor. Under it she had on ankle-length hazel pants that looked like silk pajama bottoms. These pants were plainly visible because the skirt of the girl's dress was slit as high as her haunch.

The insurance salesman said something to her, leaning toward her as he spoke because the girl made no effort to lean toward him. I sensed from the look on his face that this was a breach of etiquette, and from the girl's straight spine that it was meant to be. The insurance salesman waved her away, and she turned, her head thrown back, giving me a glimpse of a face only a chromosome more Oriental than the blond hostess's, with a nose that, though vaguely flat, was unexpectedly narrow at the bridge. Narrow, too, was her jaw, which was clenched in defiance, her eyes bright with a fire that the insurance salesman had fanned, eyes that were hot but no darker than her pants, the silk no doubt sighing as she strode out of sight.

A moment later the girl reappeared carrying a pitcher of ice water. She went up to the insurance salesman's table and with a clatter of cubes topped off goblets all around. The salesman modified her technique with a hand on her wrist, speaking to her in a tone that was less than fatherly, his eyes glancing down disapprovingly at her New Balance running shoes. She ignored him and padded over to what looked to be a pair of graduate students in the booth adjacent to mine, righting their water goblets and filling them with perturbed efficiency, nostrils flaring. Something about the impatient contempt she showed for the mundane details of her work reminded me of Joyce.

A waitress came up behind the Eurasian water girl and perkily asked the grad students if they were ready to order. The water girl stepped over to my booth and sluiced ice water from the sweating pitcher into my glass, not looking at me. I said, "Excuse me. Do you know if Hung speaks English?"

The girl looked down at me in the same way she'd looked down at the insurance salesman a moment ago. Then she shook her head. "Hung no speak English." She started to move off.

"Wait," I said. "I'd like to speak to Hung. Would you translate for me?" I nodded across the room. Hung had just come out of the kitchen, a wiry little man who was clearing dishes from a booth across the way. He seemed to sense my interest in him, because he turned then, giving me another look at the sweeping scar that ran from under his nose to what was left of his right ear. It resembled a smiling second mouth.

His congenital mouth, however, was a down-turned gash, and his black gaze, as it passed from the girl to me to the hand that I realized I'd placed on her thin wrist, contained not an iota of Oriental inscrutability. He was glaring at me with an expression of undisguised hatred, as if I were a lecherous barbarian breathing beery depravities into the ear of innocence.

41

He started across the room, a black plastic basin propped on his slender hip, the dishes inside it rattling as he came at us, his starched white busboy smock smeared with Saigon sauce, his eyes so filled with anger that he seemed upset not only with me, but with the goblet girl, too. He said something to her in a language of high-pitched, singsong syllables shaped mostly in the rear of his throat by the pressure of his tongue against the roof of his mouth. The girl replied in the same language, and not pleasantly if the expression on the busboy's face meant anything. I'd let go of her, but he was still glancing at her arm as if I'd soiled her sleeve. He spoke to her again, something rapid and sharp that I could have sworn included the name Sue Ann. Xuan?

The girl had moved on, but I called after her. "Xuan?"

She paused and turned, her expression puzzled but expectant.

Hung, shaking his head at me, shouted, "No Xuan! No Xuan," as if he'd never "Xuan-ed" in his life, not once.

Glances were darting in our direction. The waitress had ceased taking the grad students' orders and the blond hostess was on the verge of inquiring as to our difficulty.

"No Xuan!" the busboy snapped again, emphasizing the negation with a swift slicing movement of his small but hard-edged hand: bluish calluses were prominent along the length of the little finger and the outer edge of the palm. It was a gesture of finality, of the closing of the subject, its termination. It also seemed to imply that any failure to let the subject drop might result in my termination as well.

"Is there problem?" It was the Oriental insurance salesman. He was smiling sedately, but with a hint of anticipation, as if maybe the busboy's chopping motion had got me in the mood to think about providing for my loved ones.

I said, "Do you speak Vietnamese?"

"I am owner of Nguyen Nook."

He said this as if, being the owner of Nguyen's Nook, he was capable of a good deal more than speaking Vietnamese. I said,

"The busboy keeps shouting 'Xuan, Xuan.' Can you tell me what he's saying?"

"Xuan? Why, *xuan* mean spring."

Maybe *Xuan* meant spring. And maybe the busboy was simply irked at the weather. I said to the owner of Nguyen's Nook, "I think I've upset the busboy by touching the girl who was pouring the ice water. His name's Hung, I believe? Would you please tell him I'm sorry? I meant no disrespect. And the girl, too."

The owner accepted my impeccable apology with a smile and a slight bow, and spoke to Hung. Hung said something in reply, and the two of them appeared to discuss at length Hung's impression of me. Then the owner said to me, "Hung accept apology."

"And the girl?"

"She, too, accept apology."

I said, "How could she have done that without opening her mouth?"

The owner still smiled, but his black eyes suggested sharp depths: tiger traps studded with pungi stakes. He said, "It is same from me."

"You speak for her?"

"She cannot speak for self. She is without English."

"Oh? She just spoke to me in English."

The owner, friendly but firm, said, "She is without English."

"Then please ask her if she left her apartment voluntarily yesterday, or if Hung forced her to go with him."

That was the last I saw of the owner's smile. He said, "May I ask what business you have?"

"Notice I did not ask if Hung and Xuan have green cards and work permits. I asked only if she left her apartment with Hung voluntarily."

The owner swallowed dryly. "Xuan leave voluntary."

"Again she speaks without moving her lips."

The owner bowed curtly and spoke to Xuan. Xuan answered in Vietnamese. Hung objected. Hung and Xuan carped at one another in undertones, their whispers—a kind of sibilant warbling—growing in volume, rising angrily over the reggae.

The owner stepped between Xuan and Hung and said to me, "Please understand, in Binh Nghia Xuan live nineteen year, but in America one year. Here she is only small child. Like many Vietnamese father, Hung is not approve of Vietnamese woman have so much freedoms as American woman. Hung has make rule Xuan live home with Hung."

I could believe Xuan's father would be worried about her future in America. She exuded the same bold sullenness one saw on the faces of fashion models. And street whores. What I couldn't believe—seeing them together—was that Hung was Xuan's father. I glanced from one to the other, seeking a genetic echo of the busboy in the water girl, whose face reminded me very much of a tune nature had played once before and that Hollywood had entitled "Jennifer Jones." I said to the owner, "Xuan doesn't look at all like Hung. I'd like an official explanation of that, if you don't mind."

The owner eyed me coldly, trying to decide something. Then he said, "When Communist take over, they say Xuan mother have American child, is American whore. Hung say no, Xuan his child. Communist know Hung protect Xuan and Xuan mother. They put him in reeducation camp, call him puppet soldier, but say to Hung, 'You confess Xuan not daughter, you leave reeducation camp.' Hung say Xuan his daughter. Communist very mad. They keep Hung in reeducation. Hung eleven year in camp."

"So she's not his daughter?"

"No."

"Her father was an American?"

"I do not know."

"Xuan owes Hung a great deal," I said, "yet she does not seem to like him greatly."

"Xuan life in Vietnam very bad. Steal food. Much lie. Here life easy. But Xuan believe nothing. Live only for Xuan. Getting trouble. So, Hung make Xuan live home with Hung and Xuan mother."

"Xuan's mother is living with Hung, too?"

"He say so."

"Ask Hung why his wife returned to live with him."

"Sorry," said the owner, stiffening, "you have official identification for ask these question?"

"Let me explain something to you, my friend. Xuan's landlady saw Hung snatch her from her apartment yesterday. She reported the incident to the local police, who brought it to the attention of our field office. Further investigation of Xuan's background has led us to her employer, a woman Xuan worked for as a housekeeper and a baby-sitter. It so happens that that woman's baby was kidnapped yesterday. At the time it happened the baby was under Xuan's care. And then Xuan doesn't show up for work at the woman's house this morning. Are you beginning to appreciate our interest in Xuan, and her sudden change of employment?"

The owner appeared to appreciate it acutely. He took in my three-piece suit with a look of defeat, as if my wardrobe, being equal to his, were sufficient to trigger a long-dormant servility. He turned to Xuan and began questioning her in Vietnamese. She answered in monosyllables, her eyes on the floor. The owner turned back to me. "Please, what you want?"

"I want to speak to Xuan."

"Xuan no speak English."

"Then I want you to translate. Please sit down."

The owner hesitated, then slid into the booth. He spoke to Xuan, and she sat down beside him.

I said, "Tell Hung to go away."

The owner said something to Hung, but Hung hung in there, speaking his mind, accentuating his unease with precise slices of his hard little hand.

The owner said sharply, *"Di!"*

Hung came briefly to attention, did an about-face, and stiffly resumed the busing of chicken bones, peeking over his shoulder from time to time.

I pulled out my notebook and said to the owner, "First, what is your name?"

The owner said, "Fuck."

"What?"

"My name Fuck."

There was not the slightest twinkle of amusement in the owner's eyes, no suggestion that he had toyed with better men than Jack Bodine. I said, "Spell it."

He said, "Spell is P-h-u-c."

I wrote it down.

With just a hint of I-know-my-rights in his tone, he said, "You have name, please?"

I stuffed my notebook back into my breast pocket while looking at him. "Sherlock Javert."

Mr. Phuc gave this a moment's analysis, but did not share his conclusions with me.

Xuan was shooting frequent glances at Hung, whose efforts at clearing the nearby table were decidedly painstaking.

Before I could start in on Xuan, the waitress who had been tending to the grad students bubbled up to our table and asked with a sparkle if we were ready to order.

Mr. Phuc waved her away.

Feeling my oats, I stayed her with a raised hand, turned my menu toward Mr. Phuc, and opened it. "What do you recommend?"

Mr. Phuc said, "All thing on that menu suitable to American taste."

"There's another menu?"

"For Vietnamese."

"With dishes different than the Vietnamese meals listed on this menu?"

"Yes."

"I'd like to see it."

"It is not written. Cook devise new menu each day according to ingredient available. I write menu here." Mr. Phuc pointed at his head.

"What are today's selections?"

"Things you are not like, I am sure."

"Such as?"

"Great delicacy." There was something of a dare in Mr. Phuc's tone, a certainty mingled with irony, as if it were well known to Vietnamese that we Americans had our limitations, and not only in matters of gastronomy.

Joyce had long ago developed my taste for exotic fare. I'd eaten snails and squid and oysters raw. And other things, thanks to Joyce: tiger paws stuffed with gecko livers. I said, "Mr. Phuc, I wish to order the rarest of your delicacies." I snapped shut the tourist menu and handed it to the coed.

Mr. Phuc smiled at me, and said to the waitress, "Hung will take order to kitchen. Thank you." Having dismissed the waitress, Phuc called Hung over. Hung approached tentatively, his narrow gaze sliding in my direction as his boss spoke in rapid Vietnamese. Hung's expression revealed nothing. I smiled at him. His scar smiled back at me. Then he departed for the kitchen. Xuan looked worried. Mr. Phuc sat back and stared at me.

I said to the girl, "Now then, Xuan, the woman whose baby was kidnapped told me she thought you knew the man who took the child. Is that true?"

Mr. Phuc said something to Xuan in Vietnamese. For a moment Xuan seemed to be contemplating defiance. Then she looked at me and shook her head.

I said, "Please describe the man."

"She speak no English," Mr. Phuc repeated.

"Then ask her to describe the man in Vietnamese."

Phuc spoke to Xuan and Xuan said something to Phuc. Phuc said to me, "She say he American man."

"Was he a white American, a black American, a Spanish-

American, a Native American, or an Asian-American?"

They conferred. "White with gun."

"Young? Old?"

They talked. "Middle."

"Beard? Mustache? Bald?"

"She does not remember."

"What was he wearing?"

"She does not remember."

I said to Xuan, "If we are to find the woman's baby, we must know what the kidnapper looked like."

Phuc explained this to Xuan. Xuan listened to Phuc. Phuc listened to Xuan. Then Phuc, eyeing me coldly, said, "She say man look like you."

I sipped my Vernor's. "I feel I am being lied to, Mr. Phuc."

Mr. Phuc shifted uncomfortably. "I feel you lie to me."

"Your instincts are serving you well. My instincts are alert, too. And they tell me that truth is not a specialty of this house. Therefore Xuan is going to sit with me and you are going to go away. And if she truly cannot speak English, then we will drive over to Walnut Street together."

"Walnut Street?"

"Yes, to the Asian Refugee Community Center. I will find someone there whose translations please me."

Mr. Phuc sat back and marshaled his hands in his lap. "I am not permit Xuan go with."

"I am intent on finding the woman's baby."

"Xuan say you take baby. You leave."

"Not without Xuan."

"Then Xuan leave."

"Not without me."

Mr. Phuc leaned forward, his hands beneath the table. "Without you."

I felt something hard tap my knee.

Phuc said, "Pistol, nine-millimeter. You stay, Xuan go."

Phuc wasn't kidding. I wasn't either, but Phuc had the pistol.

Or at least he had hold of something under the table that was heavy and metallic and immensely undetrimental to his self-confidence. I said, "You would shoot me right here in your own restaurant?"

"Yes."

"I can see the headline: RESTAURATEUR RIDDLES GASTRONOME. Don't you think that would be bad for business?"

Phuc said, "Letting man kidnap employee daughter very bad for conscience." He said something in Vietnamese, not looking at Xuan, who hesitated, frowning. Phuc snapped at her, and she jumped up and hurried toward the rear of the restaurant, pushing through the swinging door that opened into the kitchen.

I let her go. I figured I could find her again easily enough, more easily than I could find a new knee. I said, "Anyway, it's a nice place you've got here, Mr. Phuc."

"Be most careful show all identification for display."

"I bet Michelin rates it three bullet holes." I dug down into my left rear pocket, pulled out my wallet, and dealt my credit cards one by one down the center of the table as if setting up a game of solitaire.

Without taking his eyes off mine, Phuc called the hostess over and asked her to read the cards. The girl obliged him eagerly, grinning at the little game Phuc and I were playing, her eyes glittering with intrigue as she informed Mr. Phuc that my name was Bodine, B-o-d-i-n-e, and that I was, according to the document she held in her hand, a private investigator. She was about to feel my triceps when Xuan, wearing jeans now, came hurrying through the archway, heading for the front door. The hostess flagged her down and, making points with her boss, explained to Xuan in pidgin English that employees of Nguyen's Nook always exited through the delivery door at the rear of the restaurant.

Xuan, tossing her head as if to say she'd had about enough, whirled around and headed for the rear of the restaurant, zipping up her down-filled jacket and scooping her hair out from under its high collar. She pushed through the door to the kitchen just as Hung was coming through it the other way. He steadied his tray and gave her a quick piece of his mind before delivering my lunch, sliding the serving dish onto the table and uncovering it, displaying a glistening farrago of meat and vegetables, the dark slivers of flesh intertwined with bright green shreds of complex carbohydrates. It smelled of perfume.

Mr. Phuc said, "Eat."

I plopped a glob of sticky white rice onto my plate.

"Glutinous rice," said Phuc. "Very popular in Vietnam."

I smothered the rice with the aromatic stew and paused before inserting my laden fork into my fatuous face. "Won't you join me, Mr. Phuc?"

Mr. Phuc said, "No."

I ate the food. "It's good. Have some."

Mr. Phuc shook his head. "Not since I have taste my first Big Mac have I dine on cat."

I swallowed, scooped up another forkful of food, and said, "Actually, it tastes a great deal like crow."

# 6 ◂◂◂

At three fifteen sharp the kids exploded out of school and bunched up behind the crossing guard. I didn't see Eddie in the first gaggle to cross the street, nor in the second, but then he was suddenly there, almost abreast of my car, his face obscured by the hood of his sweatshirt, the shape of his body hidden under his thick down jacket. He was walking home with his buddies, Tory Zukovich and Howard Slackmeijer.

I watched him a moment more, feeling the usual blend of tender protectiveness and self-censorship. It was hard to explain, but in my mind Eddie was innocence incarnate, and not just any innocence, but my own, that which had been lost but was born again in him. It had taken me quite some time to figure this feeling out, but as soon as I realized it was nearer to self-love than anything else, I always tried to repress it, for it had very little to do with Eddie Bodine himself. He was a different ball of ear wax altogether. I tapped my horn.

Eddie saw me and brightened, but that lasted as long as it took him to realize how geeky it was to have your father waiting for you outside school. At the same instant Howard Slackmeijer, noticing that Eddie was distracted, leaped sideways and tried to kick Eddie in the testicles. Eddie saw the kick coming, turned away, and took Howard's foot on the haunch. He kept turning in a kind of pirouette, pivoting in a full circle, kicking out as he whirled, the heel of his shoe catching Tory Zukovich square in the gut.

I jumped out of the car. "Eddie!"

Eddie trotted over to me. "Hi, Dad."

"Why are you guys kicking each other like that?"

"I don't know. How are we supposed to do it?"

"You aren't supposed to do it at all."

"It's karate, Dad." Eddie knew I wanted him to feel guilty, aghast, and ashamed, but he succeeded only in looking extremely pleased with himself.

"You guys could seriously hurt each other."

Eddie glanced at his friends. Howard was laughing at Tory, who was writhing on the sidewalk.

I said, "Go see if Tory's all right."

Eddie, his shoelaces dancing around his feet, ran over to Tory, said something obligatory, then ran back to me. "He's okay."

"Then why is he still laid out?"

"I don't know. He's faking it. What do you want, Dad?"

"I want you to get in the car. Tory, are you all right?"

Tory groaned.

"Howard, is he all right?"

"Yeah, he's okay."

"Well, help him up."

Reluctantly, Howard leaned down over Tory and held out his hand. As Tory reached upward his foot shot out and caught Howard in the groin. Howard doubled over and Tory jumped up and ran off.

"Howard? Howard, are you okay?" I started around the car.

Smirking, Howard jumped up and ran off after Tory.

I got back into the car. "Why do you guys do that?"

Eddie, his seat belt buckled as per Michigan law, shrugged. He had his feet propped on the dashboard and was staring impassively at his grimy white leather high-tops. A drool of snot glistened on his lip. I pushed his feet off the dashboard, opened the glove compartment, and found a packet of tissues. "Blow your nose." Eddie blew.

I sat there glowering at innocence incarnate, wondering what was going on in his eight-year-old mind, wondering why I was wondering. What did I expect him to say? *We were working on our pecking order, Pop, nothing to worry about, you did it when you were a kid.* I said, "Answer me."

"What?"

"Why do you guys do that?"

"Do what?"

"Kick each other."

Eddie shrugged.

"Don't you know it's dangerous?"

"Everybody does it."

Possibly. Before school had been dismissed I'd noticed a couple of safety patrols kicking each other, *aieeee, thud!* I said, "Well, why does everybody do it?"

Eddie shrugged. "Mr. Hoto's been telling us about it in gym."

"Mr. Hoto?"

"Yeah."

Surely Mr. Hoto had dwelt on the spirituality of karate, the yin and yang of it, its essential self-defensiveness. Or was I thinking of Buddhism? "What exactly did Mr. Hoto tell you in gym?"

"He said to keep blocking the other guy till he runs out of moves. Then you nail him."

"I don't think I've met Mr. Hoto."

"He's new."

I knocked my Chrysler into gear. I'd changed back into my jeans and jacket and was sitting on a full tank of gas.

"Where are we going, Dad?"

"To a restaurant."

Eddie said hopefully, "McDonald's?"

I shook my head. "No, this is a stakeout."

Eddie groaned and slumped back against the seat.

"What's the matter?"

"I don't like steak."

I said, "A stakeout means we're going to a restaurant so we can watch it."

"But why can't we go to McDonald's?"

"Because the man I want to follow doesn't work at McDonald's, and I'm in a hurry to get back to watching for him."

"I'm hungry."

I turned onto Michigan Avenue and the wind hit us broadside. I tugged on the wheel and said, "There's food in the backseat, apples, a couple granola bars, Fruit Roll-Ups. I nuked some popcorn before I left the house, too."

"I thought I smelled popcorn." Eddie grabbed for his seat belt.

I said, "Wait till we get there."

"Why can't I have some now?"

"Because it's snowing again and I'm driving in traffic and if I hit the brakes your head will hit the window."

"Snow's not even sticking."

"I know. But it makes it hard to see other cars and I might have to slam on the brakes."

"I'm thirsty."

"I brought a thermos of milk."

"Can't we stop at McDonald's?"

"I brought your spelling book, too, which you forgot to take this morning. When we get where we're going I want you to finish up the assignment you didn't finish yesterday."

"Geez."

"Before you do anything else. Okay?"

"Geez, can't I have some popcorn?"

"You can have popcorn while you do your sentences. When we get there."

• • •

We got there.

I'd subcontracted some help, of course, and the first thing I did was cruise Nguyen's Nook, making sure he was still on the job. He was parked at one of the metered spaces out front, a kid-trainee my partner, Ed Quinn, and I had hired a couple months ago. I preferred working with Ed and not his gofer, but Ed hadn't been feeling well lately and was having some tests run at a hospital, so the youngster was it. Eight bucks an hour. As I drove past him he waved and stuck the aerial of his transceiver out the window. I motioned for him to give me a minute, and drove around to the rear of the restaurant.

After the admonition the hostess had laid on Xuan about leaving by the back door, I was betting Hung would exit that way, too, which was why I decided to personally stake the rear of the place. The problem was I couldn't simply park a safe distance down the street from the back door and watch it through my binoculars because it opened into a courtyard that was bounded on all sides by buildings. There were alleys leading out of the courtyard, two of them, one from Linden Street and the other from Ann, but I couldn't watch both alleys from one street. There was also a walkway between the Catholic Students' Center and the building that housed the 54-B District Court, which meant if Hung left by the back, he had his choice of three exits out of the courtyard, all of them going in different directions. And there was only one of me. So I'd decided to watch from the courtyard itself.

I pulled back into the courtyard and parked in a corner next to a garbage-filled dumpster, pulling in nose-first and adjusting my mirror so I could keep an eye on the rear door of Nguyen's Nook through the rear window of my car. There were other vehicles parked in the courtyard, too, cars and a couple delivery vans, so I didn't feel particularly conspicuous.

I cracked the fly window, fed the transceiver's aerial outside, and checked with the kid in front. He came on and said he'd gone into Nguyen's Nook for a second cup of coffee and that

55

the mark was still there. Hemmed in like I was, it wasn't a five-by-five conversation, but we could hear each other well enough. I told him we were set, and signed off.

Eddie wanted to say something on the radio, but I didn't want to confuse my young associate out front, so I said no. This made for hard feelings. Insisting that Eddie start his spelling assignment made for harder feelings, but eventually he got to work.

At one point he asked me how to spell *popcorn*, his mouth full of it.

When he finished his spelling, he began rooting around in his Lego case, talking to himself with a chaw of watermelon Roll-Up bulging in his cheek. I could smell it.

I watched my mirror.

Eddie asked if he could try out my binoculars, and he played with them for a while.

I continued to watch my mirror.

Eddie gave the binoculars back to me and began perusing his collection of "Far Side" cartoon books.

The walkie-talkie sat silent on the dash.

Eddie would show me an occasional cartoon and we would laugh.

By four forty-five we were laughed out. Eddie's thermos was empty, his food gone, and his interest in Gary Larson, me, and his Legos had been exhausted. He was slouched down in the seat, sullen with boredom.

I started up the car and flipped on the blower.

Eddie jumped up. "Is it him?"

"No. Just warming up the car again."

"You said I could start it next time."

"I forgot. You can wipe the window, though." I pulled a tissue out of the packet and handed it to him. He ignored me. At the start of the stakeout I had instilled in him a deep desire to keep the rear window free of condensation. It hadn't been very long, however, before his sense of purpose and the window had begun to cloud over. "Come on, Eddie, I can't see."

Eddie emptied his lungs with an impatient sigh, snatched the tissue out of my hand, and wiped the right half of the window.

"Wipe it all."

"When's Mom coming?" He said this as if Joyce were an emissary of the Red Cross.

"I don't know. I told her secretary where we'd be and I left a message on our answering machine at home. Last I talked to her she said she had a lot of work to do."

"Geez."

"Get that patch of steam there."

"Dad?"

"What?"

"Why do you want to follow this man?"

"Do you realize, Eddie, that it's taken you over an hour to get around to asking me that?"

"But why do you want to follow him?"

"Because he may have something I want."

Eddie stuck his finger up his nose. "What?"

I held out the packet of Kleenex. "You want a tissue for that?"

"No. I can get it with my finger."

"Use a tissue."

Eddie took the packet. "What's the man got?"

"A woman's baby. She hired me to find it."

"He kidnapped it?"

"Somebody did."

"She didn't see who took it?"

"No."

"Then why does she think he took it?"

"She doesn't. She thinks another man took it."

"Who?"

"A man who helped her get the baby in the first place."

"Her husband?"

I took a pause on that. "No, a man who helps women adopt babies."

"Why does she think he stole it?"

"Because he said he did."

Eddie thought about this. "What's his name?"

"Agnew."

"Why would he help her get the baby, then steal it back?"

"Because she didn't pay him enough money for it. Don't wipe that on the seat. Use the tissue."

"Dad? If he said he stole the baby, how come the police didn't arrest him?"

"The woman doesn't want the police to know about it. That's why she hired me."

"What's he doing so long in the restaurant?"

"He's not in the restaurant."

"Then why are we here?"

"Because I want to follow the man who *is* in the restaurant."

"But the other man said he did it."

"I know what he said. I just want to be sure the man in the restaurant didn't do it."

"But Dad, why would the other man say he stole it if he didn't?"

"So he could trick the woman into paying him the money she owes him."

Eddie slumped back against the seat, wadded up the tissue, and tossed it onto the floor.

I said, "I'm just playing out a hunch, that's all. You know what a hunch is?"

"Yeah."

"What is it?"

"I don't know."

I said, "A hunch is when you feel sort of sure about something even though you don't know it for sure."

Eddie said, "I've got a hunch."

"What's your hunch?"

"You'll get mad if I tell you."

"Why don't you read me another 'Far Side' cartoon?"

"Can't we listen to some rock?"

"I already told you, if we listen to rock, I can't hear the walkie-talkie."

"You want to hear my hunch?"

"Sure."

Eddie said, "We're wasting our time."

"You want to hear my hunch?"

"I want to go home."

I watched a bag lady totter through the courtyard. She looked frail enough that a sudden gust of wind could send her rolling down an alley like a tumbleweed.

Eddie said defeatedly, "Okay, what's your hunch?"

I said, "I think the man in the restaurant stole the baby from the woman who hired me."

"Why would he steal it?"

"He's the baby's father."

"So how do you know he took it?"

"I don't. But I do know the baby disappeared yesterday. I also know that the baby's mother suddenly went back to living with him, and that he got her older daughter and made her live with them, too. Yesterday. So it's my hunch that the baby's at his place right now."

"Why don't we go there?"

"Because I don't know where he lives."

"Why don't you just go into the restaurant and ask him?"

"I tried that earlier."

"What happened?"

"Well, let's say I had a hard time speaking his language."

"Where's he from?"

"Vietnam."

"Can I look through the binoculars?" Eddie asked.

"You've already looked through them."

"Yeah, but I didn't know what to look for then."

"What are you looking for now?"

"A Vietnamese man."

"What do Vietnamese look like?"

"Like Mr. Hoto."

"Mr. Hoto's from Vietnam?"

"I don't think so."

"Where do you think he's from?"

"I don't know."

"Then how do you know he's not from Vietnam?"

"He speaks English."

"Eddie?"

"Yeah, Dad?"

"Just don't get fingerprints on the lenses, all right?"

I felt sorry for the kid. Probably Joyce's secretary had failed to give her my message. I ought to call her. In a while I ought to call my answering machine again, too, see if Agnew had left his sitters' names and addresses.

Eddie, peering through the wrong end of the binoculars, said, "This is boring. Aren't you bored, Dad?"

Not any more bored than I would have been sitting home waiting for Agnew to call. I had a hunch he wouldn't come through anyway, a hunch that had dovetailed with the hunch that Hung had snatched Nora Toland's baby. Problem was that my hunch presupposed something of a reconciliation between Hung and his woman, Thanh Chi. Or the possibility that Hung had snatched the baby in order to lure her back home. Which would mean—

"Dad?"

"Yep?"

"What if the Vietnamese man's not in the restaurant?"

"My helper said on the radio that he was in there, remember?"

"Yeah, but what if the Vietnamese man left and he didn't see him go?"

Possible. He was a novice, after all, an earnest but spacey kid.

"Why don't you ask him to go in again and check?" Eddie said.

"I don't want the mark to get suspicious."

"What's a mark?"

"It's what I call a person when I'm interested in him. Professionally."

"What do you mean?"

"You know, if I'm watching him for some reason, or following him."

"Is the Vietnamese man a mark?"

"Yep."

"Well, what if he isn't inside the restaurant?"

"Then I guess we are indeed wasting our time."

Eddie said, "So it's possible, right? He could've left?"

"It's possible, Eddie." It was possible, too, that we were sitting here behind Mr. Phuc's restaurant only because I'd let Xuan get away, and that my hunch was nothing more than an excuse to return to the scene of an earlier defeat. Like Rambo, returning to Vietnam.

"I see him, Dad, I see him!"

# 7 ◄◄◄

Eddie had his eye on a Vietnamese man, all right, and he was Hung's size and age, but he was going into the rear of the restaurant and not coming out of it. And he wasn't Hung. I said, "That's not him."

"Are you sure?"

"Yes." I killed the engine.

"Geez."

"I sure appreciate your help, though. I'm going to make you my partner."

"Big deal." Eddie slouched down, cheek to the seat, eyes glassy with disappointment and boredom.

"Cheer up," I said. "The man who just went in is probably our mark's relief."

"You think he'll be coming out soon?"

"Yes."

"But you don't know for sure?"

"Nobody knows anything for sure."

"You don't even know if he's in there."

I pulled out my notepad and entered the fact that I'd seen an unknown Vietnamese male enter the rear of the restaurant at four fifty-nine P.M.

"Why do you write so much stuff down, Dad?"

"I want to be able to tell the woman who hired me what I did to earn her money. If I don't write things down, I sometimes forget them and they don't get into my final report. And if I don't get in all the things I did, she might not want to pay me."

"She didn't pay Mr. Agnew, did she?"

"You've got a good memory."

"Why do you want to work for somebody that might not pay you?"

"Because Mom asked me to help her."

"Is the lady nice?"

"Yes."

"Do you like helping people?"

"Sure."

"Will she have to pay you a lot of money?"

"Not so much."

"Maybe you should do something for her besides a stakeout."

"You know, I think you got a future in the legal profession."

"What's that?"

"Being a lawyer."

"What do lawyers do?"

"They help people, too."

"Do they make a lot of money?"

"Some do."

"More than you?"

"Sure."

Eddie said, "If you want to help people, why don't you be a lawyer?"

"This is more interesting."

Eddie thought about this. "Lawyers must really get bored."

"Hey, when the Vietnamese man comes out of the restaurant it's going to get exciting."

"Maybe for you."

. . .

Fifteen minutes later we were still sitting in the courtyard. The only development had been a marked decline in the quality of our air supply. I rolled down my window several more inches. "Are you sure you don't have to go to the bathroom, Eddie?"

"Who cares?"

"If you have to go to the bathroom, we'll work something out."

"You care about that lady's baby more than me."

"No, I don't."

"Then why do we have to sit here all day?"

"Because I promised the woman I'd help her."

"Why do you like to help people so much?"

Eddie's question, like the corrupt air of his bowels, hung in the air. "Well, I'll tell you, my man, I help people because it's the only thing I can do that's special. I can't paint great pictures, or sing songs or invent things. And yet I want to feel like my life is important. I don't want to waste it." Eddie was staring at the door handle as if it made more sense than I did. I said, "So I help people. I do things for them they can't do for themselves. And when I help them, it makes me feel worthwhile." I thought of Agnew and remembered his little speech about delivering a baby into a childless couple's arms and wondered if I sounded as flaky as he did.

"I don't ever want to help people," Eddie said.

"You don't have to help people if you don't like helping them. The trick is to find something to do with your life that you like. And that people will pay you for."

Eddie was silent a moment, then he said, "But what if the woman doesn't pay you?"

"I'm sure she will."

"But she didn't pay the man for the baby."

"She thought she did, but there was a mix-up."

"But what if she doesn't pay you?"

"All right, Eddie, the truth is I don't care if she pays me."

"But you just said—"

"I know what I said. The truth is I do this work because I want to know what's going on. I want to know what people are up to, especially bad people. That's why I'm sitting here in this cold car, bored blind, because something bad's going on and I'm damn well going to find out what it is." I was surprised at myself. I'd never thought of my work in the way I had just explained it to Eddie, and it gave me something to think about, a reason, maybe, not to find a new line of employ, which was what I'd been halfheartedly planning to do since the death of my father.

We sat in silence a moment, then Eddie said, "Dad?"

"Yes?"

"Do Vietnamese restaurants have fortune cookies?"

"I don't know, Eddie. I don't know much about Vietnamese restaurants." All I knew was that Mr. Phuc hadn't offered me a fortune. Maybe he could tell I didn't have any future.

Eddie said, "Can I borrow your notepad?"

"Why?"

"I want to write something."

"Use your spelling book."

"It's full up."

"That whole book's filled with sentences?"

"Yep."

"You've been working hard, boy."

"Got my brain to the page."

I ripped a half dozen leaves out of my notepad. "Here."

"Thanks, Dad."

Eddie set to work, asking me from time to time how to spell certain words.

I said, "What are you writing?"

"Fortunes. How do you spell *rich*?"

I helped him sound it out.

"How do you spell *candy*?"

"C-a-n-d-y. What kind of fortune are you writing, anyway?"

"This one says, 'You will get rich and buy a lot of candy.'"

I said, "How about, 'You will spend the night on stakeout'?"

"Forget it."

I watched people, mostly students, take shortcuts through the courtyard. Like the bag lady, they all looked gray and cold and unhappy. It was five thirty.

"I'm hungry, Dad."

"I'm getting that way, too."

"What do they call it, that stuff I had the other day at the Apple Jade?"

"Moo shu pork."

"Do the Vietnamese have moo shu pork?"

"The Vietnamese have moo shu cat."

"Really?"

"That's what I'm told."

"I wouldn't want to eat a cat. Can you imagine eating Pearl?"

Pearl was our cat. I said, "Yes."

"But do they have moo shu pork?"

"I don't know. Why?"

"I like moo shu pork. I was thinking I could order some to go, and then, while I was waiting for it, I could look around and see if the Vietnamese man was still there. That way we could get something to eat and know we weren't wasting our time, too."

I said, "It's possible you'd make a better private eye than a lawyer."

"What's a private eye?"

"You're looking at one."

"Can I do it?"

"Order moo shu pork?"

"Yeah."

"No."

"Why not?"

"Because you got some moo shu pork at home in the icebox, remember?"

"Yeah, but that's not helping me here."

"Anyway, it's not a carry-out-type restaurant."

Eddie said, "How about if I go in and ask people if they want to buy one of these fortunes? Then I could look around for the guy, and if I saw him—"

"No, Eddie."

Eddie stuffed his fortunes into his pants pocket. "What's he look like?"

"The Vietnamese man?"

"Yeah."

I ran my finger from the lobe of my ear to the wing of my nose. "He's got a scar that big."

Eddie grinned. "Come on."

"I'm telling you the truth."

Eddie said, "I don't believe you."

"He's only got one ear, and he's the meanest-looking man I ever saw."

"Cut it out!"

"Wipe the window, will you?"

Eddie sighed and wiped the window.

"Dad?"

"Yes, Eddie?"

"Did you check the phone book? You know, the way you showed me you could find somebody's address if you knew their name?"

"Yes, but there wasn't anybody named Hung in the book."

"*What's* his name?"

"Hung."

"Hung?"

"Yes."

"Dad?"

"Yes?"

"I have to go to the bathroom."

"I thought so." I got out my pad and started writing.

"I really got to go bad."

"Just a minute."

"What are you writing?"

I said, "See that little gap between those two buildings there?"

"Yeah."

I tore out the leaf I'd been scribbling on and gave it to Eddie. "Go through there and make a right turn. You'll see a printing shop and a beauty parlor and then a place with a sign that says '54-B District Court.' You go inside and show this note to the woman who works there. Her name is Mrs. Thurston. She'll let you use her bathroom."

"Okay." Eddie pushed his arms into his down jacket and grabbed the door handle.

"Wait a minute. When you get done in the bathroom—"

"I know, wash my hands."

"Right. But when you come out you stop and see Mrs. Thurston again and she'll have a note for you. Maybe. And you bring it back to me."

"She gonna tell you if I washed my hands?"

"No. That question you asked? About looking for the man's name in the phone book? That was a good idea and it got me to thinking that Mrs. Thurston might be able to check through her records and find the name and address of our mark."

"Okay. But Dad, what if he comes out of the restaurant and I'm still in the bathroom and you have to start following him without me?"

"I won't do that. I'll have my helper out front follow him. I'll be here. You just hurry up, okay?"

"Okay."

"You sure you understand?"

"Yeah." Eddie got out, slammed the door, ran across the courtyard, and disappeared into the passage between the buildings.

Twenty minutes later he hadn't come back, and I was starting to get worried . . . mainly because I had half a notion what he was up to. So I got on the walkie-talkie and asked the kid out front what was going on. He said nothing was going on, just customers entering and exiting the restaurant, but no sign of the Vietnamese guy with the scar. I gave him a description of Eddie and asked him if he'd seen a youngster like that going into the restaurant. He said he thought so. "Around five forty-five. Hey, he just came out."

"The kid or the mark?" I said.

"The kid. Say, didn't I see him in your car when you drove by earlier?"

"Right. Which way is he going?"

"Around the corner."

"Thanks. Out."

A minute later Eddie tugged the door open and climbed in, his cheeks rosy, his eyes bright, his nose running. He said, "Hi."

I said, "Hi. How'd it go?"

Eddie said, "The lady in the 54-B place said she couldn't find nothing. Here."

Eddie handed me the sheet of notepaper on which I'd written my message to Madge Thurston. On the back of it she'd written that she was sorry she couldn't help and that I should try checking with the INS. She added, "Your boy's a doll."

"Dad?"

"Yes, Eddie?"

"You better be watching." Eddie was wiping condensation off the rear window.

"Oh?"

"Yeah. He might come out any minute."

"You seem pretty sure of that."

"Yeah. I don't know. I'm just guessing."

I said, "Well, I'm tired of this stakeout. I think we ought to go home."

"Dad, the guy's in there! I saw him."

I gave Eddie a long, knowing look. "You went into the restaurant after I told you not to?"

Eddie said hopefully, "It's a neat-looking place. A man bought one of my fortunes, too. For a dollar. And he gave me a little egg roll, too."

"Eddie—"

"That guy's scar looks just like he's smiling at you."

"Eddie—"

"I know, Dad. But, geez, you said I was your partner. And I just got tired of sitting here doing nothing." Eddie started to cry.

I said, "There he goes, partner. There he goes."

# 8 ◂◂◂◂

Hung slammed the rear door of Nguyen's Nook and turned into the alley that led toward Ann Street. He looked even angrier than he had earlier, in a near rage. A Michigan spring could have that effect.

I checked my watch—it was five fifty-five—and noted the time in my notepad. Then I fired up the Chrysler and backed out of my slot, watching Hung walk down the alley. He was leaning into the wind, his fists driven deep into the pockets of a thin, thigh-length brown jacket of what looked like imitation leather. He wasn't wearing a hat and the wind streamlined his thick black hair and made his jacket billow. He looked like a hunchback.

"You're letting him get away, Dad!"

Hung turned the corner. I keyed my young associate on the transceiver and told him to follow my car in case I needed him to double me. Then I drove the length of the alley and eased to a stop half in and half out of it. Hung was walking along Ann toward Abbott. He crossed Abbott and turned toward Grand River Avenue.

"Why aren't we following him, Dad?"

"Are you buckled up?"

At Grand River, Hung turned the corner at the Bank One

building and I pulled out onto Ann Street, took a left at Abbott, and stopped at the light at Grand River. I nosed the car out into the crosswalk and took a peek around the corner.

Eddie shouted, "There he is, Dad!"

Hung had doubled back and was crossing at a run right in front of us, head down, face tensed against the wind. I raised my hand and scratched my forehead. Eddie snaked onto the floor of the car.

Hung reached the other side of the street and skipped up onto the sidewalk. The light at Grand River dropped to green. I accelerated into the intersection and drove onto campus, stopped at the curb, and got out of the car with the binoculars in hand. My young helper pulled up behind me. I focused on Hung, who was across Grand River, waiting at a bus stop with a half dozen students. A bus was just arriving. Hung must have seen it coming and realized he had a better chance to catch it there rather than at the next stop down the line. I noted the number of the bus, motioned to my helper to continue following me, and jumped behind the wheel.

Eddie wasn't in the car. The rear door was open and Eddie was on the sidewalk, standing on his toes, squinting across the street. "Eddie, get in!"

"Do you see him, Dad?"

"Yes, get in."

Eddie hopped into the backseat and struggled to shut the door. "Pull!"

He gave it everything he had, but the wind was too much. I reached over the seat and slammed the door.

"Thanks, Dad."

"Buckle up." I leaned the Chrysler into a U-turn and stopped at the light at Grand River. The bus with Hung on board was crossing our bow, heading west toward Lansing as it veered off Grand River onto Michigan Avenue, spewing fumes. Eddie was in the backseat with his nose in the air, craning over the long hood of the Chrysler.

"Did we lose him?"

"No."

"I think we lost him."

"We haven't lost him till I say so."

"Okay, okay."

"Now, buckle up."

The light changed and I made a left in front of on-coming traffic and gave the Chrysler a gulp of gas. The engine made a deep-throated gargling sound and a cloud of sooty black smoke boiled out of the tailpipe. We were moving.

Then we weren't. I had to pause at the curb half a block behind the bus, watching through the glasses as it discharged passengers. Hung wasn't among them.

The bus pulled away from the stop and I eased along behind it, keeping a half block distant. I checked my mirror. My backup was right on my bumper. He was driving a clunker, too, a '78 Oldsmobile.

The bus stopped.

I stopped.

The bus started.

I started.

A couple of times I leapfrogged the bus and watched for Hung from ahead of the stop, using the binoculars through the rear window, which Eddie kept well wiped. He was into the chase. We were having fun. It didn't last long, though. Hung got off the bus across from Omar's Showbar—BOYS NITE OUT THURS —crossed the street, and went in.

I radioed my backup to watch the rear of the place and Eddie and I U-turned and parked at the curb just down from the front door. I killed the engine and Eddie asked if we were on stakeout. I bet him he couldn't guess how long it would be till we saw Hung again. Eddie, slumping down, bet it probably would be all night. I bet a half hour.

· · ·

Only ten minutes later Hung pushed through the front door of Omar's and proceeded east on Michigan, away from us, the wind knocking him into storefronts as he trudged along. I entered the time in my notebook, and called my backup. For some reason I couldn't raise him on the transceiver. Hung was three blocks down Michigan, so I gave up and pulled into traffic. I tried a couple more times to get ahold of my help, but eventually we were out of range and all I could hope was that he'd miss me sooner than later and head home. At eight bucks an hour I didn't want him sitting out back of Omar's all night watching the wind blow trash.

Eddie was craning over the seat again. "Do you see him?"

"Plain as vanilla."

"Dad, what's that man doing over there?"

"Where?"

"Over there."

"I don't know, Eddie."

"Is he throwing up?"

"I think he's just tired of winter."

"Jimmy Hurwitz threw up in gym yesterday."

"How'd Mr. Hoto handle that move?"

"He called the custodian."

A traffic light jumped to yellow.

"Dad?"

"Yes, Eddie?"

"What's n-o-v-e-l-t-i-e-s spell?"

"Novelties."

"What are novelties?"

"Unusual things."

"Like what?"

"Little toys."

"Could we go to that store someday?"

"What store?"

"That one. See? Velvet Fingers. They got female models, too. They got . . . Dad, you didn't wait for the light to turn green."

"I don't want our man to get too far ahead of us."

"Why don't you use your binoculars?"

"I can't drive and use binoculars."

"Can I use them?"

"Sure." I handed the glasses over the seat.

Eddie adjusted them until he had the lenses smeared just right. He said, "I wonder if that store's got airplane models, too. Hey, look at that neat old train station."

"That's Clara's. It's a restaurant."

"Can we go there?"

"Tonight if you want, soon as we're done with Mr. Hung."

"What about Mom?"

"We'll give her a call and she can meet us there."

"He just went into a store, Dad."

"It's another bar." A neighborhood joint. I drove by, U-turned, and parked so I had a view of the side street and the entrance to the alley that passed by the rear of the place. I killed the engine and slid over into the passenger seat.

"Think he's had a lot to drink, Dad?"

"He wasn't long at the other place. Maybe it was just the wind blowing him around." Then again, ten minutes was plenty of time to knock back a couple doubles, maybe three.

"You don't drink, do you?"

"No."

"Don't you like it?"

"I like it."

"Then why don't you drink?"

"Because I don't ever want you to see me drunk."

"Why?"

"Because I don't ever want to see you drunk."

"Mom drinks wine."

"Yes, but she never gets drunk."

"Did you ever drink wine?"

With the exception of gasoline, I used to drink anything the government taxed. I said, "Some."

"Dad?"

"What, Eddie?"

"How's Mom going to know where we are?"

"You know, if I had one of those phones in my car I could call her from right here. You ever see those car phones?"

"But you don't have one."

"No."

"Are we on a stakeout again?"

"Yes."

Eddie slammed himself against the back of the seat, stuck out his lower lip, and folded his arms with Napoleonic defiance. "I'm tired of staking out."

"But you're my partner."

"I don't want to be your partner. I want to go home."

"I do, too."

"Then why don't we?"

"We will when Mr. Hung does."

"Why do we have to wait for him?"

"Remember the baby I told you about?"

"So what?"

"Come on. If you were kidnapped, wouldn't you want somebody to find you?"

"You said it's the man's baby."

"Right."

"So how could he kidnap it if it's his?"

"I'll bet you could ace the bar exam right now."

"What's the bar exam?"

"It's where they have you breathe into a straw."

"What straw?"

"Want to make a bet how long he stays in that bar?"

"No."

I wrote down Hung's time of entry in my notebook. "I'm going to bet fifteen minutes."

"I don't want to play."

"All right. Can you tell me what's purple and flies?"

"I don't care."

"I'm just trying to cheer you up, Eddie."

"I know, but you're cheering me down."

"Speaking of down, why don't you stretch out on the seat? Just shove your stuff onto the floor and take a little nap."

"No!"

"Eddie!"

"All right, Super Grape."

"There you go. Okay. What's purple and rules the waves?"

"Grape Britain!"

"Okay. What's—"

"Dad, if we can't talk to your helper anymore, could we listen to rock?"

Eddie listened to rock.

I peed in a bottle.

At six forty-one I made a note in my pad.

"What are you writing, Dad?"

"Our mark was just invited to leave the bar."

"Huh?"

"They just threw Mr. Hung out the door."

"Already?" Eddie jumped up and goggled at the door of the pub. It was filled by a bald, beefy gentleman who was demonstrating his dislike of Hung.

"Look, Dad, that guy just gave him the finger."

Hung was in his shirtsleeves. The wind plastered his shirt and pants to his body. He was a very wiry man, Mr. Hung, wiry and wound up. The fat man threw Hung's jacket at him and slammed the door in Hung's face. Hung let out a howl and nailed the door with his foot. At the instant of impact his body was six feet off the ground and parallel to the pavement.

"Did you see that, Dad?"

"Just like Mr. Hoto, huh?"

"Look, he did it again!"

"Strong door."

"You think he's drunk?"

I noted that the subject, having exited the bar at six forty-one, was continuing east on Michigan Avenue. "Yes, I'd say he's drunk."

"Look, he's talking to himself."

Actually he appeared to be having words with the Runcimen Funeral Home. He lodged complaints with Shattuck's Office Supplies, the House of Chin Chinese Grocery, and Anthony's Party Store, too.

Then he staggered onto Clifford Avenue and advanced on the first house on the east side of the street, a white frame bungalow with a brown roof, green trim, and a little porch out front. He entered the house at six fifty-five. I laid the binoculars on the seat and wrote down the time in my notepad.

"Is that his house, Dad?"

"He didn't beat it up, so it probably is."

"Can we go home now?"

"Soon." I drove past Clifford and pulled into a lot that was shared by a hospital equipment sales and service outfit on one side and a small printing company on the other. I rolled to the rear of the lot, slid into a space between a yellow Chevette and a van with the name of the printing outfit on the side of it. From there I had a clear view of the rear of Hung's house. There was an aluminum awning over the back stoop.

"Are we on stakeout again?"

The awning looked as if it had been tacked on by a handyman. Just about every house in Lansing had something tacked onto it by a handyman. Come to think of it, the entire town gave the impression of having been built by handymen who had three plans between them . . . which is more than you could say for a lot of towns these days, the neighborhoods giving way to builders who all used the same plan and the same names for their so-called developments: Briarwood, Boxwood, Bramblewood, Balsawood. I stuffed my notepad into the glove compartment, killed the Chrysler, and got out. "You stay here, Eddie."

"But it's getting dark!"

"Lock the doors. You'll be all right." I shut the door without slamming it and motioned for Eddie to thumb down the lock stems. He looked as though he were about to cry. I gave him a wave and left him there. I felt guilty about it, but this wasn't going to take but a minute.

I skirted the front of the Chrysler and worked my way down a shallow decline to the level of Hung's backyard. It was indeed getting dark and the wind was roaring through the high old trees that seemed to hover over the neighborhood like a Greek chorus. Dry leaves swirled up at me like a swarm of wasps.

I ducked between two wind-whipped forsythias, darted across the yard to the house, and came to a panting halt under a side window. I took a peek. The curtain was pulled. I pressed my ear to the dirty glass. I didn't hear anything but the wind. Then I caught what sounded like a baby's cry, heard it again and realized that it was a woman's voice, high-pitched and full of urgency. Or fear. She was speaking the same singsong language I'd heard Xuan use when she'd had words with Hung at the restaurant. I heard a man's voice, too, speaking Vietnamese. He cut the woman off and started giving it back to her.

There was a second side window up toward the front of the house. I ran over to it in a crouch and peeked, but its curtain was down, too. The voices inside the house were much louder now, Hung's and the woman's. Their argument had become fierce, or at least Hung's end of it had turned mean. The woman's voice was full of pleading and panicky hysteria. I listened hard for a baby, trying to filter out the adult entertainment, but I didn't hear one. If there was a baby inside, it would definitely be awake. But there was no crying. Just screaming.

I left the window and crept around the front of the house, climbed the steps, and eased across the front porch. I took a look through the front window, but it was covered with a gauzy material. I could see just enough to make out that the living room was in shadow and that there was a light on in the rear of the place. I moved along the porch, opened the aluminum storm door, and laid my ear against the paint-caked panels of the front door. Hung and the woman were really going at it now. I heard a crash. The woman was sobbing. Something heavy hit the floor.

"Dad?"

"Eddie!"

"I'm scared, Dad."

"Eddie, I want you to run over to that house across the street. See the one where the lady's watching me from the door? I want you to tell her to call the police. Tell her we've got a serious domestic disturbance over here."

"A what?"

"Tell her a man's beating a woman. Go!"

Eddie clopped down the old wooden steps and darted across the street. A sudden gust filled the hood of his sweatshirt like a wind sock. The wind was loud in the bare trees, but I could still hear Hung hollering.

I pounded on the door. "Police! Open up!"

No one opened up.

Eddie was talking to the neighbor lady. I made hurry-up motions and she ducked into her house.

I pounded on the door again. "Police!" My idea was to distract Hung and give the woman inside a breather till the cops arrived. I could find out later if they happened to notice an infant inside, make it sound like a curious question from an anonymous bystander. But I knew I couldn't wait for the cops. In my mind I saw Hung hammering away at Xuan, using his hard-edged little hands on her fragile face. I grabbed the doorknob and stepped into his unlocked lair.

It was quiet now. The living room was dark and deserted. I cocked an ear toward the rear of the house. Nothing. I told myself to keep an eye out for baby stuff while proceeding with deliberate haste to the woman's rescue . . . but not so fast as to walk into a karate chop. I glanced around. A gray, dusk-dim light filtered in through the dingy gauze curtains, enough light to convince Captain Clue there weren't any rattles or blankets or bottles lying around. Otherwise the room looked as though it had been furnished with Beal Street refuse: a couch covered with food stains and a carpet that looked dead in spots, like my lawn after the neighborhood dogs had spent the winter relieving themselves on it. There was an end table rimmed with cigarette burns and a hassock mended with duct tape. The Formica table in the dinette was also decorated with cigarette burns.

The kitchen was opposite the dinette and at a glance it looked devoid of baby bottles or formula or anything you might expect to find, nipples, that kind of thing, just a wheezing fridge and the greasy stove and the cupboards. They had old-fashioned glass doors on them and I could see that the shelves were stocked mainly with rice and a lot of food in cellophane bags. Not one jar of Gerber's mashed carrots.

The house was desperately quiet. I was aware of the wind whipping around the eaves and of the wail of an approaching siren. But in the house of Hung all was very, very still, as if I were standing in the eye of a storm. I headed down a narrow hall that led toward the back door, glancing into the empty bathroom as I passed by. There weren't any Pampers under the washbasin. I leaned into a bedroom across the hall and saw a wool army blanket stretched over a single twin-sized bed.

The siren was just outside the house now, grinding down. We'd recently got a 911 system in Lansing and the taxpayers' money had evidently been well spent. I could hear car doors slamming. I didn't want to be found in Hung's house. As soon as the cops found out I was a PI they'd ask me what I was up to and I didn't want to tell them why I was looking for Nora Toland's missing baby, which would definitely put her in hot water with the Department of Social Services. So I decided to duck out the back door, collect Eddie, and beat it. I went for the knob, glancing through an open door on my left.

It was a second bedroom and it was a major mess. There were fist-sized holes in the plaster. A dresser was lying on its side, drawers spilling out of it, some of them shattered as if by a sledgehammer. A table and a lamp were on the floor, too. There wasn't any baby in the torn-up room, nor any sign of one, just an unmoving Asian woman laid out on a sunken mattress. She wore frayed canvas sneakers, a pair of cheap slacks, and a loose print blouse. Her thin arms were at her side and her long black hair was splayed across a pillow. She looked a lot like Xuan, but I was sure she wasn't. She looked dead, too, and although I didn't see any blood, I was sure she was.

That appeared to be Hung's impression, too. He was standing over her, his fists clenched, his mutilated face fierce with rage. He let out a howl and gave me a look at the soles of his black high-topped court shoes. I pulled the door shut and jumped back as Hung's right foot, face-high, exploded in a fury of splinters clean through the hollow-core door.

Given the situation, I didn't blame the cops for drawing down on me.

# 9 ◄◄◄◄

It was a quiet night in Homicide. Eddie and I had a desk to ourselves. We had a deck of cards, too, and we were playing war.

The detectives had stepped into a glassed-in office to talk over the preliminary reports of the arresting officers. The big bald dick had his back to me. He was on the phone, writing as he talked, nodding, gesturing with his pen. I couldn't hear what he was saying. The little dick had his hands in his pockets and was standing opposite the big dick's desk, leaning back against the glass, gazing at me. He had a head of thick wiry hair, and a mat of pelt showed above the knot of his slackened tie. His face, raw-looking from the razor he dragged across it twice daily, was a wise-guy face, wry, perpetually smirking, sly, and satirical. Satyrical, too, although he looked nothing like a goat. He was wearing a blue blazer and gray slacks, but that was just a trick of his, something to camouflage the fact that he was a predator, a prowling, sniffing, stalking carnivore, the kind that waited for the perfect moment and then, when every circumstance was in its favor, went for your throat. Even after I'd quit looking at him I was aware of his gaze. I felt as though I were being watched by a preternaturally intelligent wolf.

As for Hung, he was cuffed to a desk by the door. An old

Vietnamese woman, her hair pulled back in a bun, was whispering to him. Hung didn't appear to be listening.

"Your turn, Dad."

I turned over a five. I said, "What did that old woman say when she was in the police car with you, Eddie?"

"Nothing." Eddie took my five with a nine.

"The police didn't question her?"

"They tried to, but she didn't understand anything they said." Eddie laid down a three.

The old woman leaned toward Hung, whispering fiercely. She glanced once at me, then edged even closer to Hung, her long bony fingers worrying the rolled cuffs of her coat. I turned over a two. "Do you have any idea who she is?"

"Uh-uh." Eddie gathered in the cards and played a jack.

The old woman's coat was the color of a grocery bag. It was stuffy in Homicide, but she had the coat buttoned up to her chin. It was a cloth coat, a Pat Nixon original.

I flipped a four onto the desk. "Why did the police bring her in with you?"

Eddie scooped up the cards and snapped down a six. "I don't know, Dad. When's Mom coming?"

"When did you first notice the old woman?"

Eddie shrugged. "When she came around the corner."

"And then what?"

"She stopped where all the police cars were parked and watched. When they brought the Vietnamese man out she said something to him. And when they put him in a police car she tried to talk to him through the window, but he wouldn't say anything to her. It's your turn."

I laid down a queen. "She should be here any minute."

"Who?"

"Your mother."

"It's a battle!"

Eddie had also turned over a queen. I peeked at my next card.

Eddie peeked at his. We looked at each other. I said, "I'm going to bet three." I set aside my hole card and laid three cards, face down, onto my upturned queen.

Eddie counted six cards off his pile and said, "Your three and three more."

I slid three cards off my depleted hoard and placed them on top of my queen. I had four cards left. I stacked them on top of the queen, too. "Your three, and four to call. I'm going for broke, partner."

"You're betting all your cards?"

I tapped my hole card. "I can't be beat."

"You got a ace?"

"You've got to meet my bet to find out."

Eddie thought this over, peeking once again at his hole card. "Okay." He matched my four with four of his own.

"You ready?"

Eddie reached for his hole card.

I said, "We turn them at the same time, right?"

"Right."

I turned up a queen. Eddie showed a queen, too.

"You lose, Dad!"

"No, I don't. It's another tie."

"Yeah, but if the battle ends in a tie and you're out of cards, you lose the war." Eddie looked up over my shoulder. "Isn't that right?"

I turned. The detective who'd been watching me from the glassed-in office was standing behind me now, staring at me with those wolfish eyes of his, smirking at me as if I were prey without a prayer. He said, "How come you weren't at the school-board meeting last night, Bodine?"

I said, "You were in Vietnam, Zook. What's she saying to him?" I nodded at Hung and the old woman.

"I don't speak gook," Detective Zukovich said. He turned to Eddie. "Where was your father last night, Eddie?"

"He fell asleep on the couch, Mr. Zukovich."

Zukovich looked at me. "We voted, Bodine. On issues that are going to affect your kid's future in the district."

"Two tours, seems like you'd've picked up a little of the language."

Zukovich said, "What was your duty station in the Nav?"

"Morocco."

"Too bad the guy's not an A-rab. You could take his statement."

"So how are you going to get it, send him to college?"

"We got a guy coming."

"What's gook?" asked Eddie.

Zukovich said, "Gook is what gooks talk."

"What are gooks?"

"Gooks," said Zukovich, "are about the best soldiers in the world."

"Did you fight gooks?"

"I fought gooks."

"I mean, did you kill any?"

"As many as I could."

Eddie stared at Zukovich.

I said, "I bet you breathe a lot of life into those school-board meetings, Zook."

Zukovich said to Eddie, "I'd say it's your game, by the way."

"See, Dad?"

"He doesn't know anything," I said.

Zukovich said, "Not nearly enough."

"Go on, Eddie, shuffle."

Eddie gathered in the cards, glancing up at Zukovich.

"Is your father a good cardplayer, Eddie?" Zukovich asked.

"Not as good as me."

"He teach you this game?"

Eddie nodded. "Mr. Zukovich?"

"What?"

"Tory says you were in Vietnam."

"I was."

"Did you kill people in Vietnam, too?"

"Sure, Eddie. That's where the gooks are."

Eddie stopped shuffling and looked over at Hung and the old woman. "You haven't killed any since then, have you?"

"Nope. Since then I've concentrated on perps."

"What's a perp?"

"A bad guy."

Eddie stared at Zukovich again.

Zukovich said, "I'm a cop, Eddie. If I wanted to play it safe, I'd be a private eye."

Eddie looked down at the cards.

"Is your father as good at being a peeper as you are at playing cards?"

"My dad's a private eye."

"Sure he is, but is he any good?"

Eddie nodded.

"He ever show you how to do it? You know, spy on people? Follow them around, see what they do?"

Eddie glanced again at Hung. "Yeah."

"Is that what you were doing with your father, Eddie, following that man over there with the scar on his face?"

Eddie glanced at me. I shook my head.

"What about it, Eddie? Was your father following that gook?"

I said, "You don't have to answer him, Eddie."

"But, Dad, Mr. Zukovich's a policeman."

"Technically. Let's keep everything technical, Zook, and wait till my lawyer gets here."

"You're holding out on us," Zukovich said. "That could result in an arrest."

I rattled the cuffs Zook had used to secure me to the desk. "What's this, liberty and the pursuit of happiness?"

"That's what happens to guys that don't make the school-board meetings."

"It was a new couch. I had to break it in."

"Excuses are like assholes, Bodine."

"I know. Everybody's got one."

Zukovich hauled his hands out of his pockets and leaned on the desk. "Listen, Jack, Fats just found out we're neighbors and that we hang around together. He expects more from you than you're giving."

"I'm making you look bad?"

"I've looked worse."

"Right. Your reputation will survive. I give away a client, mine won't." I waved at Joyce.

Zukovich turned toward the door. He waved too, then turned back to me, scowling. "You shit. You said you called a lawyer." He unlocked the cuffs, shielding this act of emancipation with his body.

"I want my lopping shears and my telescoping tree pruner, too," I said.

"You shit." Zukovich dropped the cuffs into his blazer. "Hiya, Joyce."

"Hello, Zook." Joyce was wearing walking shoes, jeans, and a waist-length red wool jacket with a gray scarf and matching gray wool gloves. Her cheeks were rosy from the wind.

Eddie, snickering, said, "Mom, Mr. Zukovich handcuffed Daddy to that ring on the desk."

Zukovich laughed nervously. "You know how hard it is to get this guy to sit still."

Joyce knelt and studied Eddie with professional concern. "Are you all right, Eddie?"

"I saw a dead lady, Mom." Indeed, Eddie had somehow got into Hung's house and was right there when the cops pushed open the door to the bedroom and jumped on Hung. It was as if the dead woman had been placed on the bed just to make a lasting impression on little Eddie Bodine. Eddie added, "She looked like she was asleep, but she was dead."

Joyce looked to me for corroboration. I nodded. Joyce hugged

Eddie. I wanted a hug, too. What I got was a scowl that said, *You shouldn't let your son see dead ladies!*

If I didn't know better, I'd have thought Zukovich was suddenly sympathetic to my case. His normally lupine smirk bore traces of canine humility, the kind of grin a dog displays when it's done something stupid and knows it. Zukovich hadn't done anything stupid, of course, nor was he sympathetic to my dilemma. He was simply uncomfortable in the presence of mother love.

Both of us were happy to be distracted by the diffident entrance into the squad room of a familiar figure, the natty Mr. Phuc, owner of Nguyen's Nook, still dapper in his silver-gray suit. He had on a matching gray overcoat, too, with a black velvet collar.

"Is that your perp's mouthpiece?" I said.

"Nah. We got a call to the public defender's office for the gook. That's a translator. Owns a gook restaurant down in East Lansing. Best we could do on short notice. Nice seeing you, Joyce." Tongue lolling, Zukovich stalked across the squad room, nose to the ground, ears twitching with anticipation.

I said to Joyce, "Did you call Nora Toland?"

She nodded, sitting now in Eddie's chair, having dragged him onto her lap. I'd seen her do this many times, haul Eddie onto her knees, but for some reason having it happen here in a squad room of the Lansing Police Department made me realize just how much Eddie had grown since . . . since the night I'd seen him slide glistening out of Joyce's body. She said, "Did you tell Zook you were looking for Nora's baby?"

"No. But I'm under pressure. What did Nora say?"

"Her husband, Dirk, answered. I told him what you told me over the phone and he said he'd take care of it right away."

"Meaning what?"

"He said for me not to bother calling a lawyer. He said he'd come here to the station and clear you with the police."

"What did he say about the fact that Nora hired me?"

"It didn't come as any surprise to him. Nora and I had a long talk after work, which is why I didn't get your message to come get Eddie until it was too late. We stopped at Clara's and I advised her to take Dirk into her confidence, tell him she paid off Agnew, hired you, all of it. When I left her she was in the lobby making a call to her husband to have him meet her for dinner so she could fill him in on what she'd done. That's why, when I called later and told him you'd been arrested, he knew who you were and why Nora hired you. What really seemed to bother him was the news about the woman, the surrogate mother."

"What's a surrogate mother?" Eddie asked.

"I'll tell you later, okay?"

"You got cold cheeks, Mom."

Joyce said to me, "Sam Agnew left a message on your machine, by the way. He came through with the names and addresses of two women. He said we could drop by their homes any time after ten tomorrow morning."

The big bald dick emerged from his office. He was shaking hands with Mr. Phuc. Zukovich was making a point of keeping his hands in his pockets. The old woman, meanwhile, was taking it all in, her face lined with a thousand troubles, a face we'd all seen a thousand times in a thousand pictures: refugee.

I said to Joyce, "Time to take Junior home. He's bushed. Had a big day, didn't we, Eddie?"

Eddie said, "Boring day."

"Will you be all right, Jack?"

"Sure."

"You want me to try for a baby-sitter and come back?"

I shook my head. I said to Eddie, "You cooperate with your mother."

"Okay."

"I don't think I'm going to get back in time to get a bedtime kiss, Eddie, so give me one now, okay?"

He reached up and hugged me and kissed my cheek. I kissed him back. While I was in the neighborhood, I gave Joyce a peck, too. I pulled Eddie off her lap and squeezed her hand as she stood. She glanced across the room at the cops and at the three Vietnamese people and leaned toward me, whispering, "Who's that?"

I said, "He owns a Vietnamese restaurant out by the campus."

"No, I mean the one with the scar. Did he kill her?"

"I found him standing over her body. I don't know who the old woman is."

"She's the killer's mother," said Joyce.

"How do you know?"

"I can tell."

As they left me I heard Eddie say to Joyce, "Mom, do you know why excuses are like assholes?"

# 10 ◄◄◄

Hung, meanwhile, still refused to speak. Mr. Phuc, who did not seem to recognize me without my three-piece suit, cajoled and wheedled, but Hung had nothing to say. The old woman was another matter. I couldn't hear Phuc's translations of her comments, but I could watch her make them, and when she raised her arm and extended the long bony finger of her left hand the heads of Fortner, Zukovich, and Phuc swiveled around as if she were pulling strings with the fingers of her right. I might have found it amusing if the old woman hadn't been pointing at me.

Detective Norman "Fats" Fortner levered his vast ham off the desk, aimed his belly in my direction, and followed it to my desk. He stopped and stood over me, observing the game of seven-card solitaire I'd laid out. He said, "Black Jack."

I glanced at my cards. "Where?"

"That's what Zukovich calls you: Black Jack Bodine."

"I never heard him call me that."

"Maybe you never heard a lot of things people call you."

I gathered in the layout and tucked the deck into the drawer where Zukovich stashed his candy bars. Leaning back in Zukovich's squeaking chair, I gazed up at Lieutenant Fortner, whose bald, pockmarked, slightly lopsided face reminded me of a gibbous moon. I said, "What did the old woman just call me?"

Fortner, a smile waxing, gazed down at me. "Ain't got the faintest idea, huh?"

I glanced over at Hung's mother. She wasn't looking at me with hostility or disdain, or with anything but a kind of placid antiquity, nothing personal in her accusation of me. "She said I killed the woman."

"You got good ears."

"Lucky guess."

Fortner said, "She told the translator you were tossing the house. The victim came in, caught you at it, and you started knocking her around. Then Bruce Lee shows up and tries to feed you a foot sandwich."

It occurred to me that Mr. Phuc, who seemed now to have recognized me without yet having mentioned me to Zukovich, might have encouraged the old woman's lies. But I wasn't free to suggest that to Fortner. It would point his questioning in a direction I didn't want it to go: toward the kidnapping of Nora's baby. As to why Phuc hadn't said anything about our earlier encounter I could only guess his nine-millimeter was unregistered, which meant our conversation at the restaurant wouldn't get registered either. I said, "If I was the guy's mother, I'd say the same."

"How'd you know she's his mother?"

"Thing is, she wasn't in the house, so how could she know what I did or didn't do?"

Fortner sat on the edge of Zukovich's desk. It did not tip over. He said, "Maybe her son told her what happened."

"He hasn't opened his mouth since he got here."

"Maybe he told her in the car on the way to the station."

I shook my head. "They were driven here in different cruisers."

"Not bad, Bodine. Question remains, what were you doing at the scene?"

"We're at the interview stage, correct?"

"Do you see a tape recorder? Hell, this is a grounder. The Vietnamese guy karate-chopped the woman and killed her. Course, we got to wait for the ME's report. Only thing has me scratching my head is what you were doing at the scene."

I shrugged. "Simple. I happened to be in the vicinity when I heard the sounds of an argument. So I went up to the house—"

"Hey, *you're* simple. I talked to the arresting officers, so I know what you told them. What I want is the truth."

"They didn't believe me?"

"Yeah, they believed you. Hell, I'm all set to throw this Vietnamese slugger out at the plate when one of the uniforms reminds me you're a private investigator. Suddenly there's this lump in the infield, name of Bodine, and the case takes a bad hop. Now, why were you following the Vietnamese guy?"

"How about if we come back to that?"

"You mean when your lawyer gets here?"

"My wife figured the old woman for the guy's mother, by the way. Just a guess."

"You got a nice-looking wife. You got a nice kid, too."

"Nice of you to say so."

Fortner said, "Hey, I'm a nice guy."

"Then what are you doing in a place like this?"

Fortner leaned toward me. "I'll tell you. I'm in a place like this because I look like I look. I mean, I look like a cop, so I ended up being a cop. But I shouldn't be a cop, Bodine. I just got done looking at a real pretty woman dead from a crack on the head, and I didn't want to have to see her that way. I hate looking at dead people. They upset me. They frighten me. And I don't like to get frightened, big man like me. It's embarrassing. So what happens, I get angry at the guy who's responsible for making me look at a scene of death. You understand? I want to make the guy pay for putting me through it. It gets personal with me. I want to get the guy for personal reasons, for smearing my soul with the filth of his work. Am I getting through to you, Black Jack?"

"We're kindred spirits."

94

"Good. Because I don't want to include you with the guy I'm mad at right now, the guy with one ear who won't talk and his old mother who won't stop talking. I don't want to associate you with him in my mind. What I want is for you to help me get even with him for making me look at that dead woman, that's what I want from you."

In the door of the squad room, directly behind Zukovich and the cluster of Vietnamese, stood a tall man in a black coat. He was six-three at least, had dark brown hair, a dark brown mustache, bright brown eyes, and a broad face that would brown nicely in the summer sun. He looked a lot like me. Even had presence, everything I could ask for in a double except perhaps the joie de vivre I brought to my version of myself.

He was frowning at the Vietnamese. He gave Zukovich a good going-over, too, his impatience rising a notch as his eye skimmed the grim congregation of desks, file cabinets, telephones, and chairs, and lighted at last on Fortner. Or maybe it was more correct to say that Lieutenant Fortner attracted the guy's gaze. Being as big as he was, Fats Fortner drew stares the way the moon compelled the tides. Fats turned and said, "Can I help you?"

"I'm looking for a man named Bodine."

Fortner pointed at me. "This's him. You his lawyer?"

My double pondered Fortner's question as he angled through the maze of desks, sizing me up as he came. He said to Fortner, "Does he need one?"

Fortner snorted. "Wild abandon! Love that in a lawyer."

The man in the black coat said, "I'm not a lawyer. My name's Dirk Toland. I understand you're holding Mr. Bodine in connection with the death of a woman named Le Thanh Chi?"

Fortner gave Toland's question a moment's thought and said, "How is it you know her name, Mr. Toland?"

"The night-shift supervisor at my shop phoned me and said the police just called asking about her, said she'd been killed. Mr. Bodine's wife called too and said you had him under arrest, something to do with a dead Vietnamese woman."

"And you think they're one and the same?"

"Have you charged Mr. Bodine?" Toland said stiffly.

Fortner shrugged. "Remains to be seen. At present we're waiting for him to explain his presence at the scene of a homicide. And seeing as how you're not his lawyer, I'm also waiting to hear about this shop of yours and what it has to do with Bodine and the dead woman, assuming we're talking about the same individual."

Toland said, "May I ask your name?"

"Detective Lieutenant Norman Fortner, Homicide."

Dirk Toland turned to me. "What exactly have you told Lieutenant Fortner?"

I glanced at Fortner, who nodded, giving me permission to answer. I said, "I told him I happened to overhear a violent argument between a woman and the Vietnamese man sitting at that desk over there, the one with the scar. I had a neighbor call the police and then I made an effort to intervene, but too late. Lieutenant Fortner believes I was following the Vietnamese man. I've said nothing to suggest that I was. Or that I wasn't."

As I made this statement Dirk Toland scoured my demeanor for signs of allegiance. Then he drew a deep breath and raised his eyebrows as if he'd told himself he had no choice but to trust me. He said to Fortner, "Mr. Bodine's working for me, Lieutenant. He's a private investigator. I'm general manager of Midwest Micrographics. We've got a large number of Vietnamese on our payroll, good people, but lately we've had a problem with stock shrinkage, film especially. In other words, employee theft. Mr. Bodine has been observing Le Thanh Chi as part of his investigation into this matter. I'm certain he's not responsible for her death."

"You're saying Bodine was tailing the dead woman?"

"Yes, from the shop."

Fortner nodded vaguely, his lips pursed in thought. He seemed to think this wasn't the worst explanation he'd heard. Not the best, but not the worst, either. He said to Toland, "See that old woman over there?"

Toland glanced at Hung's mother. "Yes?"

"She insists she saw Bodine hanging around her son's house just prior to her going out to the store at around four twenty this afternoon. She says the dead woman wasn't at home at that time. If Bodine was tailing the deceased, how could the old woman have seen Bodine in the vicinity?"

Toland said, "She's made a positive identification?"

Fortner nodded. "She's the guy's mother, so I'm taking what she says with a grain of salt. Still—"

"You mind if I have a word with her?"

Before Fortner could refuse, Toland turned toward the old woman and fired off a rapid series of questions in what I assumed was Vietnamese, walking over to her as he spoke, standing over her once he reached the desk, glaring down at her, emitting from his perfectly American mouth those warbling, singsong phrases with an ease that was almost shocking.

The old woman glanced over at me, then up at Toland, answering in a sharp, high-pitched voice. Mr. Phuc got into it then and the three of them, with Hung still staring glassy-eyed at the desk, eventually came to some kind of understanding.

Toland turned and said to Fortner, "She's mistaken. The man she saw loitering near her house looked like Mr. Bodine, but she's convinced now that it wasn't him."

Fortner said to Mr. Phuc, "Is that an accurate reflection of the woman's change of mind?"

"Yes, Lieutenant." Mr. Phuc bowed toward Toland. "This gentleman speak very fine Vietnamese. Hung mother change mind."

Zukovich was eyeing Toland with an interest bordering on astonishment. He said to Toland, "Where'd you learn to talk gook?"

"I went to the horse's mouth."

Zukovich said, "I did, too, but the horse puked on me." There was a shade of contempt in Zukovich's tone, as if Toland's facility with Vietnamese somehow invalidated his experience of the horse. He said, "Where were you in-country?"

"Quang Ngai. A little village named Binh Nghia."

"Army?"

"Marines. Combined forces."

Zukovich nodded. "I heard of you guys. A lot of you went native."

Toland turned away as if he didn't care what Zukovich had heard. He was a man with an agenda, and I was it. "What about Bodine, Lieutenant Fortner? Is he free to go?"

Fortner, still teetering like a soft boulder on the edge of Zukovich's desk, was gazing at Dirk Toland. He said, "What kind of work did the dead woman do at your company, Mr. Toland?"

"Le Thanh Chi was a camera operator. The night-shift supervisor said he already told your people that. Or maybe you don't believe I'm who I say I am? You could call the shop and have the super corroborate—"

"No need for me to do that, Mr. Toland. A paycheck from Midwest Micrographics, signed by you, was found in the woman's house. If I asked to see your driver's license I'm sure we'd get a match, wouldn't we?"

"What about Mr. Bodine?"

Fortner shrugged. "I appreciate your candor in clearing up his connection to this case. He's free to go."

Toland motioned toward Hung. "What about him?"

"He stays. Neighbor across the street from his place says she saw him threaten the deceased with a butcher knife late last summer. Chased her out of the house into the street. Everyone in the neighborhood saw it, too. She moved out on him after that. Should have stayed out, but that's moot. We're going to charge him, and that's not. Beat it, Black Jack."

I got up.

Fortner stayed me with a finger that looked like an articulated bratwurst. "You know Lieutenant Smith over at the state police?"

"I know of him."

"Well, I'll be informing Smitty that our paths have crossed."

Dirk Toland said, "What do the state police have to do with this?"

"Nothing as yet. But Lieutenant Smith is the acting commander of the Private Investigation Division. He monitors PIs statewide and he'll certainly be pleased to know that private investigator Bodine has been cooperating with officials of the Lansing Police Department." Fats Fortner winked meaningfully.

I winked back. Or maybe it was a nervous tic.

# 11 ◄◄◄

As we left the squad room and walked over to the elevator, Toland told me what he thought of creeps who took advantage of distraught women like his wife. He wasn't talking about Agnew, either, but that wasn't why I suggested he shut his mouth. Toland refused to stop venting his opinion of me, however, so I nudged him and nodded at the guy wearing the plain-toed shoes and the plain gray poplin raincoat who was plainly listening to Toland's estimation of my character. He was a plainclothes dick and he was waiting for the elevator, too. After a second glance at the cop, Toland shut up.

The elevator showed up and the three of us got on and stood in silence. The light from the elevator's fluorescent fixture made the dick's face look as gray as his raincoat. His eyes, however, remained as shiny and black as his shoes. Neither Toland nor I looked at him, but the dick looked at us—me, then Toland—back and forth, his head oscillating like a radar dish. From Homicide it's only five floors to the street, but it seemed like we were sinking to the center of the earth.

When we hit the ground floor Toland followed me out of the station onto Michigan Avenue. The dick had taken the elevator down to the basement, so we were alone on the street. It was after nine and quite dark, but I could see Toland just fine in the light reflecting off the illuminated dome of the capitol. He still hadn't warmed up to me.

"I don't care if your wife is Nora's boss," he said, picking up where he left off. "I saved your ass in there, so as far as I'm concerned we're even."

I said, "The lie you just told Lieutenant Fortner is far larger than my ass. I could lose my license."

"The way you've handled this, Bodine, maybe that's a good thing."

Two oversize garage doors seal off the bowels of the Lansing Police Station from the outside world. While Toland and I were busy squaring off, the right metal door rolled up with a clatter and a gray sedan nosed up out of the basement. The driver paused at street level and stared at us. I was pretty sure it was the gray-faced dick from the elevator. I gave him an all's-well wave and offered my hand to Toland, turning so the dick in the cruiser could see us making up. Toland shook my hand grudgingly.

The dick wasn't impressed. He continued to sit there, the cruiser's exhaust condensing around the car in a cloud.

I nodded at the greenhouse windows of Jim's Tiffany Place just down the street and suggested to Toland that we stop in for a cup of coffee.

Toland said, "I've got to get home to Nora." He pulled his hand free of mine and started to turn away.

I said, "Toland?" I probably should have called him Dirk, just to show there weren't any hard feelings, but I didn't like his name. Nor did I like it that anyone who looked so much like me could be so unpleasant to a fellow as handsome as himself. "We've got to have a talk."

"About what?"

"About what happened tonight."

Toland said, "Look, your wife told me what you said to her over the phone, that you were working on the theory Agnew lied about kidnapping the baby. You had the idea that her Vietnamese father grabbed her and that Agnew was taking advantage of that to extort more money from Nora. Correct?"

"Yes, although that's not what I want to talk about."

"But the baby wasn't at Hung's house, was she? So you were wrong, weren't you? And now the police have got my name, don't they?" Instead of slugging me, Toland took a deep breath and expelled it through clenched teeth. "So, Nora and I appreciate the effort you've put into your investigation, but it hasn't worked out. Let's leave it at that. Send us a bill."

Toland's contempt for me was as thick as the dick's exhaust. I said, "What about the baby?"

"What about the baby?" Toland shouted.

The dick in the cruiser pulled out onto the street and drove past us, slowly. I didn't look at him, but I knew he was watching us with the same cold glare Toland was giving me. I said, "I can have your baby back for you tomorrow."

Toland, glancing at the cop, held up his hands as if he were trying to keep me at arm's length, waving them back and forth between us, warding off my good intentions. "You just keep out of this."

"What are you afraid of?"

Toland let me see that he wasn't afraid of anything, least of all me. "Did you hear me? I don't want you bothering Agnew about the baby."

"Have you got a way of getting the baby back without bothering him?"

"We're not getting the baby back!"

"What do you mean?"

"I am not using my father-in-law's money. I'm seeing Agnew tomorrow morning and he's going to refund the old bastard's dough."

"And the baby?"

"The baby stays with Agnew. He can get twenty thousand for her easy."

102

I said, "I'm trying hard to fathom you, but I just can't reach bottom."

"Listen to me! Nora's father is the most miserable prick who ever lived. When I told him I wanted to marry his daughter he told me to my face I wasn't good enough. You know why? Because he was West Point and I wasn't anything but a grunt. I had my dress blues on. He looked at my uniform like I was wearing vomit. A couple years later he told me we lost the war because we weren't as good as his generation. He won the big one, beat Hitler and Tojo, and all we had to handle was some guys in black pajamas and we couldn't do it. When Nora found out she shouldn't get pregnant her father said to me I was responsible for him not having any grandchildren because I'd made Nora sick, as if I'd infected her. He's humiliated me like that time and again and always in front of Nora. I've had to compete for her ever since the day I met her. She's worth it, believe me, or I wouldn't have put up with her father all these years. But it's been war. That man has tried to defeat my marriage, my pride at being Nora's husband. He's tried to displace me, to steal her from me. Time and again. You hear me?"

I nodded.

But Toland wasn't finished. He pounded his fist into his hand as he spoke, his voice cracking. "Four years ago the shipping outfit he runs in Maryland bought the microfilm company I managed here. He did it so he could make a misery out of my professional life, too. Having to report to him, it was hell. It was worse than Vietnam. Last year I had a chance to move to a rival company and I grabbed it. I had to take a cut in pay, but it was worth it to get out from under Nora's old man. I don't ever want to be under him again, and I'm not going to be. That money Nora borrowed from her mother, it's going back."

I said, "A guy like that, what do you care what he thinks, or if you use his money and not your own?"

"If I let Agnew keep my father-in-law's money, Mai won't be

mine. She'll be his because that old man's money will have paid for her. And as long as he lives he'll be telling me I couldn't have got a baby without him. His money would make him the father of my child, not me. Do you understand?"

Toland's eyes were watering. I knew the gray-faced dick had driven off, but I looked around for him anyway. I didn't want to see the tears that were threatening to spill down Toland's cheeks. "No," I said finally. "I don't understand."

Toland, his voice choked, said, "Mai was a sweet kid. I feel . . . I feel like I did in the war. I lost guys. They were only a couple years younger than me, but they were like my kids. I got over it, though. And Nora will get over Mai. We're not weaklings, Nora and I. So that's it, Mr. Bodine." Knuckling his eyes, Toland turned away and headed toward his car, a subcompact he'd parked in the restricted zone in front of the station. The hazard lights were flashing.

I said, "Toland!"

He paused with the door open. "What?"

"You'll be heading right past my car. How about giving me a lift?"

He hesitated. "Where is it?"

"East out Michigan where the woman was killed tonight."

Toland hesitated, then nodded and got into his car.

I walked over to it—a slice of sushi called a Toyota Tercel —and packed myself in. Toland made a U-turn just as the gray-faced dick from the elevator cruised the station again, looking for us.

We headed out Michigan, Toland driving in silence, Omar's and Velvet Fingers blurring by.

I said, "You planning on getting a refund on the seven grand you gave Agnew at the hospital, too?"

"I don't know, Bodine. I guess he'll keep the seven for services rendered." Toland added morosely, "Speaking of services, exactly how much do I owe you?"

"I'll let you know when it's all over."

"It's all over right now."

"I don't think so," I said. "We've got a pretty good police force in Lansing. And there's been a murder—"

"I know there's been a murder," Toland cried. "I know that," he said again, lowering his voice. "Thanh Chi has been killed. I know that."

"How well did you know this Thanh Chi?"

"She worked for me. I make a point of knowing all the people who work for me. Otherwise we weren't personal friends or anything. She didn't see us often during the pregnancy."

"My wife said she thought you were particularly upset to hear of her death."

"Of course I was upset. But we weren't what you'd call personal friends."

"Do you have any idea why she went back to her husband after being separated from him for almost a year?"

"I've been paying her way ever since she had the baby, but I told her I couldn't afford to keep on doing it, that she'd either have to come back to work or get a job somewhere else and start taking care of herself. So she decided she'd try Hung again, see what he could do for her."

"When did you talk to her last?"

"This afternoon. She took a bus to the shop to get some back pay she had coming to her. I wrote her a check, and we talked briefly. Then I called a cab for her and she left."

"How come she never returned to work at your shop after having the baby?"

"I don't know. I think she had a hard time gaining back her strength after having Mai. She was thirty-eight years old. I think, too, she was worried about what the other Vietnamese women would say at the shop, her being that old and having a baby. She's not married to Hung, either."

I said, "You've got other Vietnamese working for you?"

"No big mystery, Bodine. Micrographics is a very competitive business. One place you can undercut your competitors is in labor costs. The Vietnamese I hire are all dependable, hardworking people who turn out quality fiche. They do this even though I pay below scale. They know I'm paying them less than they could make elsewhere, but it's not that much less. They're loyal to me because I guarantee them jobs so they can get their citizenship. They owe me, in other words, but I don't take advantage of them. They know I'm a fair man. It helps, too, that I speak their language and treat them with respect. They're good people."

"What about this character, Hung?"

"I don't know Hung. He doesn't work for me."

"What did you say to his mother back there at the station?"

"I told her I had some suck in this country and would see to it Hung would get off if the old woman took back everything she said to implicate you."

"How do you expect to get him off?"

"I don't know yet."

I said, "Have you got any idea why he dragged your baby-sitter out of her apartment yesterday?"

"When I talked to Thanh Chi this afternoon she said she told Hung she was worried about Xuan living alone, so he went and got her, fixed her up with a job in a Vietnamese restaurant."

"Why exactly was she worried about the girl?"

"I don't know. I think she just missed her."

"Like Nora misses her baby?"

"Don't get on that again."

I said, "My car's up ahead on the right, in that parking lot."

Toland swung into the lot between the wheelchair outfit and the print shop, his headlights glaring off the pitted chrome of my Chrysler. I said, "What if Hung tells the cops he's the baby's father and that you and Agnew worked a deal to get the child?"

"I made it clear to him his freedom depends on keeping his mouth shut about that."

"What about the translator? He heard everything you said to Hung in Vietnamese."

"He won't be a problem."

I said, "Let me tell you something, he's no egg roll. And then there's Hung's mother."

"She'll cooperate to save her son. You getting out, or what?"

"They'll be performing an autopsy on the dead woman soon and they'll discover she recently delivered a baby."

"It's been almost three months."

I said, "The guy at Sparrow Hospital is very thorough. There's no baby at Hung's house, so the cops'll check the records. When they come up with Mai's birth certificate they'll see the dead woman listed as her mother, and you as her father."

"They aren't going to look for any birth certificate."

I gestured beyond my car toward the house in which Hung and I had been arrested and which now was cordoned off with a yellow crime-scene tape. Lights were on inside and there were figures moving around. I pointed them out to Toland. "That's the house where Thanh Chi was killed, and those are evidence technicians inside."

"So what?"

"So what if there's a copy of the birth certificate on the premises?"

Toland watched the figures moving around in Hung's house.

I said, "They'll be knocking at your door wanting to know what your name is doing on that document. You'll explain that the woman was a surrogate mother for you and Nora, and they'll want to know why you didn't mention that fact tonight at the police station. And while they're at it they'll ask you where the baby is. And what are you going to say? Are you going to tell them the guy who arranged the surrogate deal repossessed the kid?"

Toland rubbed his face. "I'll tell them Nora took Mai to Maryland. That's where Nora's parents live."

"Is she going to be visiting them the rest of her life?"

Toland had a hard grip on the steering wheel. He sat there staring at his knuckles as if they were memories of Nora.

I said, "Anyway, all they have to do is put in a call to the cops in Maryland and they'll check to see if she's got the baby."

Toland sighed and squeezed his eyes shut. "I'll think of something."

"It seems to me you've got to get the baby, no matter what. There are three ways to do it. One, you can come clean with the cops, tell them you faked the surrogate deal, that Agnew kidnapped your baby and that you want them to get it back for you."

"No."

"It'll be a mess, but not nearly the mess you'll be in when they find out you tried a cover-up. You'll be looking at jail."

Toland said, "If I go to the police about Agnew, I'll lose my job."

"You can always find another job. And it'll be a lot easier without a prison record."

Toland, his emotions barely under control, said, "This place I manage, business depends on government contracts. You got to have a security clearance to handle those records. If they ever find out about the deal I made with Agnew, I can kiss my career good-bye."

"Who's going to tell them?"

"Agnew."

"Why would he do that? He's crooked. He's got as much to lose as you do."

"I don't want to risk it. And even if I did, the courts wouldn't give us the baby."

"You don't know that."

"Don't you get it? I'm not her father. I haven't got any legal claim to her."

"Agnew sure doesn't. And Hung doesn't either. Nora said he's not married to the woman. When I talked to Agnew earlier today he said a man not married to a woman who bears his child hasn't got a legal claim on the baby. As I see it, the baby's up for grabs. With any luck you might get a judge who's sympathetic to your obvious love for the child. The fact that she's lived with you and Nora for the past three months, and that you spent all this money and effort to get her, might just work in your favor."

Toland shook his head. "No."

"All right. Your second choice is to let Agnew keep the thirteen thousand from Nora's parents and to borrow another ten grand to pay him off."

"Don't you think I've tried that?"

"I don't know. But if you truly can't come up with the money, your third choice is to let me have a free hand to look into Agnew's operation. I can almost guarantee you'll get back the thirteen grand from Nora's father and the seven you paid Agnew up front. Not to mention the baby. With a little luck, and Nora's help, I can have her for you tomorrow."

Toland slammed his fist down on the dashboard. "I said no! I've made up my mind. All you have to do is stick with the story I gave the police at the station. You think you can do that?"

I said, "I do windows, Dirk, but I don't do perjury."

Toland stared at me.

I stared back.

He said, "What good is it being a private detective if you don't protect your clients?"

"You're not my client. Your wife is."

"What's the difference?"

"I'm beginning to think there's a world of difference."

Toland, his voice a menacing whisper, said, "I've had a very hard time convincing Nora that it's got to be my way and not some other way. I don't want you screwing that up, Bodine. Now get out of my car. And stay out of my life."

I got out of his car.

# 12 ◄◄◄◄

I got out of my car and stepped into my life, the locus of it, anyway, a three-bedroom ranch-cum-carport, lawn, kid, cat, and wife. The wife and the cat were curled up on the new couch waiting for me. Mercifully, the kid was not.

I shouldered the door shut and thumbed the dead bolt. Joyce set aside her *Barron's* and studied my expression, intent on reading my mood. It was like trying to read a sphinx, though. I said, "Hi there."

"You had a bad time with Nora Toland's husband, didn't you?"

I regarded Joyce enigmatically. "What makes you say that?"

"You want to talk about it?"

"If it will make you feel better."

She was silent a moment, then she said, "Can I fix you something to eat?"

"I'm not hungry."

"Can I call you an ambulance?"

I dumped my wallet, my change, and my keys into a coin basket in the top drawer of the buffet, pegged my jacket in the foyer closet, and made for the bathroom. As I tiptoed past Eddie's bedroom I was hailed drowsily. I paused and leaned in and asked him in a whisper why he was still awake.

"I got insomnia." He said this tiredly, but with a trace of pride, as if mastering adult skills were hard work, but nothing he couldn't handle if he put his mind to it.

"It's late and you've got school tomorrow."

"I been waiting for you to give me a bedtime kiss."

"I gave you a bedtime kiss at the police station."

"That didn't count."

"It's really late, Eddie."

"Dad!"

"What?"

"Where are you going?"

"To the bathroom."

"Will you bring me a glass of water?"

"Sure."

"Will you bring me an apple, too?"

"There aren't any apples in the bathroom."

"Come on, Dad."

No apples, just Eddie's inside-out clothing lying in piles on the bathroom floor. A wet towel was heaped under the sink and a sopping washcloth had been sucked into the bathtub drain, creating a scummy puddle into which the shower dribbled.

I flowed and flushed and stuffed Eddie's clothes down the laundry chute, gave the washcloth a twist and hung it up to dry. Then I rinsed out the tub. I snugged the shower fixture, but it continued to drip. The toilet was running, too. I set the tank top on the toilet seat and fiddled with the flapper and the tank began to fill.

Joyce leaned into the bathroom. "Your choices are Swedish meatballs, vegetarian lasagna, or stuffed cabbage."

"Whatever." I replaced the tank top and washed up.

"Jack, should I have called a lawyer instead of letting Dirk Toland handle it?"

I turned the water off. "What's Eddie said to you about the dead woman? You know, his reaction to it?"

"He was wired after we left the police station, but a million

111

words later I still can't say for sure what's going on inside him. You really don't care what I fix you?"

"How about braised loin of cat?"

"Don't let Pearl hear you say that."

"Pearl's deaf," I said. "I'm going to talk to Eddie."

He was lying on his side with his arm around his snow-white Santa Bear. Hudson's had been hawking Santa Bears a couple Christmases ago, ten bucks a bear with every fifty-dollar purchase. The bear was almost as big as Eddie and he loved it shamelessly. His other stuffed animals had been relegated to the foot of the bed. I sat next to him and said, "You bothered about what happened today?"

"I'm just hungry."

"It's very late, Eddie, and if I bring you something to eat, we'll have to go through the brushing-of-the-teeth routine and all the rest of it, and I know you're tired. Here's your glass of water, by the way. Sit up and hold it with both hands so you don't spill it."

He sat up and slurped at the glass. I took it from him and set it on the dresser. "Now, I want to say something to you."

"I know, go to sleep."

"What I want to say is . . . well, it's awful to see somebody dead, isn't it?"

"I guess so."

"It's even worse if you see somebody dead who's been killed by another person. Right?"

"'Cause that's murder."

"Yes. And that's what you saw today, somebody who'd been murdered. And I'm sorry you saw it."

"Was it the first time you saw somebody that was murdered?"

"No, it wasn't."

"How old were you when you did?"

"I don't remember. But I was a lot older than you."

"How old?"

"The point is that even though I was older than you, I still think about it. And I know I'll think about it for the rest of my life. And the lady I saw this evening, I'm going to think about her, too. And so are you. The two of us are going to have that sad and scary thing between us forever. But even so, it's not going to keep us awake at night. You know why?"

"Because if it does, we'll just get something to eat?"

"No. Because as soon as I find out why the lady was killed, I'm going to tell you all about it, everything. You'll get the truth from me. And then, when you understand why it happened, it won't seem quite as scary and depressing."

"But the Vietnamese man did it. He—"

"We don't know that, Eddie. We don't know that for a fact. And even if he did do it, we don't know why. And that's what I'm going to find out. Because I don't let things fool me, especially bad things people do. I figure them out. And when I do, those things lose their power over me, and I can sleep at night."

"Even if you're hungry?"

"So, until I figure out why the lady was killed, I can't do much for you except tell you that I love you, and that you've got to be brave and close your eyes and snuggle up to Santa Bear. And if anything bothers you or Santa Bear, Mom and I will be right out there in the kitchen, and you can call us. Okay?"

"Okay."

I leaned down and hugged him and kissed him. He hugged me and kissed me and I hugged and kissed Santa Bear and headed for the door.

Eddie said, "Are you guys having popcorn?"

Joyce had turned on the microwave a few minutes ago and Eddie could hear the blower. "No," I said, "no popcorn."

"What's Mom making?"

"A frozen dinner."

"For you?"

"Yes."

"What kind?"

"I don't know."

"Don't you care?"

"I'm not really hungry."

"I am."

"Please try to sleep, Eddie."

I went into the kitchen and sat down behind a sheet of paper toweling that had been folded in half and sprinkled with utensils. Joyce, globbing a spoonful of cottage cheese onto a plate, said, "How'd it go?"

"You think I ought to get him something to eat?"

"We had popcorn and an apple just before you came home."

"Yeah, but he really seems—"

"Topped off with a tin roof sundae. This is after a nine-piece chicken McNuggets and a large fries."

"It just came to me what I want for dinner."

"How'd it go with Dirk Toland? Did he tell the police anything about the dead woman being a surrogate?"

"No."

"Did Agnew get mentioned?"

"No."

"The baby?"

"Nope."

"Then how did Toland explain the fact that you were following that Vietnamese man?"

"He told them he hired me to tail the guy's wife, said she worked for him at his microfilm shop, and that he suspected her of employee theft."

Joyce glanced at me. "And the police bought it?"

"I'm here, aren't I?"

"Mostly. There seems to be a little something missing." She tapped her temple.

"I'm still pondering the menu."

The microwave beeped. "Too late to change your mind." Joyce plucked a plastic pouch out of the oven, slit it open with a knife, and shook a tangle of steaming parsleyed noodles onto a plate. She knifed a second bag, poured lumpy brown gravy over the noodles, and set the plate in front of me.

114

I hesitated, remembering my meal at Nguyen's Nook. "These are Swedish meatballs, right?"

"Imported from Stockholm." Joyce sat down across from me and wiped her hands on a dishtowel. "Do you think the police will find out Toland lied to them?"

I picked up a fork and nudged the noodles. "Depends."

"On what?"

"Lots of things."

"What about the Vietnamese man they arrested? Won't he tell them he's the baby's father, and not Toland?"

I toyed with a meatball. "Toland assured the guy he'd get him off if he kept his mouth shut."

"How can he possibly get him off?"

"I don't know. And even if he does, the autopsy will most likely show that the dead woman recently gave birth. I explained to Toland that the cops will check the records, find his name on the birth certificate, and ask him why he didn't tell them he was involved in a surrogate arrangement with the victim."

"The police will realize you lied to them, too, won't they?"

"Yep."

Joyce studied me. "You aren't worried about that?"

"I can't be."

"Jack?"

"Yes?"

"Do you want to lose your license?"

"No."

"I mean, I'd feel terrible. I got you involved in this and I just—"

"Don't worry about it."

"What I'm worried about . . . I mean what I'm really worried about is that you'll lose your license . . . sort of on purpose."

"Ah."

"I'm not trying to pressure you. I'm just—"

"You're just worried about me."

"Yes."

"I understand. I appreciate that. And believe me, I don't want to lose my license."

"But still, you let Nora's husband put you in a hell of a position with the police."

"Joyce, you remember last year when we had those windows replaced, how the guy who did the job said the whole secret to doing it was not to be afraid of the windows?"

"Yes?"

"You know what he meant, right? Windows break if you drop them. There's a risk. But you've got to take the risk and be in charge of the windows or they'll be in charge of you. If that happens, you'll take forever to get the job done and in the end you'll probably drop one anyway. Right?"

Joyce nodded. "But what does this have to do with the police?"

"In my line of work it's not bad guys you have to worry about. They're not, so to speak, the windows. It's the police. You can't be afraid of them. You respect them, but you aren't afraid of them or you'll never get your work done. Just like a matador who's afraid of bulls, or a wide receiver who's afraid of cornerbacks, you get afraid of cops and you're done."

Joyce didn't say anything, but I knew what she was thinking.

"And I haven't been hanging around the house because I'm afraid of cops," I said. "That's not it. It's just that I didn't think I was accomplishing anything doing the work I've been doing, you know, taking the kind of cases we used to take, Dad and Ed and I. Dad's dead now, Ed's sick, and I'm tired of helping people get out of one bad marriage so they can get into another, or of finding people who don't want to be found. That kind of work, I was doing it for other people, not for myself. And I realized today, talking to Eddie, that I like the work I do, but I've got to be doing it for me."

Joyce gave this speech a shrug, as if to say, So what's the problem?

"What I'm getting at is this," I said. "From now on I won't be

taking every case that comes down the pike. Only those cases
—like Nora Toland's—that interest me. Even if I never get paid.
Which puts a lot of the burden on your shoulders."

Joyce said, "We can manage on what I make."

"I know we can. I just wanted you to know what's going on up
here." I touched my forehead. "I'd have told you a long time ago,
but I just never got it thought through till this afternoon with
Eddie, thinking out loud."

"Maybe you should try thinking out loud more often."

"I'm going to take you up on that right now."

"Nora's case?"

I nodded. "There's—"

Eddie called to us from the bedroom.

Joyce started to get up.

I said, "I'll check on him." I went into Eddie's room. "What's
the matter, partner?"

"What's *autopsy* mean?"

"Well . . . that's something doctors do. Why?"

"I heard you and Mom talking about it."

"You want me to close your door so we won't bother you?"

"No. I just wondered what it means."

"It's kind of a grown-up thing to talk about, but I'll make you a
deal. You get to sleep, and I promise I'll tell you about it in the
morning. Okay?"

"Do they really cut you open when you die?"

"Where'd you hear that?"

"Tory Zukovich. He said when you die they cut your guts out
and saw off the top of your head."

"You believe everything Tory says?"

"Do they really do it?"

I hesitated. "Sometimes."

"Why?"

"In order to find out why a person died."

"Are they going to give the lady an autopsy?"

"Yes. If somebody's been murdered, they have to. It's the law."

"Dad?"

"Yes?"

"It's too bad you didn't go into the lady's house a little bit sooner. Then maybe she wouldn't have been murdered and they wouldn't have to cut off the top of her head."

I heard the flooring creak and knew Joyce was listening from the hallway. I said to Eddie, "I guess you're right."

Eddie said abruptly, "Good night."

"Good night." I adjusted his blankets, gave him another kiss, and stepped out into the hall.

"I'm sorry I gave you that look at the station," Joyce whispered. We went into the kitchen. "Did you hear what he just said?" I asked.

"Yes. But it's not your fault."

"I mean about autopsies. He still doesn't get it that when you're dead, you're dead."

Joyce said, "I don't either."

I glanced down at my plate. It was empty. "Where's my food?"

"You ate it."

"What are you talking about? I'm not even hungry."

"Not now, you aren't."

I snatched a Kaliber out of the refrigerator. Guinness Kaliber is a miracle of modern brewing. It contains virtually no alcohol, but tastes nearly as good as regular beer. If only the boys at Jack Daniel's could do the same for Tennessee whiskey. I keyed off the cap and took a long pull. The foil around the neck of the bottle was rough against my lips.

"You wanted to talk to me about Nora's case?"

I said, "All my tough talk about the cops aside, I meant what I said about not wanting to lose my license. And if ever I had a case where it might happen, it's this one. You see, I don't think Mr. Hung killed the woman."

"Mr. Hung?"

"The Vietnamese man I found standing over that woman's body."

"But you told the police he did it."

"No. I told them what I saw, which was Hung standing beside the bed, his fists clenched, the woman lying on her back, arms at her sides."

"But you said over the phone he was some kind of karate freak, and that he was drunk."

"Right. But the dead woman just didn't look like she'd died taking karate chops."

"Because of the position of her body?"

"It's not how she would have ended up if Mr. Hung had been knocking her around," I said.

"Unless he suddenly regretted what he'd done and picked her up and laid her on the bed."

"True."

"You also said you heard him arguing with her just moments before you went into the house."

"I heard him arguing with a female who was speaking a foreign language, possibly Vietnamese."

Joyce went to the counter. There was an open bottle of Pinot Noir next to the microwave and she poured herself a glass. She said, "Eddie told me that the man's mother showed up at the scene a short time after the arrest?"

"Right."

"You think she could be the one you heard arguing with her son?"

"I don't know. Maybe the woman I saw on the bed was still alive and shouting when I heard the voices. But if she wasn't, then it could have been the guy's mother or even the Tolands' baby-sitter, Xuan. Or someone else altogether. And that person would have heard me yelling that I was the police and could have made an easy exit out the back door. By the way, how did you know the old woman was Hung's mother?"

Joyce shrugged. "The same way you know he's innocent."

"I'm not a hundred percent sure, that's why I didn't say anything at the station. All I know for certain is that I had a glimpse of the woman lying there and I didn't see any marks on her. I also know that the same day Nora Toland's baby was kidnapped, Mr. Hung hauled Xuan out of her apartment and took her to live with him and her mother, who just happened to move back in with Hung almost a year after having left him."

Joyce watched me finish my beer and said, "That's why you acted on the hunch that it wasn't Agnew who kidnapped the baby?"

I nodded.

"But you said you didn't see any evidence of a baby at the woman's house."

"Maybe I missed it. Or maybe the killer took the kid and all its things, too."

Joyce thought this over. "Why do that?"

"Because you wouldn't want the cops to know it had been there. They'd start looking for it and if they found it in your possession, you'd have some difficult questions to answer."

Joyce asked uneasily, "When you say 'you,' who have you got in mind?"

"I have a very bad feeling about Dirk Toland."

Joyce cocked her head to one side. "You're thinking that he . . . what are you thinking? That he killed the Vietnamese woman?"

"Let's don't forget Nora."

Joyce scoffed at this. "She was with me all afternoon."

"Till when?"

"Till five thirty, when she called her husband from Clara's."

"And afterward?"

"I don't know. I left. But I know you're on the wrong track."

"Because you like her?"

"Yes, I like her. But the point is, I've worked with her long enough now that I just can't believe . . . I mean, she's a rational, sensible, straightforward woman who just would not commit murder. Anyway, there are other explanations for the woman's death that make more sense, a burglar or . . . what about Agnew? Maybe the Vietnamese woman decided to blackmail him. She would have known he was involved in the phony surrogate deal."

"True. But the thing I keep coming back to is the fact that the baby disappeared the same day Hung brought his stepdaughter and his wife back home to live with him."

"Maybe that's just a coincidence."

"I hate coincidences."

"If Agnew didn't kidnap the baby," Joyce said, "then doesn't it qualify as a coincidence that someone stole it just when Agnew happened to pay his visit to Nora?"

"You know," I said, "if they stop making this beer, it'll be called ex-Kaliber."

"Answer my question."

"Look, Joyce, I can't see a couple of Vietnamese refugees who can barely speak English attempting to force a blackmail deal with Sam Agnew."

"But you can see them stealing back their baby from the Tolands?"

"Yes."

"All right," Joyce said, "let's say the Vietnamese did kidnap the baby. That doesn't mean the Tolands are involved in the woman's death. After all, Agnew would have to assume that eventually the Tolands would pay him what he asked for the baby. In fact, Nora tried to do just that. And he took her money and said she owed him more. Why? Because he didn't *have* the baby. But he knew he had to come up with it. He couldn't keep putting the Tolands off indefinitely."

"But why would he figure the Vietnamese had it?" I said.

"Because Dirk Toland went to him and accused him of kidnapping it. But Agnew knew he didn't take it . . . assuming he didn't. So he would have asked himself who else would be motivated to steal the baby, and he would have come up with the Vietnamese. Don't forget, that's exactly the same line of reasoning you used when you decided to follow the Vietnamese man from the restaurant."

I thought about having a second Kaliber. The nice thing about guzzling Kalibers was that you could drink and think at the same time, all night long if you wanted to. I said, "You've got a flair for this, Joyce."

"Anyway, Agnew found out where the Vietnamese people lived, and . . . Jack, we know he's a crook."

"I thought you rather liked him."

Joyce ignored this. She said, "It could be that when Nora went to him this morning and gave him her parents' money, Agnew stalled, telling her she had to come up with more. Then, later in the day, he went to the woman's house and tried to take the baby away from her. He's a powerfully built man. The Vietnamese mother resisted, and he hit her and ran out with the baby. When you got there she'd already been dead a while. This man, Hung, he found his mother in the house and . . . who knows, maybe he thought she killed the woman? They argued and the old woman ran out when you knocked on the door." Joyce raised her eyebrows. "Well?"

"Possible, but unlikely."

"Why?"

Joyce watched me peel the foil off the neck of my Kaliber. I said, "Because as an explanation it's too complicated."

"The simplest explanation is that Mr. Hung's guilty."

I nodded. "Let's just say I'm keeping an open mind."

Joyce was flushed, and not from the wine. "So, what are you going to do?"

"I'm going to call Ed's gofer and make sure he's not sitting behind Omar's. Then I'll sack out before testing the various hypotheses."

"Test them how?"

"Early tomorrow morning I'll pay Nora a surprise visit. If the baby isn't there, then I'll proceed on the assumption Agnew's got it. But if it is there—"

Joyce said abruptly, "There's a good chance it will be. Nora told me Dirk's going to pay off Agnew and get the baby back."

"When did she tell you that?"

"I talked to her on the phone just half an hour ago. I was worried about you, so I called her to see if Dirk had gone downtown yet, and she said he had and that he promised her before he left that he would let Agnew keep her father's money and do whatever was necessary to raise the extra ten thousand. She said Dirk vowed he would get the baby back as soon as possible, maybe even as early as tomorrow."

I shook my head. "Half an hour ago he told me he was going to see Agnew and demand a refund of his father-in-law's money."

"Oh, dear."

"There were tears in his eyes, Joyce. He meant it."

"But what about the baby?"

"Toland assumes Agnew will sell the kid to someone else. He said Nora's already agreed to let that happen."

Joyce shook her head angrily. "That's not what Nora's expecting at all." She leaned toward me. "Nora said this afternoon at Clara's that she never felt better than she did during those three months when she had that baby. It was almost like a wonder drug. But the day Agnew kidnapped the baby she started getting pains again. I told her to take tomorrow off, she looked so pale. She needs that child, Jack. You can't let Dirk Toland deprive her of it because of his silly pride."

I balled up the foil I'd scratched from the neck of the beer bottle and tossed it toward the wastebasket. "Dirk Toland told me to keep out of his life."

"What did you tell him?"

I watched the ball of foil skitter toward the floor register. "I told him he wasn't my client. His wife was."

Joyce looked both worried and relieved.

I said, "Are you sure I ate my dinner?"

# 13 ◄◄◄

Early the following morning, a sunny Thursday, I drove over to East Lansing and found a spot from which to watch the Tolands' Tudor, a cul-de-sac some ten doors down that offered a secluded if distant view of the left rear fender of Dirk Toland's Toyota. Daffodils were everywhere, yellow as the sun.

A few minutes after eight a tall man wearing a coat and tie left the Toland house and backed the little red Tercel into the street. A quick look through the still-smeared lenses of my Bushnells confirmed that the driver was Dirk Toland. I sat tight, polishing the lenses of my binoculars.

By nine o'clock I felt pretty certain Toland was gone for the day, so I left my car, walked up the tree-lined street, and rang Nora Toland's doorbell.

Nesting sparrows chattered at me from the Baltic ivy that clung thickly to the broad chimney towering over the slate threshold.

I pushed the bell a second time.

On the third ring Nora Toland answered. She was wearing an off-white Pierre Cardin robe with piping the same color as the circles beneath her eyes. Her complexion was off-white, too. I said, "Good morning."

Nora smiled.

A sparrow shat on my shoulder.

Nora groaned and said, "Oh no! Oh, Jack, come in. I'll take care of it."

I went in.

"Quick, give me your jacket."

I took off my suit coat and followed her down a tiled hallway that led directly to the kitchen at the back of the house. Nora dabbed at the sparrow splat with a damp sponge, muttering apologies, water hissing from the tap. "Dirk said that was bound to happen what with those birds nesting up there, but I'm so fond of that ivy I just couldn't bear the thought of getting rid of it."

I said, "Sometimes we get attached to things and regret it later." This remark wasn't a gem of subtlety, but it was more or less to the point.

Nora, scrubbing furiously at the dollop of doo, stopped and glanced up apprehensively. "What do you mean?"

I nodded at my suit coat. "When you get the baby back you and Dirk both better be prepared for fallout of the kind you're attending to there. Or have you already got her back?"

"No, but we will. Dirk's seeing someone this morning about a loan."

"Did he say who?"

"No. Just that it was an old friend."

"Did he mention the talk we had last night?"

"Yes. Briefly. Mostly we talked about the money I'd borrowed from Mom and Dad. It was hard for him to accept the fact that I'd done that, but he stuck to his promise to let the loan stand." Her voice faltered. "I love him very much. And we're going to get Mai back. He said he would arrange for the extra ten thousand this morning. Everything's going to be all right." Nora smiled through her fatigue, and I saw that she was in a pretty good mood, tired yet fulfilled, like a woman who'd just given birth. She said, "And Jack, I want to thank you from the bottom of my heart for all you've done. Especially for not mentioning our involvement with Mr. Agnew to the police."

126

"Are you sure Dirk changed his mind about accepting money from your parents?"

"Yes."

"He told you that? Specifically?"

"Yes. Last night. Before he left to go to the police station, and then again after he came home. He said this morning that we'll have Mai by the end of the day. Tomorrow at the latest." She gave me a second look and frowned. "Why do you ask? Specifically?"

I took a deep breath. "I'm sorry, Nora, but that's not what Dirk told me he was going to do."

Nora stopped scrubbing my suit coat. She stopped looking fulfilled, too. Nor did she look very much in love with her husband. "You're saying Dirk lied to me?"

"I suppose he could have had a change of heart, but last night he made a very emotional statement of his intention to leave Mai with Agnew and demand your parents' money in exchange."

Nora shook her head violently. "When Dirk left this morning he said Agnew could keep Mother's money. He said he was going to see a friend to get the extra ten thousand dollars. He promised!"

I said, "Maybe that's what he's doing. I feel like a terrible tattletale, but you're my client and I want you to know what I know. Or what I think I know."

"Which is?"

"Well, once he gets your mom's money back from Agnew I'm guessing he'll tell you that the refund is the money he's supposedly out borrowing this morning. Then, when you see Agnew to make the ten-grand payoff, you'll discover the baby's been sold to someone else. That will leave Dirk free to reimburse your parents while claiming he did everything he could to finance the baby's return, but too late. I hope I'm wrong, Nora, but I feel obliged to tell you what I suspect."

Nora Toland sagged against the sink and stared at my suit coat, cradling it in her arms as if it were her lost child.

I didn't know what to say, so I didn't say anything.

After a moment Nora gave the suit coat back to me and went to a cupboard and brought out a bottle of orange pills and a three-inch-square packet of something called Questran. She ripped open the packet, dumped the contents into a glass of water, and stirred. The water turned yellow and thick and she drank it, washing down two of the orange pills, grimacing as she swallowed. She set the glass down and breathed a deep, tension-filled sigh. "I wonder what she said to provoke him."

"Who?"

"The Vietnamese woman. I'll never understand why she went back to that man."

I didn't see any reason to mention my hunch that Hung was innocent. I said, "I don't know, Nora. He was drunk, full of anger." I put my coat on, smoothing the damp shoulder and tugging the lapels. I said, "Anyway, that's the bad news. The good news is I've got the names and addresses of Sam Agnew's sitters. They're expecting Dr. Joyce O'Connell, M.D., and her lawyer, barrister Bodine, any time after ten this morning. By the way, did you mention to Dirk the little scam Joyce and I worked on Agnew yesterday?"

"No."

"Good. What I want is for the two of us to pay those women a visit. Agnew won't be with us, so we'll gain entry to his sitters' homes with you pretending to be Joyce."

"I—"

"Listen to me. You're interested in becoming a surrogate mother, but you're not all that keen on this business of Agnew's one-week waiting period. So you've insisted on meeting his sitters to make sure they're competent. We don't have to carry it too far. All we want is to find out if the baby's on the premises. I want you to accompany me because you know what Mai looks like. We don't want to kidnap the wrong kid, do we?"

"Kidnap?"

"I don't suppose it's really kidnapping. In any case, we'll take possession of her and I'll drive you directly to the airport. You'll spend some time with your mom and dad. I'll handle Agnew. And Dirk."

"But . . . the police?"

"Agnew's up to his ears in a scheme to extort money from you. He won't call the cops. The main thing is to get the baby away from him before he makes arrangements with another couple."

There was a wall phone in the kitchen and it pealed. Nora flinched. The phone rang a second time and Nora said, "I'll listen to the answering machine." She left the kitchen and I followed her down the hallway toward the foyer. She turned into a study just off the foyer, a small, pleasantly book-crammed space with a Queen Anne table desk, a dark blue leather lounge chair, and an answering machine just like mine, an Answertech 500. It came to life after the third ring and a deep voice said brusquely, "This is Dirk Toland. What is your message?"

The machine beeped and the worried voice of an elderly woman said, "Nora, it's Mother. I know you told me not to get upset, but, sweetie, I just can't help it. Please give me a call. I've got to go out this morning, but I'll be home all afternoon. Daddy still doesn't know about . . . you know what, but—"

Nora picked up the receiver and tapped a button, cutting off the loudspeaker. She said, "Mother? Yes, I'm all right. Yes, everything's . . . all right." Nora glanced at me.

I said, "Tell her you want to pay her a visit."

Nora nodded.

I left the study and stepped across the hallway into the living room. It was a large room with a cavernous English-style fireplace, ashes cold on the grate. Early morning light flooded the room. Motes floated through sunbeams. I could hear Nora's voice in the study, but I couldn't make out what she was saying. I had no trouble tuning in to Zook Zukovich, however, my antenna having turned toward the future, toward a time when Zook would say, "You're a fool, Bodine."

I heard Fats Fortner add, "Just what did you think you were doing?"

Sergeant Smith at the state police remarked, "I'm going to blow my nose on your license."

My lawyer just shook his head, and Joyce dabbed at her eyes as the judge pronounced sentence.

I heard little Eddie cry out, "But Judge, my daddy did it because he likes helping people!"

And the entire courtroom exploded with laughter.

I laughed with them. After all, I didn't know Nora Toland from Debra Winger, whom she resembled slightly. I mean, if I was hot for a Debra Winger look-alike, it would all make sense to Zukovich. And maybe to me, too. But I wasn't hot for Nora Toland, who, for all I knew, would end up making a rotten mother.

"So, what did you think you were doing, Bodine?"

"I don't know, Zook. I guess I just liked her living room."

Which was true. The furniture, new but traditional, had been upholstered in a heavy, tapestry-type brocade, mostly muted patterns. The hardwood floors had been refinished recently and the walls looked freshly painted. There was a thirties-vintage breakfront buffet against one of the walls with a set of Japanese prints hanging above it. The art in the room was otherwise abstract, all by the same painter, a guy whose sense of line and color worked surprisingly well with the period furniture. Interestingly, there weren't any drapes on the windows, just miniblinds of the same color as the walls—antique white—which reinforced the sense of airiness. Several healthy and appropriately placed plants brought it all together.

"You liked her living room?"

"I admired her taste, felt comfortable with it, which coincided with my feelings toward her."

"Hey, what makes you think the hubby didn't have something to do with decorating the living room?"

"You got me there, Zook."

"That's not the only place I got you. So why'd you do it?"

"I'll tell you. I held back pertinent information from you and committed a quasi-kidnapping for her because of the way she held my coat."

"Toss this jerk in the slammer!"

"Okay, the truth is, I did it for myself. I wanted to find out what was going on. I was curious."

"You sicko."

"All right, the real reason is . . . I was the best guy for the job. It's why I was born, to do this kind of work. God made me do it!"

"Jack?" Nora Toland was at my side.

I said, "What did your mother say?"

"I told her I was coming. I called Piedmont, too. They have a three-ten flight to Dayton. I make connections there."

"Good."

Nora regarded me as if she were searching for signs of goodness. She said, "I left word for Dirk on the answering machine."

"Word?"

"Yes. That's what we do instead of leaving notes. He can call the machine from his office. I told him I was out shopping."

I said, "Okay. Get dressed and packed. What with the baby and all you'll have plenty to carry, so pack only the necessities."

Nora, thinking about it, looked disheartened by the task.

I took her by the elbow and led her to the stairs. "Come on. I'll pack the baby's stuff and you can double-check my work when you get yourself squared away. Show me to the nursery."

She started up the stairs, gathering her robe in front of her.

The stairs, carpeted with a cheap, threadbare runner, creaked beneath our feet. I noticed by the light from a window above the second-floor landing that the plaster walls of the staircase were dingy and fingerprinted. The floors of the upper level hadn't been refinished, nor had any of the rooms into which I glanced as

Nora led me down the hallway, rooms covered with peeling wallpaper and sparsely furnished with what looked like second-hand furniture.

But the baby's room was another matter. Loving attention had been paid to every aspect of the redecoration, which was clearly a professional job from start to finish, three grand minimum, for which the Tolands had got a cleverly worked-out series of Disney-character murals on three of the walls and a set of built-in cupboards and cubbies on the fourth. The cupboards flanked a dormer window that had been finished with drapes of intricate lace. The empty crib was in a corner. It had all kinds of dangling doodads, two of which I remembered with a pang from Eddie's days as an infant: a windup musical mobile with a half dozen little rubber animals hanging from threads, and a play board that had been tied to the bars of the crib and featured a little telephone dial, a horn, a mirror, and other items that would someday be of interest to a crib-bound creature.

There were smells that hit me with a pang, too, the sweet scent of baby powder strongest among them. It stirred up memories of a time I'd long since forgotten, which I had no idea I'd find quite so moving. All the details of my day-to-day life with infant Eddie came rushing back as Nora opened the bottom drawers of the changing table and pulled out the Huggies (which rode up, as I recalled) and the Wet Ones (which dried out if you left them uncovered—but not to worry, you could add an ounce or two of water and a drop of No Tears baby shampoo and be right back in business). I had no desire to be back in business. I just had no idea that I would find my recollections of those days so full of a sense of loss.

Nora showed me the baby's carryall, a small plastic-coated suitcase. It had a shoulder strap and a flap-top opening and room inside for a day's supply of diapers and miscellany. She reeled off an assortment of things she thought she might need—a teething ring, paregoric, rattles, bottle liners, nipples, a pacifier, tissues

—and I noted them, but with a look that made her pause. "Jack, are you all right?"

Thinking of Eddie's room as it was now, rank with sweat-soaked sneakers and crammed with an array of mementoes ranging from Star Wars weaponry to Bruce Springsteen posters, I almost said, "No, Nora, I'm not all right. I miss my baby, too." But us private eyes don't ever think such things, much less voice them, little things I hadn't thought of in years, the way I used to make a point of putting Eddie to sleep on his stomach so he wouldn't choke if he burped up. Or how I always made sure his ear, like a plump little Sunmaid apricot, was smoothed out and not doubled up under his fuzzy skull, which, leaning down, I'd touch with my lips, not really kissing him, just touching him with my mouth, nuzzling him. Then I'd pull up his blanket and settle it softly over his shoulders so just his head and a minuscule fist were left peeking out from under it.

"Jack?"

I had tears in my eyes! I turned away from Nora, blinking, catching sight of a laundry basket full of baby clothes, all neatly folded. On top of the pile was the nightgown she'd mentioned at the diner yesterday morning. I reached down and picked it up. It was gray, with darker gray trim, just like the uniform blouse of a West Point cadet. Around the hem, as she'd said, were the Marine Corps and the West Point mottoes: SEMPER FIDELIS and DUTY, HONOR, COUNTRY.

I cleared my throat and said, "This is a nice gown. I'll pack it. Your mom will like that. Maybe your dad, too. Now go on, get ready. Wear something doctorish."

She turned to leave.

I said, "By the way, what about the formula?"

"Blue cans in the kitchen cupboard next to the range."

"Six-packs?"

She nodded.

"Smart. Now get dressed. I'll take care of everything here." I did, too, and without blubbering very much at all.

# 14 ◄◄◄◄

Forty-five minutes later Nora and I were turning into the driveway of one of Agnew's baby-sitters. Her name was Mrs. Isherwood and she lived among trees. A hackberry stood tall by her rural mailbox, and a little farther down her drive I saw a tree of heaven. There was a chinquapin oak, and, just across from it, an American hornbeam. I picked out a Chinese fringe tree, too, as well as a paperbark maple, a butternut, a common bald cypress, and an uncommon umbrella Hankow willow. Nora Toland, eyeing intently what there was to see of the small cottage at the end of the rutted drive, paid no attention to the deciduous diversity. I made no effort to point it out to her, either. She was girding herself for the recapture of her child. Anyway, if she wanted to know the names of the trees she had only to read the little plaques that someone had attached to each trunk.

Or almost each trunk. Here and there a number of Mrs. Isherwood's plaques had fallen out of their frames. Others, not having weathered well, were almost illegible. Her exotic groves were littered with deadfall, too. A large pine had toppled across what looked like a gazebo. The remains of the gazebo were matted with gray-green moss. As for Mrs. Isherwood's little house, it was covered with ivy where it wasn't obscured by the overgrown shrubs that stood almost as high as the display of intricate paint-flaked fretwork—a touch of Black Forest gingerbread—that decorated the eaves. Huge pines leaned over the house, blocking out the sunlight and muting the distant sounds of traffic. We were east of East Lansing, at the edge of things. Beyond Mrs. Isherwood's little forest you could walk for miles and encounter nothing but the occasional farm, probably abandoned.

We got out of the car. It was cold beneath the pines, and Nora Toland shivered as we mounted the wooden steps and clunked across Mrs. Isherwood's shrub-shrouded porch, pausing on her dark doorstep, the air rank with juniper. We could hear a baby bawling inside the house.

"Mai!"

"Take it easy, Nora. That might not be Mai. And if it's not, we don't want to say or do anything that would cause this sitter to tip off the one we haven't seen yet."

Nora nodded and knocked, rattling the panes of the dilapidated storm door, her breath ragged with anticipation.

"Remember," I said, "you're supposed to be a doctor. You're used to examining people. That's more or less what you're going to be doing to Mrs. Isherwood, examining her credentials. You talk your way into the nursery, get a look at the baby. If it's not Mai, you don't touch it. If it is Mai, you ask to hold her a minute. That's the signal. You say you'd like to carry her around while we look the place over. You drift toward the front door, then make a break for it. I'll hold off the sitter. Okay?"

Nora nodded, inhaling deeply.

The door opened and a little black girl peeked out at us, her eyes round with uncertainty.

Nora said, "Is your . . . is Mrs. Isherwood home?"

The little girl gaped at her.

"Sweetheart, we'd like to speak to Mrs. Isherwood."

The little girl closed the door in Nora's face. Nora stood there

135

a moment, then let out a muted cry of exasperation and raised her knuckles to the door.

"Give her a minute," I said.

"I don't think she understood."

"That's just a four-year-old's way of answering a door. Give her a minute."

Nora let out a deep sigh and began worrying the tortoiseshell handles of her purse, rubbing them with her thumb. "How do you know she's four?"

I had no idea how I knew. However, on our drive to Mrs. Isherwood's place I'd come to know that Nora Toland was a lot like Joyce O'Connell. If you made an assertion it was a good idea to have the data to back it up. So I said, "She looks five, but she'd be in school if she were. Unless she's got afternoon kindergarten."

But Nora was listening to the footsteps on the other side of the door. She raised her chin and swallowed dryly as the door swung inward and a pale woman stared at us through the dusty panes of the storm. She was paler than Nora, but not because of an illness. Hers was a haggard wanness that the Michigan poor seem to acquire over the long dark stretch of the Michigan winter, no tanning spas for them, no weekends schussing down the slopes of Boyne Highlands. Truth be told, I was a little pale myself. Nora said, "Mrs. Isherwood?"

The woman cracked the storm an inch. "Yes?" There was an odd mixture of defiance and defeat in Mrs. Isherwood's tone.

Nora said, "I'm Dr. O'Connell and this is Mr. Bodine, my attorney."

I smiled.

Fortunately, Mrs. Isherwood, who was not wearing her teeth, made no attempt to smile back. She looked as though she hadn't made any attempt to prepare for our visit, either. She was wearing a faded housedress and a pair of nylon stockings that were rolled down to her ankles. Her feet were stuffed into worn high-top sneakers, the kind you wear on a basketball court. Mrs.

Isherwood didn't appear to be out of breath, however, which wasn't to say she hadn't been exerting herself. I had the feeling that before answering her door she'd made a fierce effort to purge her stark face of its habitual anxieties. "What do you want?"

Nora said, "Mr. Agnew arranged for us to talk to you. May we come in?"

Mrs. Isherwood hesitated.

I said, "You weren't expecting us?"

"No." Mrs. Isherwood said this as if her expectations counted for very little.

"You mean Mr. Agnew didn't tell you we'd be coming?" said Nora.

Mrs. Isherwood looked us over again and seemed to see something she'd missed. "You're from Sam?"

I said, "My client, Dr. O'Connell, is considering becoming one of his surrogate mothers. She wanted to be reassured that her baby would be well cared for during the period prior to its placement. That's why we're interested in getting to know you."

Mrs. Isherwood said, "He never had any of the mothers come here before."

I said, "This is a very special situation, ma'am. We'd just like to have a brief chat with you. May we come in?"

The woman thought this over, frowning. To Nora she said, "You're a doctor?"

"Yes."

Mrs. Isherwood found this doubtful, but at the same time she didn't seem capable of trusting her own skepticism. She shrugged and pushed the storm door open and Nora went in ahead of me. The place smelled of freshly baked cookies. Stale dog would have been more likely, considering the decor. There was a moose head on one wall and an elk head on the other. Or maybe it was a caribou. Could have been a mountain goat for all I knew.

Mrs. Isherwood excused herself and disappeared down a hallway that led to the rear of the house. Nora Toland and I looked at one another but said nothing. A stuffed bobcat snarled at us from the mantel. Or maybe it was a lynx. Mrs. Isherwood returned with a jawful of teeth and said, "You want some coffee?"

Nora said, "No thanks, we'll just be a minute."

"Want to sit?" Mrs. Isherwood indicated a divan that had been upholstered with a fabric that was imprinted with ducks.

"No thank you," said Nora, thumbing the handles of her bag. "This won't take but a minute. Actually, we'd just like to look around."

Looking around, I caught sight of two items I could unequivocally identify: a .410-gauge, single-shot bird gun and a 30-30 lever-action rifle. The weapons were racked on antlers over the door and were festooned with cobwebs. The cobwebs were a good sign. There was always the possibility, though, that Mrs. Isherwood's nickel-plated .357 backup was well oiled, fully loaded, and ready to hand. I looked her over, but didn't see anything in the way of revolver-shaped bulges, which didn't mean her piece wasn't strapped to the inside of her thigh. Though probably not. Probably it was in her dresser, cool to the touch, lurking just below the satinette swirl of her intimate apparel by Argenti. Gazing again at Mrs. Isherwood, a faded woman in a faded housedress, I figured the odds against a handgun equaled the odds against the intimate apparel. But, of course, one never knew. The uncertainty imbued the impending pinch with an edge, and made one's heart skip when the baby we'd heard earlier let out a howl.

Nora, pretending a professional curiosity, said, "I take it you're currently caring for a baby for Mr. Agnew?"

"Two babies."

"I see. How long have you had them?"

Mrs. Isherwood shrugged. "Been here a day or two. You want to see the room they're in, or what?"

"Why, yes." Nora glanced at me. "Yes, we would."

Mrs. Isherwood, intercepting the look that passed between Nora and me, stiffened. It was as if she'd suddenly realized what we were up to. She said to me, "There's nothing illegal about it." This was almost a question.

I said, "Would we be here if there were?" This was almost not a question.

Mrs. Isherwood said, "Sam guaranteed me it wasn't against the law. He's got a lawyer said so."

"Then I'm sure you have nothing to worry about."

Mrs. Isherwood, who was frowning and biting her lip, did not appear convinced. It was as if the moose and the elk were whispering conflicting warnings.

The baby shrieked again and Nora headed for it, disappearing down a hallway. Mrs. Isherwood hurried after her and I brought up the rear, admitting to myself that I did not feel entirely comfortable with certain complications that had waited till now to suggest themselves, the little girl who'd answered the door, for instance. I didn't want her to see what we were about to do. Not that I was worried about her pointing a finger at me in court. It just seemed like a bad idea to kidnap one child in front of another. Then, too, a component of my unease was a direct function of the masculine influence that had been exerted on Mrs. Isherwood's decor. Where, after all, was the fellow who'd plinked that moose? If I were to presume for a sexist moment that moose-plinking was man's work, was the moose murderer at home, perhaps dandling little Mai on his knee while sporting a .44 Magnum on his hip?

I followed Mrs. Isherwood through the door to the nursery. Her hubby wasn't there, although evidence of his avocation was mounted on the pine-paneled wall: a fish with a gaping, fang-studded maw that would have given a great white shark a shock. It wasn't as big as a shark, but it was meaner-looking. Probably a muskellunge. There were other fish, too, but my main interest was in the cribs in the room, two of them, one baby to a crib. Nora was staring down at the infants, not reaching for them, just staring.

The little black girl was in the room, too, her eyes as dark and as wary as a fawn's, eyes that made you remember the terrible fate of Bambi's mother. Mrs. Isherwood stood over the little girl and said coldly, "What are you doing in here, Kisha?"

"Nothing."

"You know you're not supposed to bother the babies."

"But they were crying."

"Because you were bothering them."

"No, Mama. I—"

"You are not to call me Mama. I am not your mother."

"I know, but—"

"Don't ever forget that, Kisha." Kisha's eyes filled. There seemed to be enough water welling there to irrigate the Sudan. "Now, go to your room."

Kisha made a pigeon-toed departure, head down, hands behind her back, two fingers of one hand hard in the grip of the other. Her chin was trembling.

Mrs. Isherwood, satisfied of the exit, glanced from Nora to me. She seemed strangely proud of the effect she'd had on us. She said primly, "Kisha is a difficult child, but I do the very best I can."

The babies had stopped crying. This wasn't much of a relief because I could hear little Kisha sobbing in the next room. I wanted to leave. Neither of the babies looked in the least Oriental, but I glanced at Nora for confirmation that Mai wasn't here. Nora shook her head and I took a deep breath.

Mrs. Isherwood missed none of it. Whatever suspicions she had of us seemed now to be confirmed. Oddly, she appeared to relax. She said, "Are there any questions I can answer for you?"

She was looking at me when she said this, as if I were in charge of the deception. Which I was. I said, "No, I don't have any further questions. Except one. Where is Mr. Isherwood?"

She said coyly, "Sam didn't tell you?"

"No, I don't believe he did."

"Mr. Isherwood is dead."

"I see. I'm sorry."

"Why should you be?"

I thought of the squashed gazebo and the trees that were missing their plaques. I thought, too, of the neglected little girl in the room next door. I said to Nora, "If you have any follow-up questions for Mrs. Isherwood, why don't you get into that now and I'll just take a quick look around? Would you mind if I did that, ma'am?"

Mrs. Isherwood shrugged, her expression as smooth as still waters. "Suit yourself."

"Thank you. I'll just be a minute, Dr. O'Connell." I left the nursery and checked the kitchen. The cookies, laid out on a dish-towel, tempted me from the counter. I leaned into the stairwell that led to the basement and flicked the wall switch. I took a few steps down the creaking staircase and saw hundreds of dusty Mason jars, an ancient Kelvinator, and an even older wringer washer like the one my mother used to curse at and beat with a stick. There was some broken-down furniture, too, and an assortment of neglected power tools. In one corner of the basement a herd of mounted animal heads stared back at me with dusty eyes. I hustled back upstairs and glanced out the back door and saw a Ford Maverick with a bad case of Michigan cancer parked inside an open-ended structure that was something of a cross between a toolshed and a garage. Leaving the kitchen, I cruised the dining room. It was furnished with a heavy table and a set of chairs like the ones I'd noticed in the basement. Then back through the living room and into the hallway. Kisha was in the bedroom next to the nursery. I winked at her and went in. "You like babies, Kisha?"

She looked down at her hands and nodded.

In the adjacent room I could hear Nora making small talk with Mrs. Isherwood. I said, "Babies aren't much fun to play with though, are they?"

Kisha said, "They can't help it. They aren't fully developed."

I did not smile at this burst of precocity. "Is there another baby in the house for you to take care of?"

"No."

"Just the ones in there?" I nodded at the nursery.

"Yes." Kisha looked down at her hands again. "Are you going to take them away?"

"No."

"Good."

"Was there another baby that was taken away?"

Kisha nodded. "Lots of them."

"Recently?"

Kisha stared at me.

"You know, like last night or early this morning?"

"No."

"Kisha?"

"Yes?"

"Are you happy here?"

Kisha looked suddenly afraid. "You going to take me away?"

"No, that's not why I came." Kisha didn't look disappointed to hear this. I said, "But if you want me to, I could talk to some people and maybe get you out of here. Would you like to get away from Mrs. Isherwood?"

"No."

"Are you sure?"

Kisha nodded.

"Would you like me to come back and visit you sometime?"

Kisha shrugged.

I said, "Do you like Mrs. Isherwood?"

Kisha said, "We make cookies together."

"Well," I said, "they smell like awfully good cookies."

# 15 ←←←←

Nora and I drove in silence down Hagadorn Road, heading south along the eastern edge of the Michigan State campus. Off to the right was Hubbard Dorm, a towering escarpment of glass and brick with a sprawling tangle of bicycles racked out front. From the road the students' massed ten-speeds looked like a three-acre thicket of spokes. I was hoping Eddie would someday park a bike there, too. I guess my conversation with little cookie-loving Kisha had got me to thinking about Eddie's future.

Nora said, "I can't get that poor child out of my mind."

Off to the left, near Esoteric Way, stood the new Hannah Technology and Research Center. The center hadn't been there the last time I'd driven down Hagadorn Road. Eddie was with me that day, just a little guy, as I recalled. He had to stretch to see over the dashboard. The two of us had been visiting the university's sheep. I wondered if the sheep were still free to range over their modest ranch south of campus. I sure hoped they weren't confined to cramped stalls in the basement of the Hannah Technology and Research Center. It was an odd thing to worry about, but I couldn't seem to get that poor child out of my mind either.

Nora said, "While you were out of the room I asked that

woman exactly what her feelings were for the little girl and she said she didn't have any feelings for her at all. She said she was merely providing foster care. I told her I didn't think there was much care being fostered and she said it was strictly a business arrangement. She gave me the name of the adoption agency that placed the girl with her and said if I had any complaints I should talk to them, that she was only doing her job, which was to see to it that the girl was fed and clothed, period. She said there wasn't anything in her contract about little black girls being allowed to call her Mama either, and that she simply wasn't going to tolerate it."

I stopped at a light at Mt. Hope Road and gazed across a barren field. The expanse of soil was as dry and as drab as moon dust. It was university property, perhaps one of the ag department's experimental plots lying fallow. At the far side of the field stood a huge new concrete building. It looked lunar, too, like something designed for another world. I had no idea what was taught there, but it was somehow comforting to know Eddie had a chance at finding out.

". . . it was like righteous anger, as if she held me to blame for her own coldness toward the child. When I think of what that poor little girl's life must be like I want to cry."

I continued driving and Nora didn't cry and eventually the road narrowed down to a single lane each way, trees up close to the shoulder. Suddenly there they were, a half dozen woolly specimens grazing intelligently on the sloping pasture by the road. The sign out front of the sprawl of low white farm buildings was still there, too, green with white lettering: SHEEP TEACHING AND RESEARCH, MICHIGAN STATE UNIVERSITY. I remembered reading the sign to Eddie, who'd giggled for five minutes at the thought of sheep who taught professors.

I was aware that Nora was watching me, no doubt searching my face for some sense that I shared her distress over the little girl. She said, "Why are you smiling?"

I waved vaguely at the sheep-teaching sign, which was already behind us. "I was just reminded of something."

She said, "Don't you think we ought to report that woman to the adoption agency?"

I turned left onto Holt Road. Holt Road ran east and west, which was one of two ways roads ran in central Michigan. The other way was north and south. In the Upper Peninsula nature determined how the roads ran. Up there the roads swooped and soared. Or so I imagined. I'd driven many Michigan miles and I'd never yet swooped or soared. All I'd ever done was drive north and south, east and west.

"Jack?"

"No detours, Nora. And the same rule applies: If Mai's not there, we don't spook the sitter. Okay?"

Nora was silent a moment, gazing at me. Then she said, "Okay." She didn't mention the little girl again. She continued to stare at me, though. I turned south onto Okemos Road, aware of her eyes. There was a seed company on the right, a confusion of silos and feed tubes and barns. Nora glanced at the seed company. Beyond its silos the land opened up and she looked out over the vast expanse of fields, most of which were plowed and awaiting the company's seed. It was as flat as the sea out here.

Nora said, "There."

I was already slowing down. There wasn't another car within miles of me, but I flicked on my turn signal anyway, less out of habit than out of a need to do things as I did them in places less lonely than this. I pulled onto a gravel drive and crunched to a stop near the side door of a restored farmhouse that was set back a stately distance from the road and was tucked in behind lilacs so large they reached to the second-floor windows. The lilacs hadn't got their full complement of leaves yet, so I had a clear view of the house. It had a fresh coat of paint, cream with blue trim, very tasteful. And very large, this house, but not commanding enough to dispel the sad emptiness of the flat fields that stretched away on all sides, endlessly barren in mid-April.

A matronly woman wearing leather boots, a long denim skirt,

and a tweed jacket over a cashmere turtleneck stepped out of the side door of the house. She was in her sixties, tall, her chestnut hair streaked with gray. She came at us with her hand extended.

"My dear Dr. O'Connell! I'm so glad you've come. I'm Adele Lord." She grabbed Nora's hand, beaming at her across the length of their handshake before coming in close, leaning toward Nora with her head cocked at an inquisitive angle. She said, "I was worried after what happened at Ida's that you'd given up on us."

"Ida's?"

"Ida Isherwood. We just hung up. She called me because she was deeply depressed about a surprise home-study visit she just had from an agency couple. It wasn't till she told me she was convinced they were only pretending to be there on Sam's okay that I realized I hadn't told her to expect you. The mix-up was entirely my fault and I'm so very sorry." Adele Lord was still shaking Nora's hand, as if the prolonged pumping would undo the damage.

Nora said guardedly, "You're friends with that woman?"

"I've known Ida for years. We grew up together. Her husband worked at the university as a groundskeeper. Perhaps you noticed the trees on her property? Jim planted every one of those specimens. They had a gazebo—did you see it? Jim was painting it when a tree fell and destroyed his back. She lost him several years ago. Her children are all grown and gone and she was so lonely after what happened with the adoption agency that I told Sam about her. She's really a wonderful woman. From what she said just now I know she made an entirely contrary impression on you, but that's altogether my fault. I became so preoccupied with making arrangements for your visit here that I forgot to tell Ida that Sam had given you her name as well as mine. I promised him I'd call her to let her know you were coming, but it slipped my mind entirely, so poor Ida assumed you were there from the adoption agency and were using Sam as a cover. Mr. Bodine, is it?"

The medium-length nails of Adele Lord's aged but not unattractive fingers were shiny with clear polish. I gathered them in, feeling, as I let go of her hand, that the exchange was somehow incomplete, that maybe I should have bowed and given her a peck on the knuckle. I gave her a smile instead, a little grin of forgiveness meant to assure her the mix-up was hardly cause for concern.

Adele Lord, more or less ignoring me, said to Nora, "Poor Ida was beside herself when I told her you genuinely are interested in Sam's surrogate program."

Nora said skeptically, "I explained all that to her."

"Ida said that you did, but she simply didn't believe you. You see, she lost a child last year to that adoption agency and she's no longer the trusting soul she once was. I don't think she'll ever get over it."

I squirmed. I did not want to hear about Ida Isherwood's lost child any more than I wanted to wallow in the emotional mire I'd stepped into over on Beal Street yesterday when I talked to Celia Gore, the woman who'd lost her son in Vietnam. What I wanted to do was shoulder aside the loquacious Ms. Lord and rifle her rooms till I found Nora's baby, then haul out of there with a spray of gravel and a sigh of relief. But what I did was nod agreeably as Adele Lord, walking us to the side door of her house, made fervent assurances that dear Ida ("Was she wearing her high-tops?") was the soul of motherly love, a woman who would do anything for that little Kisha of hers, even pretend to be a heartless harridan in order to hold on to the child.

Nora Toland said, "I'm sorry, but I can't comprehend her rationale."

Adele Lord paused beneath a cantilevered trellis through which dangled tendrils of budding wisteria. She said, "You see, Doctor, Ida thought you were from the agency, and she was worried that you'd get the impression she was emotionally attached to the girl."

"I still don't understand."

"Well, if you had actually been from the agency through which Ida has her foster-care contract, and if you truly thought Ida cared for Kisha, then you would have recommended they take the child away from her. That's what they did with the other little girl."

"But why?"

"It's their policy."

"To take a child away from a woman who—"

"Loves it? Yes. It happened to Ida."

Nora said, "That's very hard to believe."

"The other little girl was an abandoned child. Her name was Katie. Ida had her for two years. She loved her deeply and applied to adopt Katie. The agency dispatched a home-study team to interview Ida. The next day they reassigned the girl to another foster mother and there wasn't a thing Ida could do about it. She was devastated."

"They must have sensed there was something wrong with the woman."

"There was nothing wrong with Ida's love for Katie. They did it because government subsidies are based on the number of purchase-of-service agreements the agency has with private providers, people like Ida. They take their cut and pass on what's left to the providers, the foster parents. But if a provider adopts, then the agency loses the stipend for that child. And believe me, Dr. O'Connell, certain agencies don't like losing stipends. Foster-care kids, particularly black or handicapped children, are their bread and butter. Not all of them are underhanded, mind you. But there are those few that take advantage of the system, and cause grievous pain."

"You're saying that as long as Mrs. Isherwood shows no emotional attachment to the child, then the adoption agency will let the girl stay?"

Adele Lord nodded.

"But why doesn't she report them, or take children through another agency? Or through the state directly?"

"You've met Ida," said Adele Lord. "She's in no position to be choosy. Or to make waves. She's a wonderful human being, but that's not immediately obvious to the high-minded souls who run the child-care system in this state. They're hardworking, dedicated people, most of them, but they operate under the mistaken belief that they know what's best for the rest of us. Which is why Sam's work with surrogate mothers is so important. Or to put it another way, it's women like you who make it possible for progressive people like Sam and me to get a night's sleep." She reached for the door. "Please. I have someone inside I'd like you to meet."

Adele Lord showed us in and gestured toward a counter, encouraging us to sample a croissant. A carafe of coffee was standing by, as was a girl of about thirteen. "This is Sam's daughter, Quintina. Quintina, this is Dr. O'Connell."

Quintina Agnew, fashionably disheveled in her pegged pink jeans and oversized Ocean Pacific sweatshirt, looked as though she'd prefer to be cruising Meridian Mall with her friends. She gave Nora a smile, however, and held out her small hand. Adele Lord looked on with tense expectancy glittering in her bright blue eyes. She said to Nora, "I know you're here to get some sense of Sam's sitting arrangements, and of me in particular. I have three babies under my care at the moment, by the way, and miraculously they're all sleeping just now. I expect them to wake for a noon feeding any minute, so if you wouldn't mind speaking to Quintina in the meantime, I'd be very grateful. I went through considerable trouble to arrange for Quintina to be here this morning, and I'd like very much for her to get some sense of you."

Nora glanced at me. I gave her a don't-spook-the-sitter smile and shrugged amiably.

Adele Lord said, "Perhaps you have another appointment, Mr. Bodine?" Her tone suggested she would be only too happy to have me leave and come back later.

I said, "No."

"I see. Oh, by the way, this is Mr. Bodine, Quintina. He's Dr. O'Connell's lawyer."

Quintina showed me her braces and said, "Hi."

"Well," said Adele Lord, "why don't we sit down?"

No one came up with a reason why we shouldn't, so we followed Adele out of the kitchen, stepping up from its rustic, twelve-inch tiles into a dining room with twelve-inch, tongue-in-groove plank flooring that had been refinished in the same light-stained tones as the dining-room woodwork. It would have been a pleasant room if it hadn't been for the furniture. It was the same stuff I'd avoided in Sam Agnew's office. There was a beat-up china cabinet in the corner and four scabby-looking ladder-back chairs arranged around a table that had a warped surface and a smattering of original paint. Shaker chic. Which meant there weren't any curtains on the windows. A lot of light was trapped in that dining room, trillions of perfectly fine photons wasting themselves on all that rustic piety. It struck me that Adele Lord had odd taste in furniture for a woman who liked to compliment herself on the progressiveness of her politics. But the Shakers had been considered progressive in their time, so what did I know?

Adele Lord said, "Dr. O'Connell. Mr. Bodine. Please, have a seat."

The chair stuttered over the braided rug as I pulled it back from the table. I sat and squirmed, trying to get comfortable. Adele Lord, sitting with her spine as straight as a schoolmarm's switch, seemed to find the arrangements bracing. She said, "I'll come right to the point, Dr. O'Connell. Several of Quintina's classmates have made disparaging remarks about her father's commitment to the plight of childless couples. They seem to believe there's something immoral about the women who volunteer for the surrogate role, or that Sam has some kind of evil hold over them. Now, Dr. O'Connell, do you feel you've been in any way manipulated or duped by Sam?"

Nora looked a little stunned by the irony of her position. Not only was Sam Agnew holding her baby for a ten-grand ransom, but the surrogate deal he'd facilitated with the Vietnamese woman had been fraudulent from the get-go, not to mention the fact that his actual surrogates, from what Nora had told me, charged a healthy fee for their "volunteer" work, from which selfless Sam undoubtedly received a sizable kickback. With all that in mind, I could hardly blame Nora for the long silence that filled the room. At last she took a deep breath and said, "No, Quintina, I haven't been manipulated in the least. In fact, I was the one who approached your father. I admire him a great deal."

Adele Lord turned to Quintina. "I've never met Dr. O'Connell before, dear. This is not in any way rehearsed."

Quintina, who did not appear to have a skeptical bone in her young body, said, "I believe her. It's just that, well, how could she have a baby and then just give it away?"

"The point," said Adele Lord quickly, "is that Dr. O'Connell is not the kind of person your friends have accused your father of dealing with. You can see that, can't you?"

"Yes, but—"

"Even if she were, Quintina, it's not where the baby comes from. It's where it goes. The childless couples who rely on your father for help are people who truly want the children he provides. If you knew how many babies are born to women who don't want them—"

"I know that, Grandma."

"You're Sam Agnew's mother?" Nora asked.

"His adoptive mother." Adele emphasized "adoptive," glancing at Quintina. "I'm very proud of your father, Quintina. That pride is something I would never have known if I hadn't adopted him. Think of all the couples in this country—one in six—who are infertile, who want children desperately, but who can't have them, who will never know the satisfaction and joy of seeing their youngsters grow up to make meaningful contributions to society. You ought to be proud of your father, dear. Really, it upsets me no end to hear the lies people are spreading about him. And for your mother to suggest she believes them . . . well, Mary Beth ought to know better."

I said, "What sort of rumors are being spread, Ms. Lord?"

"I don't want to get into that. That's not important. What's important is that Quintina, and hopefully her mother, can come to appreciate what Sam and people like Dr. O'Connell are doing for people like . . . myself, women who can't have children but who want them very, very much. I was lucky. When I adopted Sam, babies were plentiful. But they aren't now, not at all. It's a terrible time for infertile women. Far from exploiting women, Quintina, your father is doing more for them than all the liberationists put together. And that's coming from me, a feminist. Do you hear me, dear?"

Quintina said meekly, "Mom's not against him. I mean, she's not going mental, or anything."

"Oh? That's not the impression I received."

"She's taking care of a baby for him right now," Quintina said. "That's not being against him, is it?"

Adele Lord raised her eyebrows. "She is? I didn't know that."

Quintina said, "It's just this once. He knows all your cribs are full, so he asked Mom, and she said okay."

Before Adele Lord could respond, a baby let out a howl from upstairs and Nora Toland almost cried out in answer.

I stood. "Well, now that Quintina has had a chance to meet Dr. O'Connell, it might be fun to have a look at the babies."

# 16 ◄◄◄

Twenty minutes later Nora Toland and I were parked in the lot of the I-96 Burger King. Nora looked dangerously pale. Her baby hadn't been among the trio of infants at Adele Lord's place, and the disappointment seemed to have drained her.

I said, "I'm going to duck in there and check a phone book, find Agnew's address so we can see about the baby his wife's sitting. Can I get you something to eat while I'm at it?"

Nora's hands were lying limply in her lap. She was resting her head against the seat, staring at the sun visor. There wasn't a mirror on the visor or a schedule of the Tigers' season or anything worth gazing at. Just road dust and fingerprints. She shook her head.

"Cup of coffee? Maybe some tea?"

"No, thank you. I'm feeling a little dizzy. I'd just like to rest."

Whenever I got dizzy food and coffee worked wonders, but the problem with Nora Toland was beyond my limited repertoire of remedies. So I hit the Burger King alone, asked if they had a phone, and was referred to the Mobil station next door. I had a word with a mechanic and a moment later I was jotting down Agnew's address while wolfing a Whopper.

I climbed back into the car and held my breath as I leaned

across Nora, opened the glove compartment, and dug out my *Graphic Street Guide of Greater Lansing, East Lansing, DeWitt, Dimondale, Haslett, Holt, Mason, Okemos and Other Outlying Areas.* I sat back and held up the map so it caught the light streaming in through the window, which I rolled down a bit. I didn't want my onion fumes to betray the fact that I'd taken time out from the case to sneak a snack. No sense attempting a kidnapping on an empty stomach, after all, but even though I'd eaten on the run, I felt vaguely unprofessional, as if I'd failed to fully empathize with my ailing client's dilemma. "Here it is," I said. "Potawatomi Drive."

Nora said listlessly, "Where's that?"

"Just up the road in Okemos."

Okemos is a bedroom community. Professors, corporate execs, doctors, and lawyers snooze peacefully on the spot that had once been a favorite campsite of Chief Okemos of the Ottawas. Or maybe it was the Chippewas. Anyway, those who usurped him named their town after the chief, and its winding suburban lanes after his native rivals and any other Indian tribe they could think of, including the Arapahos and the Apaches. There was an Arrowhead Road in Okemos, too, and a Tomahawk Circle. I started the car.

It was a ten-minute drive to Agnew's house. His place was on a corner lot, and as I turned onto Potawatomi Drive I noticed a pair of shirtless laborers axing and spading in the backyard. The woman watching them had an infant in the crook of her arm and a diaper on her shoulder. I parked at the curb, cut the engine, and glanced over at Nora. She'd seen the baby, too, and the sight of it had perked her up considerably. I said, "How do you feel?"

"All right. But are you sure this is it? Somehow I thought he'd be more well-off than this." She nodded at the house.

It wasn't anything spectacular, a brick ranch with faded shutters and paint flaking off the trim around the door of the attached two-car garage. The basketball backboard was sagging and the net was a tangle of rotted twine. A Yugo was parked inside the open garage. The space for the second car was taken up with lawn equipment and enough bicycles to stock an MSU dormitory. There were also wagons, scooters, Big Wheels, and skateboards. And more, but my view was blocked by a flatbed truck from a DeWitt landscaping outfit that was also parked in the driveway. The truck was loaded with a collection of balled shrubs, nothing that would have interested the late Mr. Isherwood, just some junipers, yews, and a couple dwarf flame bushes.

I said, "Ready?"

"Jack? What if it's not Mai?"

"Then we take direct action against Mr. Agnew."

Nora gave me a sidelong look, as if I'd suggested the shattering of kneecaps, or worse. "What do you mean, exactly?"

"I'm not a thug, Nora, but if I discuss this openly with Mr. Agnew, it won't be a therapy session."

"You wouldn't hurt him, would you? Physically?"

"Does that possibility bother you?"

Nora thought about this. She had her hand pressed against her abdomen as if the thought of physical violence had caused her physical pain. I waited, watching her wrestle with a conscience that was a lot healthier than she was.

Finally she said, "I was so angry I thought about hurting him when I went to see him yesterday."

"Agnew?"

"Yes."

"But you didn't?"

"No, of course not."

I said, "Okay, how about if I limit myself to verbal abuse?"

"I just . . . I hate the thought of violence."

"Snatching that baby out of Mrs. Agnew's arms is not going to win us the Nobel Peace Prize."

"I know. The tension is giving me a flare-up."

"I'd do it myself, Nora, but you've got to come along and verify that it's the right baby before I grab it."

"I understand." She was clutching her purse now, her thumb hard at work on the handles.

"Okay, let's go."

We headed for Agnew's backyard. I saw myself as a real-estate agent squiring a difficult client from one listing to another. I had no idea what a nosy neighbor would take us for, maybe a pair of pledge canvassers from the local church. Or a census team. As soon as we grabbed that kid, though, we were going to look like Bonnie and Clyde.

We paused at the open gate. The woman was adjusting the burp rag on her shoulder. I said to Nora, "Is that Mai?"

"I can't tell from here."

"Ma'am? Excuse me!"

The woman holding the baby turned toward us. As she did she laid the child's head on her shoulder, which meant the kid was once again facing away from us. "Yes?"

"Are you Mrs. Agnew?"

She nodded.

Mrs. Agnew had full, high-boned cheeks and a handsome, high-bridged nose. She was wearing sandals, a long denim skirt with a wide leather belt, and a colorful print blouse. If it hadn't been for her straight blond hair, she could have been Chief Okemos's great-great-great-granddaughter. Maybe she was. Maybe the good chief had cut quite a figure with the white man's squaw. I said, "May we speak to you a minute?"

Mrs. Agnew hesitated. She looked like a gregarious sort, but something about us bothered her.

I said, "Sam sent us. He said you might be able to give my client some down-home advice."

"Well, I guess so."

As we passed through the gate, one of the workers, a sweaty kid with shoulders that had got their definition muscling more than the occasional arborvitae, glanced over at us. His partner was in his fifties and uninterested in anything but the end of his shovel. The kid, however, had energy to spare and was wasting it in

Nora's direction, his head swinging around like a compass needle in a magnetic field as she passed by. He'd bear watching. He was using an ax to dislodge a root mass. I'd hate to break his ax.

I hated having to lie to Mrs. Agnew, too. There was an ingenuousness about the woman, a general goodheartedness that was as plain as the nose on her pleasantly freckled face. But she wasn't any dummy. As we approached her she sensed the menace in us but wasn't quite sure what to do about it except to protect the child in her arms. Her large hand traveled to the baby's sparsely thatched skull, shielding it as if from the sun, except that she was standing in the shade. I said, "I'm Jack Bodine. I represent Dr. O'Connell here. She's interested in your husband's surrogate-mother program and, uh, we understand that you sometimes baby-sit for him in an overflow situation?" I nodded at the baby and smiled. "Cute kid. Boy or a girl?"

"Sam didn't say anything about this to me. Are you sure—?"

Nora edged behind Mrs. Agnew and checked out the baby. Her eyes filled with tears, and her chin suddenly crumpled as the tears spilled down her face.

Mrs. Agnew glanced at Nora and then at the baby, thinking there had to be something wrong with the child to have caused the woman to burst into tears like that . . . but no, the baby was fine. Mrs. Agnew frowned, and her speculations, developing along other lines, were plainly revealed in her guileless face. She was entertaining the possibility that Nora was a surrogate mother who had changed her mind about giving up her baby. "Oh, dear. Is this your baby, Dr. O'Connell?"

"No." Nora's face was contorted with frustration and pain. "No, it's not my baby. And I'm not Dr. O'Connell. My name is Toland and your husband kidnapped my child and I want her back. I paid him, and I want her back! Do you hear me?"

The young man with the ax heard her fine. He paused to appraise the situation, his muscle-bound chest heaving with good intentions. He said, "Something the matter, lady?"

I said, "Keep out of this."

He said, "You got a problem?"

I said, "Sure. And so do you. It's down there in the dirt, so get after it."

"Hey, pal."

Without glancing in our direction, the kid's grizzled partner said, "Dig, Kurt, and shut up."

The two landscapers conferred with intensity. I divided my attention between them and the two women. Mrs. Agnew was reacting to Nora's accusation with an expression of shocked disbelief that appeared entirely genuine. "Sam did what?" she said.

"He stole my baby."

"No."

"Yes. I didn't know we still owed him money. I told him that. I promised we'd pay, but he took my baby anyway. And even after I paid him he wouldn't give her back to me. He said I owed him another ten thousand dollars. I haven't got ten thousand dollars. I mean, I haven't got it now, but I'll get it. I just want my baby back. I'll get the money somehow. Please."

Mrs. Agnew glanced at me, her expression now a mix of anxiety and resolve. She said to Nora, "I can give you the names of the women who sit for Sam. Your baby's probably with one of them. There's a Mrs. Isherwood. She lives out past Marsh Road. It's not far."

"We've been there," I said.

"Well, try Sam's mother's place. It's just down—"

"We've been there, too."

Mrs. Agnew appeared stumped. She began jiggling the baby as if to calm it, but the kid was already asleep. Nora looked as if she was about ready to drop off herself. Her eyelids were heavy and she'd gone as white as the proverbial sheet. I said, "Are you all right, Nora?"

Nora shook her head. She said to Mrs. Agnew, "May I use your bathroom?"

"Sure. There's a half bath just inside the back door. Door's right there. See it? Sometimes I can't even find the back door myself, this place is so overgrown." Her voice trailed off as Nora went into the house. She turned to me and waved at the now sullen diggers and at the truckload of shrubs out front on the driveway. "That's my birthday present. Sam insisted on a present, so there it is, a bunch of new shrubs. Cost us two hundred fifty bucks we haven't got, but that's Sam." She gave me a searching stare. "What are you really?"

"Private detective."

Mrs. Agnew rolled her eyes and shook her head. "Sam, Sam, Sam." She sighed deeply. "What's your name again?"

"Jack Bodine."

"Right. Well listen, Jack, Sam's not a bad guy."

Now that I had a close-up look at Mrs. Agnew I saw that she was forty pushing fifty. But the wear and tear hadn't got her down. There was something in the woman that appealed to me, an earthy honesty, I suppose. It wasn't something I'd tell Joyce about, my appreciation of Mrs. Agnew's earthy charms. That was just between me and myself. And Mrs. Agnew. I could tell she liked me. Or maybe she felt for me, seeing that I was just about at the end of this day's rope. I said, "Your name's Mary Beth, isn't it?"

"Yes."

"Well, Mary Beth, bad guy or not, my client's got a serious problem with Sam."

Mary Beth Agnew's mouth turned down. "Her and me both."

I nodded. "Your mother-in-law alluded to the fact that there was some tension between you and Sam. She said he was causing Quintina a little trouble, too. At school. Something to do with Sam's business ethics."

"Quintina was with Adele? When she should be at school?"

"Evidently your mother-in-law went to some trouble to set it up. She wanted Quintina to meet Mrs. Toland. She was under the impression Nora was a doctor who wanted to become a surrogate mother. She thought it might do something to improve

Quintina's opinion of her father's line of work, you know, a doctor choosing to be a surrogate mother."

Mary Beth Agnew received this coldly. "Adele. She actually tried to talk me into giving away one of my kids once. Jimmy, my youngest. This was just before he was born. Adele said I had more kids than I needed. Called me the old woman in the shoe." Mary Beth Agnew shot a glance at her house as if it pinched her soul. "Adele's only been on the receiving end, though. She hasn't any idea how it would feel to give a baby away. All her life she's had everything given to her, including Sam. Her second husband's a money tree. A brain surgeon. Through him she supports Sam. Subsidizes his work, otherwise Sam couldn't live on what he makes in fees."

"He made a killing off Nora Toland."

"Look, I'm not saying anything about that. I mean, I don't know if he did what she says. But if he did, it's because of his mother. She's got him dependent on doing this surrogate stuff. I admit it's been the first solid thing he's got into. He's had a lot of problems, businesswise. Used to play a little pro ball, played the market after that, tried to develop real estate over by Saugatuck, owned an orange grove in Florida that the developers passed by, sold steel for Jones and Laughlin till they got bought out by LTV. He's got something steady going now for the first time ever. But he needs his mother's money to keep his head above water. I mean, two kids in college and five more to go? What with tuition and room and board and books, it costs over six grand a year per kid just to send them to Michigan State."

Mary Beth Agnew continued to jiggle the baby. Then she said, "I told Sam I was against this whole surrogate-mother bit. It's not right for a woman to give a child away. I don't know. Maybe it's different for a man to do it, you know, sperm banks and that kind of thing. But for a woman, it's different. It's asking for trouble. Later on in life you can't help thinking about that kid, wondering. It's biologically wrong, that's all. And when it comes to basic biology, man-and-woman–type biology, I've had some experience. I'm the voice of it, Jack."

"Experience?"

"You bet. And the Voice says it's wrong." She sighed, shaking her head. "The things they say about him, the Christers, it makes me want to crawl into a hole. But here I am, sticking up for the man. We do what we got to, right?"

I stood there nodding in agreement. "What kind of things do they say, Mary Beth?"

"Vicious things."

I waited.

"Sam likes to tell them the Virgin Mary was a surrogate."

"What do they say to that?"

"They get back at him by calling him a whoremaster. They say he keeps prostitutes for breeding purposes, mates with them himself, churns out babies as if it's an assembly line. Custom orders, too. Male whores with such-and-such traits banging prostitutes with such-and-so looks. You know, Nazi Germany, that kind of thing. Sick, vicious rumors."

"But groundless?"

Mary Beth Agnew nuzzled the baby with her cheek. "There was a prostitute. One. A bright, good-looking woman. She'd get a couple interested in a surrogate deal and then she'd tell them it would cost, but not to say anything to Sam. Eventually he found out about her and dumped her from the program. She vowed to get even with him. I think that's where the rumors started."

"How did he find out about her?"

"Some clients complained. So Sam hired a private detective to check her out. The guy went to see her with his wife, pretended they were interested in having a baby with the woman. Kind of like what you're doing with . . . what's her name, again? Toland?"

I nodded, wondering if the private detective had been "the white man with a gun" who'd snatched Nora Toland's baby from its basket, and if he was anyone I knew. I said, "Do you remember the PI's name, by any chance?"

"No. Just that the surrogate put the touch on him and he reported it to Sam. Beautiful girl, too. Graduated from the University of Michigan, turned to tricking. Call-girl stuff. Said being pregnant actually increased her business. Said a lot of men like it, a woman being pregnant when they . . . you know, do it. Sure is a sick world, isn't it, Jack?"

Inside the house I heard a toilet flush. I said, "Well, we keep looking for a cure."

"You going to hassle Sam?"

"Yes. You going to warn him I'm coming?"

Mary Beth Agnew said, "Maybe if I was to let you blind-side him, it'd be for the best. Thing is, you wreck Sam and you wreck us, me and my kids. Sure, I'm going to warn him. I've got my children to think of."

# 17 ‹‹‹‹

Nora was definitely sick. I drove her home hoping I was wrong about her husband. I wanted him to have borrowed the money just as he'd promised her and to have paid Agnew off. I wanted him to be waiting on their doorstep with the baby in his arms. But—no surprise—no Dirk.

So I encouraged Nora to take a nap and to rest easy in the certainty that Sam Agnew, if he had her baby, was about to hand it over. I told her not to worry about violence, either, I'd get results without getting physical. In fact, I found myself looking forward to the challenge. There had to be more than one way to break a broker. I could mess with his clientele . . . the very folks who happened to be sitting none too comfortably on his hard chairs when I arrived at his offices, three couples, all white, thirtyish, and none too poor. Of course, poor folks couldn't have afforded Sam. And anyway, if you were poor and infertile and really wanted a child, eventually you'd get one. Kids among the poor are like jugs of Gallo. They get passed around.

"May I help you?" Agnew's secretary addressed me with a smile of friendly competence. Despite this, she was rather fetching. Despite that, I found myself wondering if maybe she'd fetched baby Mai while her boss had distracted Nora.

I said, "I'd like to see Mr. Agnew."

"Do you have an appointment?"

"No, but I'm sure he's expecting me. Jack Bodine."

Agnew's secretary folded her trim hands on the Shaker table that served as her desk, her smile having become more competent than friendly. She said, "I'm sorry, but I can't get you in to see Mr. Agnew without an appointment." This was final and definitive. Her black, bunned-back hair was as shiny as her black-framed glasses. The lenses of the glasses seemed to intensify her determination not to knuckle under.

I glanced again at the faces that had turned toward me at my entrance, Agnew's clients. The cut of their hair and clothes suggested affluence; not great wealth, but mainstream success: college degrees and dual careers, mortgages, Cuisinarts, and golf. And exercise spas, no heavy drinking or eating. One's body was a Porsche, after all. As social specimens they were a notch or two above me, but they all seemed a bit uneasy, as if their self-confidence quotient was somewhat depressed. My entrance had raised the overall average considerably, but none of them seemed heartened by my arrival. In fact, their gazes slid away from mine, drifted off in a way that suggested they were guilty of something. Or ashamed. I couldn't imagine what was wrong with college, Cuisinarts, mortgages, and golf. I still aspired to those very things myself. Of course, I'd also aspired to Eddie and had got him, whereas these folks had tried for Jennifer and Jason and had not got them and were worried there was something wrong with them personally. Which was why they were here, looking like so many sinners in a church. Or maybe they looked that way to me because they were seated on old church pews, compliments of Adele Lord, no doubt. I knocked a knuckle on Agnew's secretary's Shaker desk and said, "Did you know that the early Shakers were communist celibates?"

The secretary looked at me as if I'd flopped a halibut onto her blotter. Herself, she smelled like an iris. She said, "Do you intend to make an appointment or not?"

"What I intend to make is a point . . . unless you tell me where Nora Toland's baby is."

"I don't know what you're talking about," she said knowledgeably.

"Okay. Then I'll make my point. Back in the seventeen hundreds in England there was a woman named Ann Lee. She had four children, but they all died in infancy. You can imagine how Ann felt. She wasn't too happy with her marriage, either, but the loss of her babies made her decide to give up on a family and found a religion."

The secretary said, "I'm sorry, but if you refuse to follow our procedures, then I think you should go away."

"That's what the English said to Ann. So she sailed for America with seven converts and spread the word and eventually they set up a number of self-contained communities that were really quite remarkable. I'm getting all this from my *Collier's Encyclopedia*, by the way. I couldn't sleep last night."

The secretary's buck-stops-here look was starting to show signs of mettle fatigue. That was because I was one buck she wasn't about to stop. I was Lone Buck Bodine, the two-fisted discourser.

"Now then," said I, "the Shakers did all right. They lived in neat, well-planned, peaceful villages, were progressive agriculturists, and were quite advanced in the mechanical arts. They were deeply concerned about social betterment, too. Say what you will about their furniture, they were good people, sound, sensible, serious, sober folks. They were a lot like the folks in this room here. Except they were celibate, which, along with communism, was perhaps taking things a bit too far, but the point is they accepted converts with children and everyone loved the kids as if they were their own while living happy, meaningful lives without necessarily insisting on having babies that were biologically related to themselves."

I paused, noting the glances that were being exchanged. Sentiment appeared to be against me, but that was all right.

Somewhere between yesterday and today I'd decided I wasn't too keen on surrogate mothering, and if I was having a negative effect on its future, that was fine. Meanwhile, Agnew's secretary had decided she wasn't too keen on me. She said, "I'm sorry, sir, but I'm going to have to ask you to leave."

I straightened up, stuck out my chest, and folded my hands behind my back. "All right, get it over with."

"What?"

"Ask me to leave."

"Yes, leave! Go away!"

"No." I turned to Agnew's clients. "There are worse things than not having children of your own, you know. And coming to a place like this is one of them."

A lean fellow with dark hair and soulful features spoke up, being careful not to stand up. "Why are you saying these things?" He let me see that it wasn't anything he cared to come to blows over, not wanting to stoop to my level, which, I had to admit, was very nearly subterranean. Although I could go a lot lower if I had to.

"I think it's the furniture," I replied. "It brings out the moralist in me. And Sam Agnew is a very immoral man."

Agnew's secretary punched a button on an intercom. "I'm sorry to interrupt you, Sam, but there's a person here who's saying things to upset your clients, a man named Bodine. I told him you're not able to see him, but he refuses to leave."

I leaned over the secretary's desk and thumbed the button. "Hi, Sam, it's me. I've been asking around about you, and people are saying some pretty unsavory things. Can we talk?"

I'd hardly let up on the button when the door to Agnew's office opened and Sam stepped out into the waiting room. He looked flushed, but in control. "What's the problem, Trish?"

He said this as if I weren't there. I said, "Trish hasn't got the problem. You do."

Sam Agnew faced me squarely. He was not a small man—pro ball and all that—and his drawn-back shoulders sent tremors of apprehension through his clientele. He said, "I'm busy, Mr. Bodine. I'm in the middle of a placement."

"It can wait."

"Now just a minute, fella! I work on an appointment basis." Agnew motioned at the craning couple seated inside his office. "Those people have an appointment." He nodded at the couples seated in the waiting room. "These folks do, too. But you don't. So make an appointment." He made a gesture that signified Trish as the appointment-maker.

Trish said sensibly, "Maybe you'd better talk to him, Sam."

Sam saw that he was being given serious advice, but there was something feisty in him that declined to follow it. He said to Trish, "Try to squeeze him in at the end of the week."

I said, "I'm the one who's doing the squeezing, Sam, and the question is, do you want me to squeeze you in front of your clients, or in private? I'm speaking metaphorically, of course."

Agnew turned to the couples seated in the waiting room. "I apologize for this individual's behavior."

"Well, I'm not about to apologize for your behavior, Sam." I said to his clientele, "Sure, Sam's got debts, but does that justify the use of prostitutes—clean, nice-looking young women, I must admit—to produce babies for people who can't get them on their own?"

"Now just a goddamned minute!"

The woman with the dark, soulful man said, "What do you mean by prostitutes?"

I said, "You know, women who have sexual intercourse with men for money. Sam's surrogate mothers are prostitutes. I mean, really, who's going to carry a baby for nine months just for the fun of it?"

Agnew appealed to the woman. "This is bizarre. This is completely untrue. This man is a mental case. I haven't any idea where he got any of this."

I said, "I am told, incidentally, that pregnancy doesn't really interfere with the turning of tricks till about the fifth or sixth

167

month, and even from then on there's money to be made because there are a lot of guys who enjoy fornicating with pregnant prostitutes. It's the rage."

One of Agnew's female clients—wool skirt, silk blouse, hair cut in bangs—emitted a *tsk* of disgust and stalked out the door. The man with her got up and followed her out. Neither of them said a word. The couple in Agnew's office, having left their chairs to stand by the door in order to hear me better, also made a furtive dash for the hallway. The last two couples looked more confused than revolted. I said helpfully, "The surprising thing is that even after the babies are born the hooker moms keep right on working. There are men who apparently like to nurse, you know, to suckle up some of that liebfraumilch, and who pay a premium for the privilege. The fact that the woman's vagina is temporarily off limits, being tender from the rigors of childbirth, isn't a problem, either, since there is another orifice available, and there are men, very often the sucklers I'm told, who deem this alternate orifice more desirable than normal channels. If you get my drift."

The soulful couple excused themselves.

Sam Agnew watched this with a dropped jaw and a heaving chest, his fists clenched at his sides. "What are you trying to do?"

"I'm attempting to force you to return Nora Toland's baby. The one you repossessed on Tuesday."

"I don't know what you're talking about."

I said to the remaining couple, "He works a kickback scheme with the whores. They hit you up for twenty grand, ten goes to Sam, ten to the whore. And if you don't make your payments, Sam repossesses the kid. True."

It was only a matter of moments before we were alone, Trish and Sam and I. Trish wanted to leave, too. Sam wanted to hit me. I wanted Nora Toland's baby. Of the three of us getting what we wanted, I liked my chances best.

Then I socked Sam on the nose, and liked myself less than my chances. Never mind that he'd swung on me first and that I didn't really sock him so much as nudge his face. I'd broken a promise to my client by committing an act of violence . . . although Sam's nose really hadn't taken a full-bodied blow. More of a punch lite. Still, I felt bad enough I almost got down on my hands and knees and dabbed at the surprising flow of blood that bubbled brightly from his schnork. Fortunately, his secretary performed that chore, and readily, too, using Sam's yellow power tie while nuzzling his dazed melon in just the way Sam's wife had nuzzled the baby that hadn't been Nora's. "Oh, baby," crooned Trish. "Oh, baby, baby, baby." I didn't know what to make of that, unless I'd been wrong about Trish wanting to leave. The error, oddly, made me feel a little better about myself. Trish seemed to sense this. She said, "Does it make you feel like a big tough man, knocking people out?"

Agnew was indeed out, though breathing freely through his mouth. "I just beat him to a punch," I said, "not to a pulp. He'll be all right."

"He had surgery to remove his adenoids last month."

"I thought his nose felt funny."

"It's not a joke."

"It isn't a Greek tragedy, either. He'll be all right. Assuming one of you tells me where the baby is."

"You just don't care, do you?"

"Not about him." Even so, I leaned over Trish's Tandy 1000, grabbed a boutique-size box of blue tissues, and handed it to her. "Here, pack his face."

She tugged a tissue from the box, rolled up one corner, and inserted the elongated wad into Sam's left nostril. She did it with such tender devotion I could almost believe it was Prince Andrei lying there, fresh from the fields of Borodino. Trish wasn't the Natasha type, but with her hair down and her glasses cast passionately aside, she'd make a pretty fair Grushenka. Except Grushenka had been a blonde and had lived in another book. I said speculatively, "Seems like it might be a little nerve-racking, boinking a guy who's fathered seven children."

Trish the Dish packed Sam's right nostril, ignoring me.

I shrugged. "Of course, if he knocked you up, he could always sell the kid."

"Get out of here!" There was a hint of a hiss in Trish's voice, but aside from her affection for the slime in her arms, there wasn't anything reptilian about her.

"I'll get out of here when you tell me where to find Nora Toland's baby," I said.

"I don't know anything about that."

"Just like you're not boinking Sam?"

"I'm not!"

"I'm not, either, so we've got something in common. But that isn't helping me find the kid. Now, where is she? Or do I regale Sam's two-o'clock appointment with tales of his operation? And, Trish, I'm not referring to his adenoids."

Contemplating this, Trish went through some changes, as they say. "Don't do that. It's not Sam's fault. They didn't give him any choice."

I suppose one could make the case that the Tolands had brought on their own misfortune, but I wasn't interested in hearing that argument from Sam's secretary. Anyway, there was something in Trish's voice, an overtone of anxiety mixed with outrage—as if someone had held a gun to Sam's head—that made it pretty clear she wasn't referring to the Tolands.

I said, "They?"

"Three men from Detroit. I don't know how they got in, but Sam and I were having dinner at Walnut Hills. Two of them watched us from the bar and the biggest one came over to our table and . . . I'm not supposed to talk about it." She hugged Sam's leaking noggin and didn't talk about it.

Walnut Hills was one of Lansing's several country clubs. It had a golf course. All I knew about golf was that my father had once caddied for the Purple Gang at Redford in Detroit. That had been back in the thirties. He'd reached into a guy's golf bag to get him a ball and pulled out a gat. There was a period in my youth when I kept after him to repeat that story, eager for details, but he'd forgotten most of it, couldn't even remember what kind of heater it was or what the guy looked like. Me, I could see the guy plain enough, standing there with his hard hand out, waiting for the ball, his cold eyes shadowed beneath a wide-brimmed fedora, gray with a black band. The hat matched his gray suit with the black pinstripes. I could see him sauntering into Walnut Hills Country Club, easing over to Sam's table, turning a chair around and sitting down, smiling sulkily. I said, "Was he from the Kiwanis, or what?"

"He was a gangster!"

"Really? What did he look like?"

"He looked like you."

"Really?"

"Same pushy, know-it-all attitude."

"Really?"

"He made Sam do it. Sam didn't have any choice."

I said, "Sam could have gone to the police."

"They threatened to kill him."

"The police?"

"The men at the club."

"Really?"

"Stop saying that!"

"What did these gangsters have on Sam?"

Trish paused.

"Come on," I said, "give me everything and I'm out of here, total history."

She took a deep breath. "One of Sam's original surrogate mothers actually was a prostitute. He had no idea."

"And?"

"When he found out he got rid of her, but she said she'd make trouble. Then these men showed up and forced him to take her back. Her and others. Prostitutes. He didn't have any choice. Really."

"Really."

"Don't make fun."

"I'm not. I'm just really, really, really excited by the information you've given me, Trish. The baby, baby, baby part ought to be enough to convince Sam to hand over Nora Toland's child and to forget about the money the Tolands owe him. And I'm talking about the whole debt, not just the ten-grand surcharge. But if it's not, I've got the unsavory surrogates. So you see, Trish, our little talk has made up for a long and very unprofitable afternoon. In fact, if I'd known how easy it was going to be, I might have punched Sam yesterday. Let's bring him around."

As I said this, Trish glanced over my shoulder. I turned, expecting Sam's two-o'clock clients, but it was Nora Toland who was standing in the door, her shocked gaze traveling from the bloody, prostrate Agnew up toward really excited me, her face settling into a look of sad disappointment.

Explanations, excuses, and mitigations crowded my frontal lobes. I was on the verge of assuring Nora that I'd barely touched the man's nose, a mere fillip to the septum . . . but I said nothing. I was busy developing a whole new spiel. Dirk Toland was standing darkly behind her.

# 18 ◄◄◄◄

Nora looked better than she had when I dropped her off an hour ago. Dirk Toland, with the beginnings of a beard shadowing his face, looked worse than he had when he dropped me off last night. His tired, scornful gaze took in Agnew lying on the deck, then shifted toward me as if he were a company commander who'd returned to his base after a night of combat and wasn't in any mood to quell squabbles among rear-echelon troops. I almost snapped to attention. Sam Agnew almost came to.

Nora, who plainly hadn't forgotten the promise I'd made to mind my machismo, sighed in disapproval and headed for Agnew. She knelt down and helped Trish lug him to his feet. With a woman under each arm, Agnew made a rubbery entrance into his office, the women emitting clucks of maternal concern as they sat him down behind his desk.

Dirk Toland continued to stare at me, saying nothing, not blinking, either. Tired as he was, it didn't seem as if the upkeep on the stare was putting much of a strain on his emotional budget.

I said, "Mind if I recommend a course of action?"

Silence.

I said, "Last night, when you explained your reluctance to take money from your father-in-law, you also expressed a modicum of emotion over the loss of your child. Remember? Your voice was choked and your eyes were filled with . . . emotion?"

Nothing. All I could say for certain was that Toland wasn't close to tears. "If you act on the information I'm about to give you, Dirk, you can have your kid back and a check in the mail to your father-in-law by the time Agnew's capable of picking his nose again."

Zero.

I soldiered on. "You remember the surrogate you interviewed last year, the one who wanted to nick you for twenty grand? Well, as you may have suspected at the time, Sam knew all about it. Whenever a surrogate produces a baby the money's divided between her, Agnew, and some bad boys from Detroit. The surrogates, some of them anyway, are prostitutes, not something Sam would care to have publicized, I'm sure."

Toland's stare had taken on the appearance of lukewarm curiosity.

"That's right, Dirk. With leverage like that you not only get your baby back, but you make Sam Agnew the nickee for your father-in-law's thirteen grand. You might even manage a refund on the seven thousand you paid Agnew at the hospital."

Toland shifted his weight and propped his fists on his hips. "That how much your bill's going to be, seven grand? Or thirteen? Or twenty?"

I said, "I'll give you double Green Stamps if you don't screw this up."

Toland shifted his weight again. He'd done an adequate job of it the first time and was merely thinking now, his eyes darting at Agnew's inner office. The women were still in there, ministering to Agnew's schnoz. I wasn't eager to send them another patient.

I said, "Or maybe there's some reason you want to screw this up?"

"It's like I told you last night, Agnew can leverage me, too."

"It seems to me you've got a bigger lever than he does.

And if you're squeamish, I'll be glad to use it on Sam."

Toland processed my remarks with a furrowed brow, his fists still hard on his hips.

I was trying to make it easy for him. I knew he cared for the baby. What I didn't know was whether he'd press to get her back. It was a kind of test, for it had occurred to me that Toland might have taken the infant from Thanh Chi and stashed her somewhere without telling Nora. He wouldn't want the baby around the house the day after Thanh Chi's death, not after he'd let Nora believe Agnew had taken it. He'd probably continue to let Nora think Agnew had the kid all along, too, not wanting to confess what he'd done to get Mai back. Finally I said, "Seems like you'd want to get the baby for Nora's sake, if not for your own."

I caught a flash of jealousy in Toland's eye. He said, "What do you know about 'Nora's sake'?"

"I know it's a good thing to be a father. You won't regret it."

Toland was staring at the floor now, his hands at his sides. Like most men he was a sucker for the image of himself as a daddy. Even I'd had a lump in my throat this morning, recalling Eddie's infancy. I knew if I worked at it I could have Toland in tears over the preciousness of it all. It would be an effort, though, because I knew, too, that fatherhood—if you did your share of the mothering—wasn't all it was cracked up to be. But that was something Toland would find out down the road. He'd find out, too, that it wasn't all a crock, just ninety percent of it. The ten percent that wasn't made up for the rest of it that was. And anyway, after your kids are grown and gone that ten percent is all you remember. At least that's what I'd been told, and I didn't think my mother was a liar. "What about it, Dirk?"

Toland let out a long sigh and said, "Okay, Bodine. But let me handle Agnew my own way. And in private."

I didn't like the idea of Toland and Agnew conferring alone, but I wasn't in a mood to deviate another septum this afternoon. So I stepped aside, and as Toland marched into Agnew's office I got a glimpse of Nora and Trish the Dish still doing their Nightingale number. Then the door closed and I took a pew and meditated.

Before long Trish stepped out of the office, closed the door, and sat down at her desk. She still looked her best. Her hair was sleeked back with a precision that was almost aerodynamic, and her dark blue suit—for all the squatting she'd done at the side of babybabybaby—still was as crisp and lint-free as an IBM vice president's. Emotionally, however, she was more than a little disheveled. That was understandable. She'd been in a rock fight with me and one of the rocks she picked up had exposed the sow bugs and millipedes of Sam Agnew's enterprise. What wasn't understandable was what she saw in Sam himself. But I didn't ask, and she attacked the keyboard of her computer, glaring at the material on her typing stand, ignoring me.

I glanced at the magazines spread out on the table in front of me. I had my choice of *Country Living* or *Country Living*. I leafed through *Country Living* and didn't see any outhouses, chickens, John Deeres, or foreclosed farms. When I looked up I caught Trish staring down at her unmoving hands, tears splattering on her keyboard. When she saw me looking at her she got up and hurried out of the office.

A few minutes later, with Trish still in the women's room, an uncertain young couple entered the office. The man, wearing a blue blazer and gray slacks, gazed at Trish's empty chair, then told me he and his wife had a two-o'clock appointment with Agnew. I invited them to abide on a pew. They took a bench on the other side of the room, the woman sitting down demurely, her husband perching protectively beside her, patting her hand. They did not read *Country Living*.

Along about the time they'd grown comfortable enough with their surroundings to begin speculating on my presence, Nora Toland emerged from Agnew's office. She looked even better than she had on the way in, pale but happy. The young wife on the pew across from me gave Nora a smile of camaraderie. The husband, if I read his thoughts correctly, seemed to think that as a surrogate Nora would do just fine. He managed a smile that was not a leer.

Nora smiled back at them and sat down beside me. The couple across the way looked vaguely disappointed. Nora leaned toward me and said softly, "Dirk wanted me to check on you."

"Was he afraid I'd carve my initials on the furniture?"

Nora paused, studying me. "You don't like Dirk, do you?"

I sure didn't like him talking to Agnew alone. "You think it's wise not to take part in the negotiations?"

"Everything's going to be fine," Nora said. "They're just haggling over dollar amounts, and anyway, I wanted to take a moment to thank you for all you've done."

"Agnew's still trying to stick you for the ten grand?"

"Dirk's sure he can raise five by this afternoon. Agnew wants seventy-five hundred, but—"

"If Dirk would follow my advice you could have Mai within the hour. For free."

"I know. Dirk confronted him with what you found out, but I'd rather have Agnew agree to a price. That way we won't have to live with the fear that he might kidnap Mai again."

"Where's the baby?"

"Agnew won't say."

"What about your father's thirteen thousand? Does Agnew get to keep that, too?"

"Yes, but Dirk's found someone to loan him the full amount, the five thousand to pay Agnew and the thirteen thousand we owe my mother. Hopefully, my father will never know."

"Who'd Dirk get the loan from?"

I was prying, and Nora's look told me I was. She glanced at the couple across the room. They were gazing up at the wall behind us as if the four of us were sharing an elevator and they were watching for their floor, politely disinterested in our conversation. Nora lowered her voice and whispered, "I don't think Dirk would want me to tell you."

I said, "Understand something, Nora. Dirk lied to the police last night, told them I followed the Vietnamese woman home instead of her husband. Did he tell you about that?"

"Yes, but—"

"If I go along with that lie, I risk my career. I risk jail. I'll do it, but only if I get answers from you and Dirk that make the risk seem worthwhile." I held her gaze and let her see that the terms I was laying down had strictly to do with self-preservation.

"All right," Nora said, "Dirk's borrowing the money from a man he knew a long time ago in Vietnam. He owns a Vietnamese restaurant here in East Lansing."

"Mr. Phuc?"

Nora winced. "I think that's his name. I only met him once."

"Why didn't Dirk borrow from Phuc a long time ago?"

Nora looked at me blankly. "I don't know."

I thought back to the police station last night and pictured Toland and Phuc together, but I couldn't call up anything —winks or smirks—that suggested they knew one another. If the cops found out, though, they would want to know why Dirk hadn't acknowledged a prior association with their translator. It would make them unhappy with me, too. Guilt by association. I could see Zukovich gazing at me with the same cool contempt he'd shown Toland last night when he'd found out Dirk could speak Vietnamese, as if knowing the language of the enemy meant you were guilty of collaboration. Which reminded me of what Zukovich had said about the men in Toland's outfit, that a lot of them had "gone native." Something clicked just then. Toland had told Zukovich that he'd been stationed in Quang Ngai, in the village of Binh Nghia. This was the same village Mr. Phuc mentioned yesterday at his restaurant, the village where Xuan and her mother and Hung had lived. I almost asked Nora if her husband had ever mentioned knowing the dead woman from when he was in Vietnam, but something stopped me: the suspicion that he'd known her, all right, and that it wasn't any coincidence that twenty years later Le Thanh Chi had come all the way to Lansing, Michigan, from Southeast Asia.

The door to Agnew's office opened and Dirk Toland stepped into the waiting room and closed the door behind him. It seemed to me that Toland looked satisfied with himself, as if his conversation with Agnew had gone a little better than expected.

He came over and knelt in front of us, one knee on the braided oval rug, the other serving as a prop for his elbow. He said, "Agnew's making arrangements with the person who has Mai to set up a time for the exchange, Mai for the money. I told him I'd have the cash at five thirty." Toland said this as if he were briefing his lieutenants in the field on the deployment of other units. If he had had a stick in his hand and a yard of sand in front of him he might have drawn us a diagram: Mai here, Agnew there, money in between, the exchange at 1730 hours.

I said, "Have you thought any more about what you'll tell the police when they find out you're listed on the birth certificate as the baby's father?"

Toland shrugged. "I'll just tell them the truth, that Thanh Chi acted as a surrogate mother for me and Nora."

"That she was a surrogate mother for you and Nora is not the truth, Dirk. It's a lie."

Toland, his jaws clenching, said, "Agnew agreed he'd back us up on it as long as he gets his money."

"And even if it were the truth," I pressed on, "the cops will want to know why you didn't tell them about it at the station last night. You got a reason for that?"

"I'll just say it slipped my mind, or that it didn't seem important."

"Not good enough. Not nearly."

Toland whispered harshly, "There's no reason why it shouldn't be, Bodine, unless you give them one."

"I want you to give me one, Dirk, a reason I think the cops will believe."

Toland looked at me with narrowed, knowing eyes. He said, "Agnew settled for five grand. What's your price?"

Nora said, "Dirk, don't."

Nora was right, I didn't like her husband. But that didn't mean I enjoyed hectoring him in front of her. I said, "Just tell me how you're going to explain to the cops why you never told them Thanh Chi was a surrogate mother for you and Nora."

Toland held my gaze a moment longer, then looked down, rubbing his face as he thought about my question, his hand rasping over his stubble. "I'll tell them I was afraid of negative publicity. Anyway, the fact that Thanh Chi was our surrogate, or pretended to be our surrogate, hasn't got anything to do with the fact that she's dead."

"Don't you get it? You are intimately connected with a murder victim. The police are going to eviscerate your story before they're done, and this business of who I was following last night, Hung or Thanh Chi, that's where they're going to insert the knife."

Toland, still kneeling in front of me, cracked his knuckles, thinking. Then, in a whisper, he said, "Look, we'll just say you were hired to keep an eye on Xuan as well as on Thanh Chi. I'll explain that Xuan worked for me as a housekeeper and I suspected she was stealing from us at home. It just so happened that Nora called you and told you there was some jewelry missing from our house and that Xuan hadn't reported for work. I'll say that when I was at the station last night I didn't have any idea Nora had called you about Xuan, which is why I told the police you were tailing Thanh Chi. I'll say I just assumed that's what you were doing. I didn't know you'd figured out Xuan was working at a restaurant and that you went there to talk to her. All you have to say is that you lost her, and that you followed Hung home from the restaurant hoping to get a line on Xuan again through him."

I had to hand it to Dirk. He could think on his knees. I said, "What happens if Hung tells the cops he's the baby's father?"

"Like I already told you, I promised Hung I'd get him off if he kept his mouth shut. As far as the baby's concerned, he could care less."

"Then why was he at the hospital the night she was born?"

"How do you know about that?"

"Nora told me yesterday morning."

Toland made a pleading gesture with his hands, opening them to me. "It's not important that three months ago Hung showed up at the damned hospital. Believe me, Hung doesn't care about the baby. I'm the one who cares. I'm the one who's going another eighteen grand in debt. Me, not Hung."

"Speaking of your debts, Nora says a certain Mr. Phuc is going to loan you the money to pay off Agnew. Is that correct?"

Toland glanced at Nora.

I said, "With a line of credit like that, why didn't you put the touch on Mr. Phuc before you picked up the baby from the hospital? You could have paid off Agnew then and saved Nora and yourself a lot of trouble."

"Nora could have saved us both a lot of trouble if she'd never hired you," Toland said.

I stood up.

Toland stood up, too, faster than I did, but not all the way. He was facing me in a slight crouch, his left hand poised low to grab my belt and yank me within range of his knee while at the same time his right hand, higher than his left, was prepared to slam into my nose, driving the cartilage backward into my brain. The marine "take-down." As a young sailor we were dependent on the marines who provided security for our isolated base, and I used to watch them practice this maneuver and other niceties. Marines played for keeps. I played for time, backing away from Toland and motioning for him to join me at the window for a gentlemanly tête-à-tête.

Toland, glancing self-consciously at the couple on the pew across the room, eased out of his crouch. They looked away from him, and Toland, straightening his tie, stepped over to the window, breathing with emotion, his index finger hard on my chest. "When I needed the money back in January Phuc was trying to negotiate a deal to buy another restaurant. But it fell through, so now he's got cash available. You satisfied?"

I eased Toland's finger off my sternum. "Nora also mentioned that you and this Mr. Phuc go all the way back to Vietnam. I had a little talk with Mr. Phuc and his nine-millimeter yesterday, maybe he said something to you about it? I got the impression Hung and Thanh Chi were from his village. I'm just wondering if you happened to bump into them when you were over there in Binh Nghia?"

Toland's face flushed. He glanced at Nora.

I whispered to Toland, "This Mr. Phuc also told me that the Vietnamese Communists were certain Xuan's father was an American."

Toland, his whisper more of a strangled gasp, said, "Why are you busting my balls?"

"You think this is painful, just wait till the cops figure out you and Phuc and Hung and Thanh Chi were together over there in Vietnam in the same little village."

Toland thrust out his chin. "Who's going to tell them?"

"Phuc said Hung saved Thanh Chi from the Communists by insisting he was Xuan's father. The Communists knew better. It cost Hung eleven years in a concentration camp."

"So what?"

"I don't think a man who loved a woman that much would kill her."

"You saw him standing over her body!"

"That's right. And the look on his face was terrible. At first I thought he looked like a man who had just beaten his wife to death. But the more I thought about it, the more it seemed to me he looked that way not because he'd done something terrible, but because the woman he loved was dead. He was grief-stricken. That's what I heard in his voice when I was eavesdropping on that argument, grief-stricken outrage."

"You speak Vietnamese, do you?"

"I don't have to speak Vietnamese to know what Hung was feeling. What I don't know is who he was arguing with."

"He was arguing with Thanh Chi."

I said, "I think Thanh Chi was already dead."

"You're crazy."

"Get this, Dirk. The cops are going to be asking you and me a lot of questions, and the two of us better have our story straight, particularly if you intend to get Hung off the hook."

Toland was swaying perceptibly. There was an angry rhythm to the motion, like a bull getting ready to charge. Agnew's two-o'clock clients were watching us intently.

I called Toland's attention to our audience and said, "Why don't we step outside?"

Toland's eyes darted around the room. Without a word he turned and headed out the door.

I winked reassuringly at Nora, smiled at the couple on the bench, and followed Dirk Toland out of Agnew's office.

# 19 ◄◄◄

Toland headed out onto the catwalk. He stopped midway and gazed down into the lobby. I went up to him and leaned close. "First thing I want to get straight is Xuan. She's your daughter, isn't she?"

Toland started to speak, then hesitated. He appeared to be rolling replies around in his mind the way Queeg rolled those ball bearings around in his fist. Then he turned and leaned back against the tubular railing and stared at me. His eyes had a sheen that made them seem bleary and unfocused, as if he'd been drinking or had gone too long between drinks. After a moment he said, "Yes." Then his gaze slid away as if his paternity were somehow incriminating.

"You and Thanh Chi?"

He nodded again.

"In Vietnam?"

"Vietnam." Toland said this as if the word explained everything.

"It's a pretty tangled tale we're going to be telling the cops, Dirk. And an ugly one, too, accusing an illegitimate daughter of thieving from you, in order to cover up an illegitimate claim on another."

Toland lowered his head and combed his large hand through his thick brown hair, sighing. "You don't understand, Bodine."

"No, you don't understand Bodine. You can't buy me off. You can't make me go away. All you can do is tell me the truth. After that, I decide what to do about it: tell the cops what I already know or help you work out a sensible solution to this mess you're in. But I got to have the truth first."

"I already told you, Xuan's my daughter."

"You look like you haven't slept in two days."

"I haven't."

"Keeping the truth from Nora has been keeping you awake?"

Toland nodded wearily.

"You've been keeping it from her for twenty years. Why the sudden insomnia?"

Toland, sagging on the railing now, said, "It's not only that. It's what happened to Thanh Chi. I loved her once, and now she's dead."

"Right. And they've got Hung for her murderer. You said you promised him you'd get him off if he kept his mouth shut about the baby. Seems to me the only way he's going to get off is if he isn't guilty. And if he didn't kill her, then she was already dead when he entered the house. And if that's true, then who did I hear him arguing with?"

Toland looked up at me.

"Was it the old woman, Hung's mother?" I said.

"No. She was out at a store."

"Who told you that?"

"Phuc."

"Did Phuc get it from Hung or the old woman?" I said.

"Hung."

"Did Hung tell Phuc who he was arguing with?"

Toland nodded.

"All right, who was it?"

Toland took a breath so deep it must have reached to the bottom of his soul. He said, "Xuan. She killed Thanh Chi."

From our perch I could hear the soft trickling of a fountain in the lobby below. I could smell it, too, a chlorinated humidity that mingled pungently with the humus smell from the potted trees. Or maybe it was a trapped-animal scent coming off Dirk Toland. I said, "Xuan killed Thanh Chi? Why?"

Toland shrugged listlessly. "They got into an argument and Xuan pushed her. Thanh Chi stumbled and hit her head on the edge of the bathtub."

I said, "I didn't find Thanh Chi's body in the bathroom."

"That's because Hung came in a few seconds after it happened and carried her into the bedroom. But she was dead. He asked Xuan what happened. Xuan told him she didn't know. She said she'd just got there herself and found Thanh Chi. Hung didn't buy that, and began yelling at her. Xuan started yelling back. She made up a story about seeing a guy run out the back door just as she was coming in, the same person who tried to talk to her at Phuc's restaurant earlier in the day. That's why when you showed up Hung attacked you. Xuan had already slipped out the back door."

"Where did she go?"

"To her apartment. It wasn't till late that night, after you and I talked, that she called me and explained what happened."

"Which was?"

"I told you, Xuan got into an argument with Thanh Chi."

"I wish you'd quit sparing me the details."

Toland turned away from me, leaned his weight on the railing, and gazed down into the lobby. People, drastically foreshortened, crisscrossed the flagstones, their voices echoing faintly. Toland's voice was only slightly more audible. He said, "Xuan didn't like having to live with Thanh Chi and Hung. And Hung's old lady. She wanted to stay at her own apartment. But Thanh Chi was worried about her. Even when the two of them lived together there were problems, Xuan hanging around with college guys, that kind of thing. So when Thanh Chi went back to Hung she asked him to collect Xuan and bring her into the fold. Hung went

186

whole hog, insisting she couldn't work for us either. He took her to Phuc and got her a job at his restaurant. Xuan didn't like that, especially since Phuc was making her work for less than Nora and I had been paying her."

"You still haven't told me what the argument was about."

Toland drew another deep breath. "Hung and Thanh Chi had decided to leave town as soon as they scraped together some money. They expected Xuan to go away with them, but she wasn't interested. When Phuc sent her home from the restaurant yesterday she went to see a boyfriend instead, and decided to move in with him. She went back to Hung's place to get her things. Nobody was there. Hung's mother was out and Thanh Chi had taken a bus to my shop to collect some back pay she had coming. When Thanh Chi got home she found Xuan packing things that didn't belong to her. Xuan said she was moving in with an American college student. Thanh Chi wouldn't let her out of the house. Xuan tried to get past her and they scuffled and Xuan pushed Thanh Chi down." Toland shrugged and shook his head. "She's a hot-tempered kid."

I said, "Why did Hung and Thanh Chi suddenly decide to leave town?"

"When Thanh Chi went back to Hung he insisted on it as a condition. I tell you, Bodine, it's hard for me not to let that little fucker rot in jail. Ten years in Jackson, he'd be getting off light. You could call it his entrance fee into the country he stabbed in the back, the little ARVN puke."

I made a point of keeping my tone neutral, not wanting to ignite Toland's high-octane hatred. "Why did he insist on leaving town with Thanh Chi?"

Toland waved his hand as if I were pestering him with trivialities. "It's a long story."

"Tell me the short parts."

"Hell. Hung's paranoid. He didn't want Thanh Chi anywhere around me. When he first found out Thanh Chi was working for me—this was way last year—he wanted her to leave town with him and his mother. Thanh Chi liked her job and didn't want to go. So Hung started making her life miserable. He figured the two of us were seeing each other again, like the old days. We weren't, but she couldn't tell him different. He ended up kicking Thanh Chi out, which suited his mother just fine. She was constantly egging him on. She always hated Thanh Chi's guts." Toland shook his head, his gaze roving the catwalk as if the animosities of the Hung family were crowded onto it like refugees clinging to a fishing boat.

I said, "I take it you had a hand in getting them out of Vietnam?"

"Yeah, but I never told them, Hung or his mother. I didn't give a damn about them anyway. It was Xuan I was interested in. And I felt I owed Thanh Chi something."

"You knew you had a child over there all these years?"

"Yes. I mean, not exactly. I didn't know Thanh Chi was pregnant till I got rotated back to the States, six months or so after I came home to Nora. Phuc wrote and told me. But by then all I wanted to do was forget the war. I resigned my commission and stopped thinking about Thanh Chi and all the rest of it. It wasn't till just recently, when Nora and I realized we wouldn't be able to adopt a child, that I began to wonder about the kid I had in Vietnam. If we could have adopted a baby here, I probably wouldn't have fixated on Xuan, but Nora and I were so frustrated it got to the point where I couldn't get Xuan out of my mind. I didn't even know her name, just that there was a good chance I had someone over there who belonged to me. I never mentioned her to Nora because I was ashamed of what I'd done. Nora and I had been married almost a year before I went over, and I didn't ever want her to know anything about Thanh Chi. To this day I don't know what's worse, cheating on Nora or abandoning my child."

I said, "How'd you get her out?"

"Phuc. He's still connected over there. Came through with their papers, the works. Cost me everything I had, although it

188

wouldn't have busted me if it had just been Xuan. That would have been pretty cheap, since lately they've been letting Amerasian kids emigrate. But Xuan wouldn't leave without her mother. And Thanh Chi wouldn't leave without Hung, who was in a prison camp. That's what cost me the bucks, having to bribe the prison officials. Then Hung's freed, but he won't leave without his old lady. By the time I was done footing the bill for the four of them I was into Phuc for a fortune. That's why I came up short when I had to pay off Agnew at the hospital."

I said, "You're telling me Xuan wouldn't leave Vietnam without her mother, yet she doesn't hesitate to knock her head against the bathtub when the woman objects to her living with a boyfriend?"

"I can't understand it either," Toland said, shaking his head. "I guess Xuan didn't have it easy over there, being half American. She took a lot of ridicule. She's not what you'd call affectionate. She's got a big chip on her shoulder. And who can blame her, always getting put down for being different? Over there they call Amerasian kids 'dirt of the dirt.' When she arrived in America, though, she found out she looks just about like everyone else, better than everyone else, and she blossomed. It was instantaneous. Hung and his mother, Christ, they hated her for that. She was Cinderella in Vietnam, no better than the old woman's slave, but when she got here to America she was a princess. Even Thanh Chi was confused and wanted to keep her down. Phuc figured it all out the day they arrived. When he told me how it was, I had him bring Xuan to stay with Nora and me till I could find her an apartment. I told Nora she was our new housekeeper."

"Does Xuan know who you are?"

"No. I never intended to tell her. I just wanted to have her around the house, you understand?"

I said, "Sure, just as I can understand how Hung might have wanted to have his daughter around his house, too."

"His daughter?"

"Mai."

Toland looked at me as if he were on bivouac and had heard a twig snap in the night. "Listen, when Thanh Chi told Hung she was going to have his baby he refused to believe it was his kid. He thought it was mine. He still thinks I'm Mai's father."

"You sure he didn't show up at the hospital to get a look at the baby to see if it was his?"

Toland, his ear still cocked in my direction, said, "What are you getting at?"

"The possibility it wasn't Agnew who repossessed the baby two days ago, but Hung."

As I spoke, Toland began shaking his head. "No. Agnew's got Mai."

"He's already slurped up Nora's parents' money without producing the baby, and you're about to pour another five grand into his trough."

"He wouldn't try to pull something like that."

"And what would you do about it if he did? You've already decided not to use what you know about him for fear he'll tell the *Lansing State Journal* you paid him to fake the surrogate deal with Thanh Chi. You don't want to queer your business relationship with Uncle Sam, remember? What if Agnew's been playing you for a sucker?"

Toland swallowed the possibility as if it were a specialty dish from Mr. Phuc's mental menu. "I don't know. I don't know what I'd do."

"What I'd do is make sure Sam Agnew's got the baby, and not some friend of Hung's."

"How? Agnew won't tell me where Mai is till I hand over the money."

"What if I told Sam I was going to have a little talk with his mother about the true nature of his surrogate operation?"

"No. You keep out of this. You've been nothing but trouble." Toland's ire was on the rise again.

"One more thing, Dirk."

"Listen, Bodine, I've got to finish up with Agnew and get back to work. Government auditors are at the shop and I've got to be there at three for fun and games while they walk through the results of their audit with me. I haven't got any more time for this."

I glanced at my watch. "Sure you do. You've got a good forty minutes. And what I want you to explain won't take but five."

"I've already told you enough."

"Enough that I'm remembering what you told me last night outside the police station."

Toland frowned. "About what?"

"About how you were going to get your father-in-law's money back from Agnew and let him keep the baby."

"Yeah, but I changed my mind."

"How do I know you didn't change it back?"

"Bodine—"

"Get your finger off my chest."

"Then pay attention. When I left Nora last night to bail you out at the cops I had every intention of keeping my promise to her to get the baby back. But when I was driving downtown I started brooding, and I got angry at Nora. And at you. And her father. Especially him. I just boiled over. When I told you I was going to let Agnew keep the baby I guess I meant it. But afterward, on the way home, I couldn't help thinking about what you said. All of a sudden I knew it was more important to have Mai than the satisfaction of thumbing my nose at Nora's old man. So when I got home I repeated to Nora that I'd do whatever I had to do in order to raise the money. See? And if you hadn't butted in this morning and told her what I said to you last night, it would have saved us all a lot of grief."

"That's a nice speech, Dirk, but in point of fact you still haven't raised the money to pay Agnew."

"I will. I'll be leaving the office at five thirty to meet Phuc. He'll give me the money and I'll deliver it to Agnew. We'll have Mai by six thirty."

"Assuming Agnew's got her."

"Will you get off that?"

"I would if I could have a word with Xuan, ask her who kidnapped the baby."

"She said it was a white guy. He had a gun."

"What if it was Hung who told her to say that?"

"I asked her—"

"I'd like to ask her, too. Where is she?"

"I don't know."

"I don't believe you."

Toland said carefully, "Believe this, Bodine, I'm going to get my daughter out of the mess she's in. I'm not going to let her down like . . . like I did Thanh Chi."

I said, "If you get her out of the mess she's in, how do you get Hung out of the mess he's in?"

Toland leaned toward me and lowered his voice. "As soon as she's safely away Phuc will get word to Hung. Hung will break his silence and tell the cops what happened between Xuan and Thanh Chi. All I need is a few more hours."

"Where are you sending her?"

"There are lots of Vietnamese communities around the country. Phuc will get her safely established with a new identity and the police will never find her."

"All this in a few more hours?"

"Phuc says he'll have a plane ticket for her when I meet him to get Agnew's money. Nora and I will pay off Agnew, then pick up the baby. I'll take Nora home, then get Xuan and take her to the airport. As soon as she lands, she'll call me. I'll call Phuc, and Phuc will let Hung know it's okay to tell the cops what really happened yesterday at his house."

"I still want to talk to Xuan."

"Hung will be out of jail by tomorrow at the latest. The rest of it's none of your damned business."

I started to disagree with him, but the door to Agnew's office opened and Nora stepped out into the corridor. "Dirk?"

"What?"

Nora nodded toward the interior of Agnew's offices. "He wants to talk to you again."

Toland went over to her and spoke in a whisper, hooking his thumb in my direction. I knew what he was saying: Get rid of the gumshoe. I saw Nora give him a reluctant nod, glancing a little guiltily at me.

Toland, before entering Agnew's office, shot me a last look, his eyebrows raised in a kind of plea as he nudged Nora in my direction. Then he was gone.

Nora came out onto the catwalk and looked up at me with compassionate concern, as if it were Eddie who'd been repossessed and not Mai. She said, "You must be under an awful strain."

There was a note of forgiveness in her voice and I had the impression she'd been apologizing to someone for my behavior. I said, "What are you talking about?"

"Is it true? Your father died recently? He was a private detective, too, and he worked with you for years?"

"Not so many years."

"And ours is the first case you've taken since his death?"

"I've been spending a lot of time with Eddie."

"Yesterday evening at Clara's Joyce never mentioned anything about your being . . . despondent, so I had no way of knowing—"

"Who's been telling you I'm 'despondent'?"

"I just had another word with Mr. Agnew. He said that when his wife called him and told him about us going to his house looking for Mai he got in touch with a private investigator to see what he could find out about you. The investigator told Agnew he knew you. He said you're a desperate man, angry and out of work and so on, and not to be trusted to act in our best interest, Dirk's and mine. But I told Agnew I trusted you totally, and, well, I just wanted you to know that Dirk has an opening at the shop. If you need work, I'm sure he'll be glad to take you on."

I didn't say anything. I was trying to figure a way to ask Nora what, if anything, Dirk had told her about Xuan's whereabouts without giving away his dirty little secret.

Nora said, "Jack, I think everything's going to be just fine. Because of you. You've helped me get my baby back and I'll be forever grateful. It won't be enough just to pay your fee. I want to do more than that. And if you've lost your taste for this kind of work, Dirk really does have a job opening at the shop."

Remembering the demise of Thanh Chi, I was sure he did. I said, "You think?"

"Pardon?"

"You think everything's going to be all right?"

"I'm convinced of it."

"How do you know Dirk isn't in there selling Mai down the Mekong?"

She shook her head. "He wouldn't do that."

"Marines never lie?"

"I told him I'd leave him."

In an odd way I was heartened to hear this. There was a good chance Nora was going to lose her hubby to the long arm of the law, and it reassured me to know she'd already contemplated the possibility of life without him. I said, "Okay."

Nora said, "Please don't worry, Jack. We'll get Mai. I'll be all right. And so will Dirk. I do trust him. And I love him."

I was suddenly a little jealous of Dirk Toland, which was probably why I signed off as abruptly as I did. I said, "Give me a call if you have any problems."

"I will. And Jack? You won't ever tell anyone about the

arrangement we have with Agnew, will you? We'd lose Mai if you did."

I said, "I'll try not to, Nora. I'll certainly try not to."

I left her on the sun-warmed catwalk, took the elevator down, and headed out into the parking lot and got into my car. If it had been later in the day, I could have driven into a sunset.

# 20 ◄◄◄

What I drove into was the Shell station across the street. I didn't need gas. I just needed a place to lie in wait for Toland. I'd decided to follow him to Xuan. I couldn't see how the girl was in danger of being incarcerated for accidentally causing her mother's death, tragic as that was. So why disappear her forever? Toland was lying to me. Or the girl was lying to him, and he knew it. She could lie to me, too, but I'd worry about that after I found her.

I parked around the side of the station, and got out of the car. Eddie was due home from school in an hour and somebody had to be there to meet him. I had to call Joyce and have her leave work early. I headed for the station office, keeping an eye on Toland's little red Tercel. I couldn't help noticing the black Olds Cutlass Supreme angling toward me across the apron, though. It wasn't actually black. It was more the color of a Michigan woods on a dim day: a dark, very grim green. The number 41 was painted on both doors of the car and there was a flasher bar above the windshield. The two cops inside the car hopped out, and after a word or two with me they insisted I lock my vehicle and join them for a ride downtown. It was one of those invitations

—coming at you over the sights of a .38 Police Special—that you can't refuse.

Except for the occasional crash of static from the radio, the trip downtown was made in silence. The officers knew nothing of the LPD's interest in me, and as to my need to be home by three thirty to meet my son, that was something I would have to discuss with Detective Zukovich, who had issued the lookout. The driver, a rookie who was quite pleased with herself for having spotted my car, mentioned Zukovich as if she were pessimistic about my chances of ever seeing Eddie again.

But she didn't know Zook was my neighbor. Of course, I didn't expect him to act neighborly at the station. The station was altogether another neck of the woods, Zook's wolfish domain. With any luck he'd treat me as if I were a member of a related species, a large dog, perhaps, an inferior carnivore whose size and genetic similarities were all that kept him from eating my throat. In other words, he'd cuff me to a desk, disparage my profession, denigrate my ethics, and threaten to revoke my license if I didn't cooperate. Everyone in the squad room would take us for enemies. Then on the weekend he'd come over to borrow my seed spreader and we'd spend the rest of the day watching the Tigers on the PASS channel.

When I stepped into the squad room, however, Zukovich looked up and smiled as if I were not only his neighbor, but his very best and dearest friend, for whom he had nothing but respect, fondness, and affection. He actually stood up, leaned across his desk, and offered his hand. "Jack," he said, "it's great to see you. Sit down, sit down."

I sat down. I needed to.

Zukovich said, "So, how's Joyce?"

Zook's interest in Joyce had always been carnal. Unless he was dragging me downtown to boast of her defection from my bed to his, it would never have occurred to him to begin with such a vacuous pleasantry. I said, "She's got a yeast infection."

Zukovich smiled as if he hadn't really heard me, his eyes darting toward Fortner's office. I glanced over my shoulder and saw Fats sitting inside his glassed-in office, gazing out at us. I waved at him, but the lieutenant kept staring at me while listening skeptically to whatever it was Mr. Phuc was translating into Vietnamese for the benefit of the manacled Mr. Hung. The English end of it was coming from a well-dressed gentleman with graying temples who was obviously a lawyer. He wasn't from the public defender's office, either. I knew all the PDs and he wasn't one of them. I bet he was costing Toland plenty. I looked around for Hung's mother and saw her perched on a bench next to the door. She was watching me, too. I turned back to Zukovich, in whose overly friendly face there seemed to be a plea for cooperation. "Care for a smoke, Jack?"

Zook knew I didn't smoke. I said, "No thanks, Mike, but you go ahead and have one if you like." I never called him Mike. I knew he didn't smoke, either. We were preparing to play a little game. "So," I said, "what brings me here?"

"Well, Jack, I'd really appreciate it if you and me could go over an aspect of the statement you made last night."

"And what aspect would that be, Mike?"

"Well, what I'd like is for us to zero in on the exact time you saw Mr. Hung enter his home."

When answering a cop's questions, no matter how well acquainted you are with the officer, it is always a good idea to seem as ignorant as an iguana. Fortunately, this has never been difficult for me. I said, "Who?"

"The gook we took into custody last night. His name's Le Van Hung."

I glanced at the tape recorder on Zukovich's desk. The little red light wasn't lit.

Zukovich said, "This isn't an interrogation, Jack. Just a friendly chat."

"An interview?"

"Right. An interview."

"And you're interested in what time this Mr. Hung entered his house, right?"

"Right."

I knew Hung had gone in at precisely six fifty-five. If I wanted to verify that fact for Zukovich, it would be a simple matter to show him the notepad in my breast pocket. But I didn't want to do that. Agnew's name was there along with the Tolands', and at this point I was not prepared to destroy their arrangements with Sam. I said, "Well, Mike, just as I told the officers last night, the Vietnamese male presently in Lieutenant Fortner's office entered the residence at 101 Clifford Street at approximately seven Wednesday evening, maybe a little before."

Zukovich leaned back in his chair and clasped his hands behind his head. He wasn't wearing his suit coat and the armpits of his white, all-cotton Oxford shirt were soaked gray with sweat. For reasons that weren't clear at the moment, it looked like Fats Fortner was stretching poor Zook on the rack of our friendship. No doubt it would be my turn next. Zook said, "Do you think you could give me an actual, specific time, Jack?"

"I'd be glad to try, Mike. How specific would you like me to be, actually?"

"Well, you say you saw him enter the residence at a little before seven. Would that be five minutes before the hour, or ten minutes, or say, sixty minutes?"

"Sixty minutes?"

"Yes. Are you sure he didn't enter the house on Clifford just before six o'clock yesterday evening?"

"No, I'm sure it wasn't that early."

"How can you be certain?"

"Well, as you recall, I had my little boy with me. I picked him up from school in the afternoon, so he was with me on the job. And I distinctly remember that just as the suspect entered the house my boy asked me what time it was. I told him it was six fifty-five. He'd been expecting his mother to drop by the stakeout and pick him up, and he was impatient."

"I don't suppose there's a notebook where you might have written this time down?"

"Not that I recall."

"I see. So, you followed the victim home from her place of employment on South Pennsylvania, and then proceeded to stake out the residence she entered on Clifford. Is that correct?"

I'd been watching the little red light on the recorder. It definitely wasn't flickering. Nor were the little wheels of the cassette turning. Zook did not appear to be wired, either. So I said, "Yes."

"Why?"

"As Mr. Toland told you last night, he suspected her of lifting film from his micrographics shop. I decided to stake out her place in case a fence showed up."

"Was she alone?"

"Yes."

"Did you see anyone enter the house immediately after the woman went in?"

"No. But I should remind you that there was a back door to the place, and it was out of my line of sight."

"All right, you say you picked up your boy from school earlier in the afternoon?"

"Yes."

"What time does school let out?"

"Three fifteen."

"So, if you're right about the time the suspect entered the house, your boy had been with you almost four hours?"

"More like three hours and forty minutes."

"How old is he, Jack?"

"My boy or the suspect?"

"Your boy."

"He's eight, Mike. This won't go past three fifteen, will it?"

"It seems to me, Jack, that an impatient eight-year-old kid might have been making a lot of requests to know what time it was during the period of the stakeout."

"You'd be correct in assuming that."

"Well then, how can you be sure, what with your son pestering you, that it wasn't five fifty-five when the suspect entered the house and not six fifty-five?"

"Mike, it's not how often Eddie asked me what time it was that matters, but the fact that he asked me at the very moment Mr. Hung entered the house. That's what keys my memory. And that's what I'll testify to in court. Six fifty-five."

Zukovich held my gaze. "This six fifty-five is absolutely solid?"

"That's right. The six fifty-five's solid."

Zukovich continued to stare at me, saying nothing. In the depths of his gaze, however, I discerned the clear glimmer of a comment, something to the effect that I was every bit as simple as I was pretending to be. There was a glint of disdain there, too, a sneer of disrespect that was not for the benefit of the squad room, but was meant for me personally. For all I knew, maybe Joyce and Zook *were* an item.

The phone on Zukovich's desk rang. He snatched it up midway through the ring and growled his name at the receiver. He grabbed a pen and a pad and began scribbling and grunting, grunting and scribbling. I gazed around the bay, trying to clear my mind of its impurities. I discerned that life at the LPD wasn't nearly as intense as it was on "Hill Street Blues." I saw a couple of clerk sergeants poking through files. There were a few detectives muttering between themselves or plinking away at typewriters. It was quiet, contained, and orderly, with none of the convoluted hustle and bustle of the Hill. Homicide at the LPD looked fake. Even Fortner looked fake. He was too fat to be a lieutenant of detectives, yet there he was, a cross between Kojak and Jabba the Hutt, staring at me from his glassed-in office while he listened without pleasure to whatever it was Mr. Phuc was saying.

Suddenly Fortner turned away from me and with a bloated finger stabbed the middle distance between himself and Mr.

Phuc. I heard him shout, "What the hell do you mean it didn't seem pertinent at the time?"

Phuc, who was once again dressed in a three-piece suit, explained himself in subdued tones, very businesslike. Hung's lawyer put in his two hundred dollars' worth while Hung himself stared at the floor. Hung's mother, sitting across the room, was watching and listening with an intensity bordering on comprehension. After all, one didn't have to speak English in order to understand the language of bodies.

Zukovich grunted and scribbled.

You'd think if Fats Fortner's body had a vocabulary, it would fill a dictionary the size of the *OED*. But not so. His corpulence was expressive of maybe three states of mind: anger, contempt, and outrage. And threat. He was threatening Phuc as I watched, but didn't seem to be getting anywhere. Phuc just looked at him, smiling politely. All at once Fortner said something curt and made the gesture of an umpire thumbing a man out at the plate. Phuc got up, bowed, and left the office. He made a dignified passage through the array of desks and paused before Hung's mother. He bowed again. They spoke. Phuc sat down.

Meanwhile Jabber the Hulk was thrusting his fat finger at Hung's lawyer. Bodily punctuation. He articulated several more choice comments, then burst out of his glassed-in office and headed for us. Zukovich hung up and swiveled in his chair. Fortner surged up to him. "Was that them?"

"Yeah."

"Well?"

Zukovich said, "Her alibi's okay. The mama-san was at the House of Chin from four thirty to six thirty yesterday."

"House of Chin?"

"Chinese grocery and gift shop on Michigan just a couple blocks west of Clifford."

Fortner said, "You sure this is solid?"

Zukovich nodded dispiritedly. "Clerk says he's sure because the old girl came into the store and wanted to make a phone call.

She didn't know how to operate the phone, so he showed her. After the call she stood around the whole time, didn't buy anything, didn't say anything, just stared out the window at the street, killing time."

Fortner said, "Does the clerk have any idea who she called?"

"No. He couldn't understand her because—get this—she spoke English."

"English?" Fortner shot a look at the old woman, who was speaking to Mr. Phuc in rapid-fire Vietnamese. "English!"

Inside Fortner's office a uniformed sergeant was having hard words with Hung's lawyer. Two plainclothes cops had just hauled in a foul-mouthed redneck and cuffed him to a desk. Phones were going off all over the bay and the computerized teletypes were chattering crazily. I could even hear a siren somewhere in the distance. I was beginning to believe in the reality of the place.

"English! What the hell. If she was talking English, how come the clerk don't know what she said?"

Zukovich shrugged. "The clerk's Chinese and can't speak English. Just knows what English sounds like. The patrolman got this from the manager of the place. He was translating for the clerk."

"Shit." Fortner was wheezing. His eyes were darting from Zukovich to the old woman to Hung to me and back to the old woman, who appeared to be only half listening to something that was being communicated to her by Mr. Phuc. Fortner said to Zukovich, "That little zip's been slick with me. I want you to call the campus and get a Vietnamese-speaking egghead out here who ain't a zip."

Zukovich said, "What about the guy who was here last night?"

"Toland?" Fortner snorted contemptuously. "Another slick boy. Like Bodine, here."

Zukovich fiddled nervously with his pen.

Fortner said, "So what about it, Zook? What time's your private-eye pal telling us?"

"He says the gook entered the house at five to seven, but—"

"That what he said?"

Zukovich nodded. "Yeah, but—"

"That what you said, Bodine?"

"No. I said he went into the house at six fifty-five."

"Shit." Fortner said to Zukovich, "That's the best you could get from this 'friend' of yours?"

"I haven't had a chance to really get into it, Lieutenant."

"You haven't had a chance? You and your private-eye buddy been yakking ten minutes."

Zook had a thick black mustache, so I couldn't tell if he had sweat on his lip or not. He sure had plenty of it on his brow, though. He stuck a finger between his collar and his neck and tugged while glancing around the bay as if looking for a way out.

Fats Fortner leaned toward Zook and said with menacing clarity, "I'll do him myself. If the old girl really speaks English, this'll work out better'n I thought. And by the way, Detective Zukovich, when I fill out your next performance evaluation, I'm going to remember the fact you're buddies with a private eye that's been slick with me. Now, get over there and see the old girl stays put till I get done with the slick dick here."

# 21 ◄◄◄

I started to get up.

Fortner said, "Sit down, asshole."

I said, "I think we know each other well enough we can drop the fancy titles, Lieutenant."

"Sit! Down!"

I sat down.

Fats sat down. "Now get this, Bodine. I want you to correct your statement about the time you saw the dink walk into that house last night."

"Dink as in gook?"

"I talked to Smith over at the state police and your license is under review."

"Is it?"

"For making false statements to law-enforcement officials."

"Such as?"

"Such as I had a couple men talk to your kid at school this morning, first thing he got there. In the principal's office. Kid told us who you were tailing, and it wasn't the woman. And he told us Zukovich knew that, knew it last night here at the station."

"You got all that from an eight-year-old kid?"

"Zukovich has been covering your ass."

"Lieutenant, I was sitting on my ass right here at Zook's desk last night and I heard everything that was said between him and my boy and the kid didn't tell Zukovich we were tailing the Vietnamese guy. He didn't tell him we were tailing a Vietnamese woman, either. He didn't tell him anything because I told him not to. And if a cop talks to a kid in the principal's office, the kid's going to tell the cop whatever it is the cop wants to hear. You can't get reliable statements from a youngster that age. You know that."

"You're saying your own boy's a liar?"

"I'm saying Mr. Hung entered his house at six fifty-five. You do a little police work, check the neighbors, you might find someone to corroborate that. Try the woman across the street."

Fats Fortner shook his head. "All she saw was you peeking into the house. She didn't see Hung go in. And prior to that, she didn't see you on any stakeout."

I said, "I'm not surprised. I'm virtually invisible on stakeout."

Fats sat back in Zukovich's chair. The chair creaked and groaned. He said, "Last night you told me you were following the woman because she was pilfering supplies from Toland's shop."

"Toland said I was following the woman, I didn't."

"See, Bodine. That's slick. But Toland's not so slick, because the dead woman hasn't worked for him since October of last year. She's been off on maternity leave. And if she's been off on maternity leave, how could she have been swiping film?" Fortner gave me a man-in-the-moon grin. "Now, you knowingly made a false statement last night and it's gonna cost you your license, you don't change the time that dink entered the house."

"What time would you like?"

"How about five to six?"

"Why?"

"You don't ask me nothing, Bodine. Just gimme the time."

I glanced over at Mr. Phuc and the old woman and caught Zukovich staring at us.

Fortner said, "It's a shame about Zook."

"How so?"

"He ain't ever going to make sergeant."

"Lieutenant, you can't hold it against Zukovich that he's got me for a neighbor."

"What I hold against Zukovich is the fact he knew last night you were following the dink and not the woman. He's been protecting you and I won't tolerate that."

"Come on. You've been a lieutenant of police long enough to know you can tolerate anything."

"You gonna do it, Bodine, or am I gonna do you?"

I shrugged. "Depends on what you've got in mind. Wiring my stuff to a generator is one thing, but taking me up in the department chopper and hanging me out the door is another. I'm afraid of heights."

Fats Fortner gave this some thought. "You're not worried about having your nuts wired because you ain't got any, is that it?"

"You haven't got a big enough generator."

Fortner got up and leaned forward on the desk. It was one of those gray metal desks with the structural integrity of a battleship. It creaked under Fortner's weight. I quavered under Fortner's breath. He said, "I'm gonna push this record button on Zook's machine here, and you're gonna make your statement that it was five fifty-five the dink entered the house. Nice and loud, so the machine picks it up." He pushed the record/play button and waited, hovering over me.

The little red light on the machine flickered, picking up background noise, but nothing from me, the little reels of the cassette turning in vain.

I glanced over at Zukovich again. He was looking at Fortner with a kind of weary irony, as if to say, "I told you this wasn't the way to do it."

Finally Fortner cursed, speared the stop button, called to the elderly uniformed sergeant, and told him to return Hung to his cell on three. I half expected him to give the order to have me join Hung in Holding, but Fortner beckoned Zukovich back over to the desk and said, "Don't forget, call the campus about that translator. And call the hospitals, too. If the ME's right—and I've never known that gut shucker to be wrong—she had a kid recently. Means there ought to be a certificate of birth somewhere. We'll show it to Mr. Hung with his name on it, see if it don't refresh his memory." Fortner glanced down at me, then said to Zook, "Handle him your way." He said this as if he were telling Zook to clean up a mess he'd made. "Meantime, I'll set up the old girl best I can." He paused and looked back at me. "You cooperate with Detective Zukovich or Smith will feed you your papers. I mean it. And Zukovich, if he doesn't come across, you can kiss your promotion good-bye."

With that Fortner headed toward Hung's mother, holding the door open for the guard who was hauling Hung down to the cells. Fortner glared at the old woman, hulking over her. I watched him from Zukovich's desk . . . Zukovich calling the Department of Asian Languages at Michigan State University, Lieutenant Fortner calling the old woman "mama-san."

It was interesting, observing Fortner and the old woman. It reminded me of a film I saw once showing Asian children riding water buffaloes, herding the beasts left or right with the merest tap of a stick. Having seen that film, it helped me now to know why the old Vietnamese woman did not look entirely terrified of Fats Fortner, who was not as big as a water buffalo. Maybe Mr. Phuc had told her how in the United States a little lawyer could ride herd on a huge police lieutenant with the merest tap of a law. Indeed, as they hustled her son out the door, Hung's lawyer jumped all over Fortner, swatting him with one legality after another. But the lawyer's efforts had no effect on the lieutenant, who had him yanked from the squad room, too. Nor did this seem to worry the old woman greatly. Maybe she figured the lawyer failed because Fats, who was not as big as a buffalo, was not as smart as one, either.

On the other hand, Fats was not the kind of cop to be buffaloed by an old woman. He said, "You hear me, mama-san? I asked you where your son's daughter is. And I want to know now." He was leaning over the old woman with his fists on his hips, talking directly at her and not at Mr. Phuc. When Mr. Phuc attempted to translate for the old woman, Fortner told him to shut up. "I'm asking you, ma'am. Where's your granddaughter?"

The old woman, unperplexed and unimpressed, gazed up at Fats. She was still wearing Pat Nixon's cloth coat, had it buttoned at her neck, just like last night, her hair in a hard bun, her emotions in a vise.

"You better answer my question, ma'am. You don't want to end up in jail, too, do you?"

How the United States had been defeated by Vietnam was hard to figure. I'd read some books on the subject and had seen more than a few movies and all I ever got was more confused. Watching the old woman stare back at Fats Fortner, however, I wondered if the reason for our defeat wasn't as obvious as the look in her eye.

"God damn it, lady! This is your last chance." Fats clenched his impractical fists.

Mr. Phuc, sitting beside the old woman, said, "You have no right speak this way." His posture was protective, but he made no attempt to interpose his body between Fats and the old woman. He added, "She is not understand."

"She's understanding everything," shouted Fats. "I know she speaks American. You hear me, lady? I know you speak American. I want to hear you speak American and I want to hear you speak it now."

The old woman sat up straight and said, "You are crude, ignorant man."

Fats rocked back on his heels as if she'd slapped him. He glanced around the bay, which was dead silent again. Everyone was watching. Fats said, "Well, that may be, ma'am. In fact, I'm sure it's true. I'm a crude, ignorant man. In fact, I'm so ignorant

I actually believed you were telling me the truth, you and Mr. Phuc."

"I have speak no lie."

"You speak no truth, either. Which brings out the crudeness in an ignorant man like me."

"I cannot help."

"Listen, lady, your people got my son in a prison over there in Vietnam. He's there and he's alive in some slime hole and there's nothing I can do about it. But here you are. You're in my country now, and I got your son, see? And I'll tell you something. He's gonna die unless you cooperate with me. Believe it. Now, where's your granddaughter?"

The old woman said angrily, "She is not granddaughter."

Mr. Phuc said something quickly in Vietnamese.

Fortner said, "You shut up, Phuc. Now, what do you mean she's not your granddaughter? Immigration says she's listed as your son's kid."

"She is not of my family. She is of America."

Fortner waved his hand as if the old woman's distinctions were nothing more than an irksome insect. "Whatever. Where is she?"

"I do not know. I do not care."

"You don't like her?"

"No."

"Why not?"

The old woman said, "She is whore."

Fats Fortner took a pause. There was a desk a few feet behind him and he sat on the corner of it. He did this to impress the old woman either with American workmanship or with his courageous disregard for the law of gravity. He gazed at her a moment, then said, "How do you know she's a whore?"

"How else could young woman survive who does not speak language of this country?"

"She could become a telephone operator." Fortner glanced around the bay, garnering smirks.

The old woman said, "I am tire from this."

Fortner sighed deeply. "All right, ma'am. The evidence technicians are finished with your place. I'll have someone give you a lift home. Or you can go back to the hotel where Mr. Phuc took you last night. Your choice."

"I go my son house."

"Good. We'll talk again when you feel rested. In the meantime, I'm sure your son will continue to enjoy his stay in our jail." With a delicate grunt, Fortner eased off the desk and stood.

Mr. Phuc stood, too. The old woman did not. Phuc said something to her and the two of them went back and forth in Vietnamese, arguing a point. Phuc prevailed and the old woman got to her feet, not availing herself of Phuc's proffered hand.

Fortner said, "And ma'am, while you're home resting, you give some thought to the whereabouts of your son's daughter or his whore or whatever she is, and you think about the woman your son beat to death, and see if you can remember where those two females were living before they moved back into his house. I'm going to ask you about that when I see you again. I'll want to know where Mrs. Hung's baby is, too, the one she had several months ago. Remember anything about that, do you?"

The old woman said, "I do not."

"You don't now, but maybe it'll come to you after you rest up. And you, Mr. Phuc, you give some thought to why you never told me till just now that Mr. Hung worked for you at your restaurant."

Mr. Phuc said, "It did not seem—"

"Yeah, I know, it didn't seem pertinent. But it's all very, very pertinent, Mr. Phuc. It's even pertinent why you didn't tell me this old woman here speaks American. Hell, all this time you been jabbering away, she's able to speak it better'n you."

Mr. Phuc said, "This woman is not old. She is my age."

"Did you know she could speak American, or not?"

"No."

"You sponsored her into this country, paid for her, and didn't

211

know she could speak English? Oh, yeah, Mr. Phuc, I've been talking to the INS. I may be an ignorant man, but I'm getting smarter by the minute. And you, ma'am, you just keep me in mind, because the sooner you wise me up, the sooner I spring your boy. Good-bye for now."

Mr. Phuc said, "There is matter of my check."

"Your check?"

"My bill. For translation."

Fats Fortner said something to Mr. Phuc that needed no translation.

# 22 ◄◄◄

Zukovich was still on the phone. He'd evidently finished with the Asian Languages Department, because he was talking to someone now about a birth certificate. He said into the receiver, "It would have been in the last two to three months. Yes, her name is Le Thanh Chi." He spelled it out. "Right, I'm Detective Michael Zukovich with the Lansing Police. Well, I can give you my badge number, my superior's name, and a number to call back. I know you already told me that, ma'am, but let me remind you that this is a homicide investigation. Lady, it would save me a lot of time if you'd just tell me if you've got the birth certificate so I don't have to drive over there for nothing." Zook slammed down the receiver, looked at me, and said brightly, "So, how you doing?"

"How you doing" is an all-purpose male greeting. If you are fluent in the language of men, if you are truly sensitive to its nuances, you can ask your archrival how he's doing and he will understand that if he crosses you he's going to be doing a lot worse. With a slight change of tone, you can use the same phrase to elicit bleak news from your cancer-stricken best friend. Somehow Zukovich managed to suggest I was his cancer-stricken archrival. I said, "Well, I don't have rhythm, and I don't have

213

music. All I got is my license to peep, and Fats is telling me I better look for a new line of work. Otherwise, I'm doing fine."

"What he said was you cooperate with your local law-enforcement officials, you'll be all right."

"Are you fascists going to continue to insist on five fifty-five?"

Zook said, "In the spirit of cooperation, we'll let that drop. For now."

"I think Fats made a smart move, letting you handle me."

"Yeah. But don't you make a stupid one, thinking you're going to cool your way out of here because we're pals." Zukovich leaned toward me. "Now, then, assuming that scarfaced gook entered the house on Clifford at the time you say, it would be most helpful to both our careers for me to know if you were watching him before that. In other words, if you could tell me for a fact he not only didn't enter that house till six fifty-five, but wasn't anywhere near it for an hour or so prior to when you found the body, it would be very significant."

What I knew "for a fact" was that Hung left Nguyen's Nook at five fifty-five yesterday afternoon. I'd written the time in my notepad. From then on—with two exceptions—Eddie and I were eyeballing him right up to the moment he entered his house on Clifford at six fifty-five. The first exception was the short while he spent inside Omar's. But even if he had had a car out back, I was sure there wasn't enough time for him to have made it to Clifford and back. Besides, before hitting the sack that night, I had called my young backup, and the kid assured me no one left Omar's by the rear door while he was watching, and he said he had stayed in place till seven thirty. Which left the second time Hung was out of my sight, the ten or twelve minutes he spent in the pub on Michigan Avenue, the one he got tossed out of at six forty-one. It's conceivable he could have cut out the rear door and sprinted to Clifford and back in that short a span, but I was certain a word with the barkeep—who'd surely remember the one-eared, scarfaced Vietnamese he'd eighty-sixed—would verify that Hung had stayed inside the pub the entire time.

"Well?"

I could explain why I was following Hung, too, and why Toland had said I wasn't, give Zook the story Toland had concocted in Agnew's reception room about me looking for Xuan because she'd supposedly stolen jewelry from Nora. But I couldn't tell that to Zukovich. I could barely tell it to myself.

"Bodine?"

"I'm thinking."

Zukovich shifted impatiently in his chair. "*I'm* thinking I could drive over to the morgue at Sparrow and ask Le Thanh Chi why she isn't telling me who killed her, but I don't believe I'd get any more out of her than I'm getting out of you. Thing is, she's got an excuse for not talking."

"You mean local law enforcement isn't convinced Mr. Hung killed the woman?"

Zukovich sat back in his chair, and we looked at each other over a long silence. When it became obvious Zukovich wasn't going to get tired of looking at me anytime soon, I said, "This isn't fair. You're uglier than me."

Zukovich said, "Okay. You're pretty enough I'm gonna turn queer in a minute, so I'll give you this: Preliminary autopsy says the woman was conked at about five forty-five, plus or minus fifteen minutes. If you're correct about the time this Hung dude entered the house, then he didn't kill the woman. Simple as that. Unless he did it an hour earlier and came back to check his work. Which is why we want to know if you were tailing him or not, so we can fix his whereabouts from the period roughly five thirty to seven o'clock last night. Do you see?"

"'Conked'? Is that how the pathologist at Sparrow described the cause of death?"

"He called it a subdural hematoma."

"Which means?"

"Which means if you get conked on the head hard enough the force of the blow can shear an artery in the brain. Blood gets pumped into a pocket between the skull and the brain and the

215

pressure screws up the brain's communication with the vital organs. Eventually the body shuts down, resulting in death. According to the ME, the woman breathed her last shortly before Hung entered the house. He said it would only have taken about an hour for a hematoma of that severity to finish her off. Usually takes a lot longer, but Le Thanh Chi got hit hard in just the right place at just the right angle and she gushed. There was a trace of blood on the tub, so they're guessing it happened in the bathroom at about five forty-five. They figure she came to, didn't feel so hot, went to her bed to lie down, and never woke up. Or that the gook found her when he came in and carried her into the bedroom."

I said, "In either case I couldn't have heard her arguing with Hung because she was already dead. Which means it had to be some other Vietnamese female I heard."

"Or a female who speaks Vietnamese."

"You got another suspect?"

"Could be." Zook said this as if there could be lint in his navel.

"What if I was to tell you I'm positive Mr. Hung wasn't anywhere near his house at the time the woman was . . . conked?"

"Then I would tell you we got another suspect."

"Which is why Fats was asking the old woman about her granddaughter?"

"Granddaughter, my ass. Neighbor across the street saw Hung bring this fox into the house day before yesterday. It was warm enough the windows were open. Le Thanh Chi just happened to be there. This is the first time the neighbor's seen her around since she left last year, which was bad luck for Hung, who's ready to strap this fox on, but there's his old lady, and she tells him the fox's gotta go. Hung says, Hell, you're back a day and already you're telling me what to do. The fox stays. So the two women get into it and the neighbor hears everything."

"The neighbor speaks Vietnamese?"

216

"No, and I'm being a little creative in interpreting the old broad's statement, but they were definitely arguing, the two Vietnamese women, Tuesday afternoon. Wednesday evening you're outside the door and you hear Hung shouting at what you think is a Vietnamese female. Couldn't have been Le Thanh Chi, because by then she's a goner. The old mama-san still hasn't got home from the House of Chin. So that leaves the fox. She's already done Le Thanh Chi, but she's hanging around the house waiting for Hung, who comes home and finds Le Thanh Chi taking the big doze. Hung and the fox get into a shouting match. You're outside the house and you hear them at it. You pound on the door and holler and the fox hears you and slips out the back. What do you think?"

I glanced over at Fortner. He was watching us from his office like a grouper in an aquarium. "I take it the autopsy also told you the dead woman recently had a baby?"

"Medical examiner could tell by the woman's organs. Also an episiotomy scar he figured was about two, three months old."

"Did the tech boys find any sign of an infant at the guy's house?"

Zukovich shook his head. "Nope."

I said, "How's the baby's birth certificate pertinent to the investigation?"

"Hung don't admit to having a kid, doesn't know anything about Le Thanh Chi having one. We find his name on the record, maybe we got him for infanticide. They do that sometimes, if it's a girl. And if you want to know something pertinent, you'd better not say 'pertinent' around here today."

"Duck drops down on a string?"

"Baby Huey. The way he dropped down on Phuc and the mama-san, he's getting real edgy. Fats's got a mystery on his hands, and Fats don't like mysteries." Zukovich snorted disgustedly. "And you. You're cute when you're courageous, Bodine, standing up to Fats and me that way. 'I cannot tell a lie, coppers, it was six fifty-five, go ahead, shove the bamboo under my nails.'

Jesus H. Christ, you think we were really trying to suborn a witness?"

"I guess you just wanted to see if I could tell time."

Zook's ears pricked up and he raised his nose as if he'd regained the scent of a lost spoor. "That's right. That's it, exactly. When I broadcast the lookout for the uniforms to haul you down here I was hoping you couldn't tell time any better'n you can tell what side your bread's buttered on, you know, the way you're down here every once in a while asking those little favors we do for you—that *I* do for you—running license plates through the net, Xeroxing case files. I mean, think about it. You owe me, Jacky, and what do I get from you? I was sitting here asking through my teeth for a little white lie so we can put a squeeze on the mama-san, and you break righteous as a deviate preacher, telling me you aren't gonna say it was five fifty-five instead of six fifty-five, Jesus H."

"You're going to ask me again, aren't you?"

"Yeah. And we're gonna work it out, too. We could've worked it out if Fats hadn't got impatient. See, he liked the old girl, the mama-san, for conking this Le Thanh Chi woman. They didn't get along too well from what we've been told, and he liked her for it. But the old girl's Chinese-market alibi cleared her, and that pissed Fats off, because he knows she's holding back."

"What's that have to do with me and the time Hung entered the house?"

"Let's face it, we got to let this Hung guy go. The only way we can hold him is if you get temporarily vague on your statement about the time he entered the house. That way we've still got pressure on the mama-san to tell us what's been going on in that house the past two, three days, and where this Xuan fox is. You understand?"

"Vaguely."

"Great. Think vague, buddy, because that's just the frame of mind I want you in when you get around to telling me what time you saw Hung enter that house. You don't have to say it on tape.

That was Fortner throwing his weight around. Which, when you think about it, is a pretty heavy cliché." Zukovich gave me a wolfish grin. "Anyway, it's too late for the tape bit, the old woman's gone. We're moving on to plan Z."

"Z?"

"Z for Zukovich. We just got done with F for Fortner. My idea is to have you drop by her place and tell her her boy's innocent because of you saying he went into the house at six fifty-five. But then you tell her we're going to pull your ticket if you don't say it was five fifty-five. You tell her you don't want to send her boy away, but the bulls downstairs are gonna tickle his toes with their truncheons unless she gives us this Xuan doll." Zukovich paused and took a breath. "What do you think?"

I thought it was a low trick to pull on an old woman whose son had already spent eleven years in a concentration camp, every bit as rotten as the rap I'd laid on Agnew's clients an hour ago. But I liked it, even though I had a better idea, B for Bodine. I said to Zukovich, "Only a cop could come up with a callous scheme like that and sit there grinning about it."

Zukovich nodded happily. "And believe it, Bodine, Fortner'll have the state bulls pull your paper if you don't sleaze through on this. He's having you tailed, just so you know. Mess around and you're in the lockup with Hung. Fats is serious about this."

I said, "What with his kid being an MIA, and all?"

Fats Fortner leaned out of his office. "Zukovich! You get anything on that birth certificate yet?"

"Not yet, Lieutenant."

"Well, hurry up with Bodine."

"Yes, sir."

Fortner heaved back into his office and slammed the door. The glass rattled.

Zukovich lowered his voice and said, "His kid's no MIA. Lives in Delta Township, weighs three hundred pounds, and bowls a mean line of duckpins. Fats just said that to pressure the old girl. What's the matter, you think it's crude and ignorant?"

"No. I think it's slick."

"Did you see the look on the mama-san's face, like she believed it?"

I said, "You believe it?"

"What?"

"That there are still guys in Vietnam?"

"Fuck, no!" Zukovich said this as if he knew there weren't, had some inside knowledge.

"Why?"

"Why do I think it's a crock?"

"Yes."

"Because no American could be a prisoner of those people and survive, not after all this time. Without any word that their own country gives a shit, living in cages? I mean, really, Bodine, who cares, huh? Name somebody."

"I met a woman yesterday. She showed me a picture of her son in a book. She wanted to hire me to go over there and take over where Rambo left off." I got up. "You want me to call you when I get done with the old woman, or come back here?"

"What's her name, the woman with the MIA kid?"

I said, "Why? You want to drive out there and tell her to wise up?" I turned toward the door.

"Celia Gore, was it?"

I didn't answer. I wasn't making any progress toward the door, either.

Zukovich studied me for a moment, and said, "Tommy Gore's no MIA."

I said, "He's living in Delta Township?"

"Hey, Tommy and me went to Nam on the same Pan Am flight together, humped ruck together, wasted gook together, did everything together but the one main thing. Believe it."

Zook didn't look over toward the door when they brought in a woman in a yellow dress that had a huge brown blot of blood on the hem. His eyes were fixed on mine with such intensity that I knew he was utterly convinced Celia Gore's boy was a goner, and had been a goner for a long, long time.

Fortner pounded on the glass and gestured at Zook to hurry up.

"Why is he listed as MIA if you know he's dead?" I said.

"Because they never found his body."

"Then how do you know he's dead?"

"Because I shot him."

The woman with the bloodstain on her dress was sobbing quietly. I said, "I don't get it."

"I don't either. He was my buddy."

"How do you know you shot him?"

"I saw him go down. I was covering his withdrawal and he stood up just as I let off a burst. I tried to get to him, but the sergeant kicked my ass all the way back to camp. Next day we went looking for him and never found nothing. So they called him MIA. But I know different."

"You never told his mother?"

"Yeah, I told her. But she's crazy, Bodine. In her mind Tommy's over there alive."

"You sure you're not wrong?"

"I'm wrong about one thing. After all this time, some people do care. I just try not to think about them."

# 23 ◄◄◄◄

I paused outside the station, standing just where I'd stood last night when Dirk Toland, his angry breath jetting thickly in the cold night air, had said he was going to let Sam Agnew keep the baby. But Toland had had a change of heart as radical as the change in the weather, although you didn't notice the weather so much as you did the government secretaries strolling around in their spring dresses. With the sun shining, everybody looked younger and happier and healthier, everybody except the gray-faced dick. He was wearing the same gray coat he had on last night and was sitting in the same gray car, looking at me in the same gray way. He was parked a half block down the street, watching and waiting, his engine idling. I stood there a moment longer, enjoying the secretaries, giving my talk with Fortner and Zukovich some thought. Luckily, I could think and be watched at the same time.

Thinking: The cops wanted Xuan, and so did I. But for different reasons. If the ME was right that Thanh Chi had been attacked one hour prior to Hung's entrance into the house, then there was a conflict with what Toland said about Xuan knocking her down just seconds before Hung came home. Unless Xuan had lied to him. But why would Xuan lie to Toland? Or had Toland lied to me?

Plan B, step one, lose the gray-faced dick, head over to Joyce's building, and have her drop me off at my car on her way home to meet Eddie. Step two, set myself up to tail Toland from his shop to Xuan. Step three, cream Toland and grill the girl.

I'd already taken a number of steps as it was, about two dozen down the block, heading right for the gray-faced dick, striding by him, hoping he'd make a U-turn and follow me in his car instead of doing the job on foot.

Wish granted; he made the turn, his tires biting hard into Michigan Avenue just as I slipped into the same coffee shop in which I'd met Nora Toland yesterday morning and listened to her problems while watching pellets of snow streak the gray streets . . . leaving by the back door this time, stepping into the alley behind the place, picking my way through the garbage, the crushed crates, the caved-in trash barrels, and the derelicts.

I found a Tigers baseball cap near the entrance to the alley. The adjustable plastic tab at the rear of the sweatband was broken and the cap stank of mold, but I put it on anyway. It sat low on my ears and lower on my forehead. I felt like a DH who'd crowded the plate one too many times. I stripped off my suit coat and rolled it up and stuffed it under my shirt. I rolled up the cuff on one of my pant legs, too, and left the alley heading toward Capitol Street. By the time I got there I had the limp down pat, hobbling along, twitching my head. Pedestrians looked the other way as I lurched past them, talking to myself.

I staggered up the steps to Joyce's building, made a lopsided entry, and asked the guard if I could use the phone on the counter to call my wife upstairs. He asked me who my wife was. I told him, and he asked to see some ID. I showed him my driver's license and a spare check I kept tucked in my wallet that had both our names printed on it, Joyce's and mine. The guard studied the check and shrugged, said I could use the phone, go ahead, grinning at the knowledge that the director of the Bureau for Planning, Research, Evaluation, and Dissemination—that foxy chick with the red hair and the haughty manner—was married to a moron.

Joyce's secretary, Evita, informed me that Dr. O'Connell wasn't in the building, that she'd been called over to the capitol for another budget powwow with the mucketymucks. Evita added that Dr. O'Connell had said she definitely would be home late, so don't hold dinner on her account, don't even wait up for her because the doctor didn't know how long she'd be, it was a crisis. Evita delivered this message the way she had delivered so many similar disappointments in the past.

I thanked her and took the stairs to the garage. Joyce's Volvo was where she usually parked it, next to a concrete pillar just down from the door. I tucked a note in a crack in the pillar telling her to take a cab home. Then I unlocked the trunk of her car, hauled out the set of golf clubs I'd bought for twenty-five bucks at a yard sale, unzipped the cleats pouch, and dug around inside it. I had a gat in there and a white terry-cloth sun visor. I threw away the Tigers ball cap and snugged on the visor, opened the rear door of the car and propped the bag against the seat so the heads of the clubs were visible through the window. Then I rolled the front seat back, adjusted the mirrors, strapped myself in, and started the car.

At the exit I fed Joyce's magnetic card into the gate box. She always left the card in the glove compartment, and I always carried a set of keys to her Volvo. I was feeling smug. The gate swung up and I swung out onto Pine Street looking like a links-bound bureaucrat. It was easy to look that way when you felt smug. If I felt this smug tonight I might make the mistake of telling the director of the Bureau for Planning, Research, Evaluation, and Dissemination that it was a lot easier to be a bureaucrat than a moron.

I reached my neighborhood at three twenty, parked a block north of my street, and walked back, figuring the fuzz might be watching my place. I turned into the alley that ran behind my house and noted with pride that it was a cut above the alleys of downtown Lansing. I eased through the back gate and crossed the yard to the back door, not worrying much about being observed. My yard was secluded, all those weigelas and forsythias and viburnums I'd failed to prune last year.

I slipped inside, snugged the back door shut, and ran to the front door and peered up and down the street. I didn't have to open the door. I'd installed a fisheye peephole a couple years back and it gave me a wide-angle view of things. I didn't see any unmarked surveillance cars out there. The watchers might be just out of range, though. In fact, I had to assume they were. And then it hit me, the name of the gray-faced dick: Oswald V. Crack. He was a boyhood friend of my father's. Funny, the things that get repressed.

I headed for the kitchen and microwaved Eddie's leftover moo shu pork, four days old and slightly rank. The Amana beeped and I grabbed the steaming food and smeared it with hoi sin sauce—forget the rice pancakes, the microwave had turned them to leather—eating fast. Eddie wasn't going to be happy with plan B and I didn't want him to catch me with my face in his food, never mind that he'd probably forgotten all about it.

As I was rinsing my plate I heard him. He was out in front of the house trading insults with a couple of other kids, probably Howard Slackmeijer and Tory Zukovich. I slapped together a peanut-butter sandwich and stuffed it into a lunch bag, threw in an apple and a handful of Fruit Roll-Ups, too, along with two paper cartons of cranberry-apple juice. Eddie's gum stash was in the drawer where we kept the lunch bags and the Roll-Ups. I pocketed a handful of sugarless Trident, figuring to buy him off later on, when the native got restless. He banged on the door.

I left the kitchen and was about to let him in when I remembered Oswald V. Crack. I bent down, lifted the flap on the mail slot, and said, "Eddie?"

"Yeah?" He started to open the outer flap.

"Don't touch that flap, Eddie."

"That you, Dad?"

"No, it's the mailman."

"Dad, I'm not in the mood for this."

"Just listen to me."

"But I'm hungry."

"I got food for you, buddy, but first I want you to pretend nobody's home. Understand?"

"No."

"Just do what I say."

"Why?"

"Because I want to see if you're any good at pretending nobody's home."

"Yeah, but why?"

"I got a pack of Big League Chew says you're going to be great at this."

"Really?"

"Yes. And don't move your lips when you talk."

"What am I supposed to do?"

"Pound on the door."

Eddie pounded on the door. "Now what?"

"Wait a second or two, then pound on the door again."

He pounded.

"Do it again."

He pounded again.

"Great. Now ring the doorbell."

"Okay."

"Ring it again."

"Is that enough?"

"Fine. Now, you know that spare key we keep down by the knob on that rosebush right next to you?"

"The key that's in the dirt in the little can?"

"Right. Use it."

"I don't know how."

"Just get it and try."

He got it and tried. "I can't make it work, Dad." There was panic in his voice.

"You're doing fine. Keep trying."

"But I can't make it work."

"You're doing great, Eddie. All you've got to do is pretend like it's working, okay?"

"Will I still get the Big League Chew?"

"Sure."

"What flavor is it?"

"Cherry Coke. Now listen. I'm going to open the door from the inside, but you act like you did it with the key, okay?"

"Okay."

I twisted the thumb bolt and tugged on the door. Eddie and his backpack bulged through the opening. He said, "Can we do it again?"

"Don't look at me and don't talk. Just pull the key out of the lock. Good. Now shut the door." I checked the street through the peephole and saw Tory Zukovich gesture at Howard Slackmeijer in a way that would have earned him a broken finger if his father had been watching. Lucky for both of us I didn't see Tory's father watching, no dark green Oldsmobiles anywhere in sight. No gray ones, either. I said to Eddie, "You did a great job, partner." Eddie was standing there like a bellhop waiting for a tip. "I haven't actually got the Big League Chew with me," I said, "but I'll try to get some on the way."

Eddie's face dropped. It had got a little stony when I called him partner, and stonier still when he found out a jawful of Big League Chew was not imminent. But the mention of "on the way" earned me the Medusa's glare. Eddie said, "Where are we going?"

"Well, there's something I have to do this afternoon and I'd like you to come with me while I do it."

"Like what?"

"Like looking for someone."

"Who?"

"A young Vietnamese woman. It won't take long."

"We're going on a stakeout, aren't we?"

"All I've got to do is find this person and talk to her. Then, depending on what she says, I may call Mr. Zukovich so he can come and talk to her, too. Or I may not. Depending."

"What's she done?"

"That's what I want to talk to her about."

Eddie said, "Does she speak English?"

"A little. I think."

"If she doesn't, how are you going to talk to her?"

"I'll worry about that then. Now, go get your Lego suitcase and something to read and anything else you'd like to bring along."

"How come I got to bring that stuff if we're not going on a stakeout?"

"Just get ready, will you?"

"But I'm hungry."

"I've got a snack packed for you."

"Can I ask Tory and Howard if they can come?"

"No."

"But Dad, Tory and me and Howard were gonna—"

"Eddie, I want you to get ready. Now! And go to the bathroom, too."

"Geez."

Pretty cheeky for a kid who'd spilled the beans to the buttons in the principal's office. Pretty typical, too, not even to mention that he'd done it . . . not that I believed he was hiding anything. He'd simply forgotten all about it. In some ways being eight was great. In other ways it was awful. I watched Eddie stomp into his room, his slim shoulders sagging beneath the double burden of his backpack and his father's bullheadedness.

Oh, well.

While Eddie marshaled his entertainments I went back into

the kitchen, looked up Midwest Micrographics in the phone book, and wrote down the number and address in my notepad. Then I dialed.

"GoodafternoonMidwestMicrographics."

"Yes, is Mr. Toland in?"

"Thankyouonemomentplease."

I cupped the receiver. "Hurry up, Eddie."

"Geez."

"Mr. Toland's office."

I said, "Yes, is Mr. Toland in this afternoon?"

"May I ask who's calling?"

I wanted to be sure he was still at his shop with the auditors, but I didn't want to talk to him . . . although if I had to I could wing it, pretend I was Brigadier General Armageddon at the Pentagon with a basement full of pay records that needed transferring to microfiche.

"Hello?"

I said, "This is Jack Bodine. I want to talk to Mr. Toland about some money he owes me."

"One moment, Mr. Bodine."

Eddie came into the kitchen. "Dad?"

"Yes?"

"Was Tory's father really in Vietnam?"

"Yes."

"Did he really kill gooks?"

"You mean Vietnamese people? I guess he did."

"Do you think he's going to kill the ones we saw last night at the police station?"

"No."

"Why not? They're gooks, aren't they?"

The line clicked. Toland's secretary said, "Mr. Bodine?"

"Yes?"

"Mr. Toland says it's impossible for him to talk to you today, he's all tied up. But tomorrow first thing would be acceptable."

"He's there at the office?"

"Till five thirty."

"Thank you." I hung up. I said to Eddie, "I don't want to hear you use that word again. Now, are you set to go?"

"Geez."

# 24 ◄◄◄

I held the back gate for Eddie. He went through it and stopped in his tracks, staring at something down the alley. I closed the gate behind me and stared with him, looking at Oswald V. Crack. Detective Crack was in his gray Olds, his fenders flanked by barrels of trash, his cooling engine ticking faintly. He was parked at the rear of a neighbor's garage, slouched down behind the wheel of his car, smugly bored. The slouch was to let me know he'd put a lot less effort into finding me than I'd put into losing him. He tilted his head toward his open window. "You going to see the old mama-san now, slick?"

He'd probably radioed the station, got patched to Zukovich, and found out I had to meet my kid at home. Nothing to it. "On my way," I said. I waved good-bye.

Detective Crack waved back.

Eddie said, "That man gave you the finger, Dad."

"Who cares?"

"But he gave you the finger!"

I said, "People are always giving each other the finger. Remember the guy who threw the Vietnamese man out of the bar yesterday? And how about Tory? I saw him give Howard the finger a few minutes ago. It's nothing special, giving people the finger. That's why I never do it, because it's nothing special."

"Yeah, but—"

"You want to know something you can do instead of giving people the finger, something that's really special?"

Eddie gazed up at me, the high priest of gestures. "What?"

"Give them the cold shoulder."

"The what?"

"The cold shoulder. You walk away and ignore them."

"What's so special about that?"

"It's special because it's the grown-up thing to do."

Eddie looked at me as if I were speaking Finnish.

"Come on." I started down the alley. I walked a little ways, then I heard Crack's engine kick over. It wasn't a major setback, him finding me again. All that mattered was that I didn't lead him to Xuan. Xuan was a hard cookie, but if she was responsible for her mother's death, I'd get it out of her. I just didn't want Crack there when I cracked her, because Dirk Toland would be on hand, too, and I promised Nora I wouldn't involve them with the cops. Unnecessarily.

Eddie caught up to me. "Dad, he's following us."

"Not for long."

"What do you mean?"

"When the time comes, we'll lose him."

"But, Dad?"

"What?"

"I know him. He's a policeman. His name's Mr. Crack."

"Is he one of the policemen who talked to you at school today?"

"They told you about it?" Eddie said worriedly.

"I heard it from someone who works with Mr. Zukovich."

We walked in silence. Then Eddie said, "I didn't think a policeman would ever give somebody the finger."

"Not very grown-up, is it?"

Eddie didn't say anything more till we got to the end of the alley. Then he said, "Are you mad at me for telling Mr. Crack we were following the Vietnamese man yesterday?"

"No," I said. "I know you must have been pretty scared, all alone in the principal's office with two big detectives."

"They showed me their badges. Mr. Schultz said I had to tell them."

"He's the principal?"

"Yeah. I was afraid to lie."

When we got to the car I said, "It's all right. I wouldn't want you to lie to a policeman."

"But you lied to Tory's dad at the police station last night."

I opened the car door for Eddie. "Hop in."

Eddie hopped in. While I was at it, I pulled the golf bag out of the rear seat and stuffed it back into the trunk. Also, I stuck out my tongue at Detective Crack, who was idling at the corner. Then I got into the car and started it. I said, "It was wrong for me not to answer Tory's dad's questions truthfully. I saw him today and made up for it, just like you did in the principal's office."

Eddie thought about this, gazing at me. "You feel bad, too?"

"Too?"

"I mean, I told the truth," said Eddie, "but I feel bad about it. I wish I'd've lied."

"You'd still feel bad. Worse."

"Do you feel bad?"

I pulled away from the curb, watching Detective Crack's Olds swing around the corner.

"Dad?"

"Sure I feel bad."

Mostly because in years to come Eddie probably wouldn't remember that I'd been making these special efforts to be on hand whenever he came home from school, only that I'd once lied to a cop. I thought about trying to explain to him that it was okay to lie to cops sometimes but not others, but I didn't think I could honestly explain that one to myself. So I turned on the radio. At Eddie's age he was better off listening to hard rock than a lecture on soft morals. Anyway, I had to concentrate on losing Crack before I lost Xuan.

By the time I got to Hung's house, though, Crack was still behind me. But that was because I'd decided I didn't have to lose him. I figured I'd let him watch me talk to the old woman, after which I'd tell him I was convinced she didn't have any idea where Xuan was. Crack would head back to the station and report a big negative to Fortner and Zukovich. While he was doing that, I'd drive out to Midwest Micrographics and follow Toland when he left his shop to get the money from Phuc. He'd pay off Agnew, get the baby, and then lead me to Xuan. Nothing to it.

I parked at the curb, cut the engine, and waited for Crack to drift in behind me.

Eddie said, "Are we on stakeout now?"

"No. I'll be right back."

"Dad—?"

"I'll leave the key in the ignition so you can listen to the radio. Have another stick of Trident."

"You promised me some Big League Chew."

"I know, but it'll have to wait. Have the Trident."

"It's gone."

"All of it?"

"Yes."

It wasn't in his mouth. "What did you do with it?" I said.

"It's on my *Mad*. See?" Eddie pointed at the floor. Alfred E. Neuman looked as if a freshly excised tumor had been stuck to the end of his nose.

"Well, don't step on it," I said.

"Dad?"

"Yes, Eddie?"

"Who's the Vietnamese woman you want to talk to?"

"You wouldn't know her."

"Why do you want to talk to her?"

"Because she may know something about . . . the dead lady."

"What?"

"I don't know exactly."

"Then how do you know you want to talk to her?"

"Just sit tight, okay?"

"Dad?"

"What?"

"Is she in that house?"

"I don't think so."

"Then why are we here?"

"Because the old Vietnamese lady's inside. Remember her from last night?"

"Does she know where the woman is?"

"Well, Tory's dad thinks she does, and he told me I had to talk to her, so here we are."

"You're not mad at her, are you?"

"No. Are you afraid of being here?"

"No."

"Then why are you trying to keep me from going up to that house?"

Eddie looked out the window. He was thinking, making an honest effort to answer my question. He said, "I don't know. I just don't understand why you have to do this." There was a tremor in his voice.

I leaned toward him. "What's the matter?"

Eddie shrugged. "Tory's dad isn't going to make you kill the old lady, is he? You know, because she's a gook?"

"No, Eddie. I'm here only because Tory's dad thought I could help him figure out who killed the woman we found here last night."

"But why does he care? She was a gook."

"I asked you not to say that word, okay?"

"Okay."

"And believe me, Eddie, even though the woman was Viet-

235

namese, Mr. Zukovich cares about her and wants to find out who killed her. He loves this town, and he takes it very seriously when a bad thing happens to someone who lives here."

"But he already knows who killed her."

"Oh?"

"The man you got into the fight with, the one who kicked his foot through the door? He hurt the lady, right?"

"Wrong. Remember what I said last night when I tucked you in? I wasn't convinced he did it, and it turns out he didn't."

"But how——?"

"The police have ways of figuring out how and when she died. And they've determined that the man I had the fight with wasn't even home when she got hurt."

I let Eddie think this over. Then he looked at me and said, "They can tell by the autopsy?"

"Correct. That's why, even though autopsies seem awful, they're important. In this case an autopsy has saved an innocent man from going to jail."

"Did they really cut her head open?"

"Well . . . yes, they probably did. But by doing that they were able to figure out how she got hurt, and when she died."

"How did she get hurt?"

"She was either hit by something or was pushed down and bumped her head when she fell."

"How do they do it?"

"What?"

"Cut her head open."

"With a special saw that doctors use. I'm going to talk to the old lady now. I'll come right back."

"Do I have to stay buckled up?"

"No."

"Dad?"

"What?"

"You don't feel anything after you're dead, do you?"

I was studying Hung's house. The yellow crime-scene tape was gone, and the house looked just as it did yesterday when Hung went in. Even the window curtains were back down to the sills. There wasn't anything to distinguish it from the rest of the cozy bungalows on the block, those that hadn't yet hosted a murder. I said, "No, Eddie. That's the one good thing about death." I climbed out of the car.

"Dad?"

"What?"

"Be careful."

"Sure. You want me to lock the car?"

"I can do it."

I swung my door shut and Eddie locked it from the inside. He locked his door, too, and climbed between the seats and locked the rear doors. Then he squirmed back into the front seat and sat behind the wheel. I rang Hung's doorbell and waved at Eddie from Hung's porch. I gave him a thumbs-up sign and he waved back. He looked very small behind the wheel of Joyce's Volvo. I felt proud of him.

I rang Hung's doorbell again, not looking at Crack, looking instead at something I hadn't seen last night, two names that were printed in faded ink above the button: Le Van Hung and Nguyen Thi Phuc. It crossed my mind that if Nguyen Thi Phuc and Mr. Phuc of the nine-millimeter were one and the same, then I ought to get the gat out of my golf bag. This thought had hardly formed when Hung's mother opened the door. She took one look at me and started to slam it in my face.

I said quickly, "I've got good news about your son."

She hesitated and pulled the door open, but not very far. "Good news?" She said this with a frown, as if she didn't understand the phrase, or was having difficulty believing that any news coming from me could be good.

She was wearing her Pat Nixon coat, had it buttoned up to her neck. She looked as if she'd been getting ready to go out. I said, "Yes, very good news. By the way, does Mr. Phuc live here?"

"Mr. Phuc?"

"The man who was translating for Hung at the police station."

The idea of Phuc living with her struck Hung's mother as more than a little preposterous. With a vague sneer she said, "No here."

I glanced down at the button. "But here's his name. Nguyen Thi Phuc."

"No. His name Nguyen Van Phuc. I am Nguyen Thi Phuc." The old woman's tone suggested my inquiries about Mr. Phuc did not reflect well on my intelligence or on the future of our conversation. She said, "What news of Hung?"

"Are you related to Mr. Phuc?"

She made a face that implied the only thing surpassing her contempt for me was her contempt for Mr. Phuc. She said, "My name Ba Kiem."

"Ba Kiem?"

She said, "*Ba* same as *Mrs.* in your language."

"Which you speak very well."

"I go." She moved to close the door.

"Wait. Why do you call yourself Kiem if your name is Phuc?"

She said, "Husband name Le Van Kiem. Therefore I am properly called Ba Kiem."

"I see. But the fact that your maiden name is the same as Mr. Phuc's is a coincidence?"

"Phuc is name give both women and men in Vietnam."

"Phuc is a given name?"

"Yes."

"But you said your name was Nguyen Thi Phuc. Wouldn't that make Phuc your family name?"

"In Vietnam family name first, then middle, then give."

"I see." I wasn't sure I did. I wasn't sure, either, that if someone had tried to explain all this to Lyndon Johnson, he wouldn't have said to hell with it and had a barbecue instead of a war. "So, you and Mr. Phuc share both a family name and a given name?"

Mrs. Phuc—that is, Mrs. Kiem—said, "Many Vietnamese

take Nguyen for name because it was greatest and last of Vietnam dynasty. Nguyen Van Phuc is one who family take this name. He is not true Nguyen." Mrs. Kiem, adjusting the collar of her coat, said this with such proud precision I had to believe she'd been born a true Nguyen. I believed she was worthy of her lineage, too, the way she'd handled Fats Fortner at the station. She was handling me with the same kind of aristocratic disdain. Mrs. Kiem had no doubt endured many indignities in her time, probably at the hands of men who looked a lot like me. Myself, I was of two minds about her. She irked me, but I admired her, too, and just because she took pride in giving me, and everything she thought I stood for, the coldest of shoulders.

I said, "So, even though you are a Nguyen, you are called Mrs. Kiem because your husband's name was Le Van Kiem?"

"Yes."

"And Kiem was his given name?"

"Yes."

"So, if I were Vietnamese, my wife would be called Mrs. Jack?"

"It is our way."

I said, "And very interesting, too." I looked over at Oswald V. Crack. Something told me Oswald wouldn't agree, especially if he checked with Mrs. Kiem to see if I'd actually inquired as to Xuan's whereabouts. Thing was, I didn't want to ask Mrs. Kiem about Xuan because she might mention it to Phuc, who would tell Toland I was looking for the girl. Although, if Mrs. Kiem wanted to share information with Phuc, she'd have to head down to the Chinese market to call him, and Toland probably wouldn't be leaving his shop for another forty minutes or so. How long would it take her to get to the store, ten, fifteen minutes? The cops had said she left the house at four twenty yesterday and had arrived at the store at four thirty, called someone, and stayed till six thirty. But last night she hadn't showed up here at the house till almost seven thirty, just as the cops were escorting Hung and me out to the cruisers. Ten minutes to get to the store and a whole hour to get back? More important was the one question that, in his fury, Fats Fortner had never asked Mrs. Kiem. I said, "Who did you call from the Chinese grocery yesterday?"

Mrs. Kiem ignored my question. "What news of Hung?"

"Well, although the police haven't released him yet, they're sure he's not responsible for what happened to Thanh Chi. I thought you'd want to know that." I smiled.

Mrs. Kiem did not.

I said, "You see, the injury that caused her death occurred at least an hour before Hung came home last night." I continued to smile.

Mrs. Kiem continued not to.

"Do you understand what I'm saying, Mrs. Kiem?"

"Yes. Hung innocent."

"But there's a problem."

"Yes?"

"You see, I'm the one who saw Hung enter this house at six fifty-five yesterday evening. And as long as I stick to that time the police will have to let Hung go."

"Yes?"

"But the police hate Hung, and are angry at the thought of having to free him. In their anger they have insisted I change my statement."

"Change?"

"Yes. They want me to say Hung entered this house an hour earlier than he did. Which would mean the police could charge him with the death of Thanh Chi."

"Police make you lie?"

"They have threatened to take away my license if I don't change my statement. And if they revoke my license, then I will lose my job."

Mrs. Kiem gave this a moment's thought, regarding me in a new if not favorable light. She said, "Nguyen Van Phuc say you quasi-police."

It seemed to me it would be truer to say that whenever I was around police, I felt quasi. With Detective Crack watching me, I felt that way this very moment. "Ma'am, in that car there, the one with the aerials, is a policeman, a terrible man named Crack. He is watching us, and if you do not tell me who you called yesterday, he will get on his radio and the police downtown will beat Hung until he confesses to the murder of Thanh Chi." I worried I was laying it on a bit thick, but Mrs. Kiem didn't seem to think so. In fact she must have thought I was laying it on too thin, because she made another effort to slam the door in my face.

This time I stuck my foot between the door and the jamb. It seemed like a good idea, but I was wrong. I might have been wrong even if I'd been wearing a pair of Timberline boots with toes of reinforced steel. I said calmly, "I don't want to lose my license any more than I want to lose my foot, Mrs. Kiem."

"I care no about license."

"Surely you care about your son?"

"My son is my life."

"And his life, ma'am, is in the hands of hard men, many of whom have been to Vietnam as soldiers. They are bitter men. They want to see Hung suffer, and they will be pleased to believe me when I tell them he's a murderer. Even though I am a terrible liar."

Mrs. Kiem didn't seem to think I was. In any case, she stopped hurting my foot. She glared at me instead. I glared back. It was an even match, and it lasted more than a moment. Waiting, I took in facial details: her prominent cheeks with their faint freckles, the pale mole at her hairline, crow's-feet at the corners of her eyes, and wrinkles ringing her neck. She suddenly looked quite old, probably because her expression had lost its tone and had sagged into a kind of weary resignation, as if she'd known all along that it would come to this, another defeat to endure. I suddenly felt like what I was, a bully. I said, "Hurry up, Mrs. Kiem, or your son will die."

She nodded, as if to agree with me that I was a bully. Then she sighed and said, "I will tell you of call. But not because I fear you threat. You are nothing. Hung is all. And I have decide to go police and tell who I call from Chinese."

"Good. It's always best to tell the truth."

"No. Never best. Lie is best. Truth is for old women who have pain so much truth cannot hurt more."

"Who did you call, Mrs. Kiem?"

"I call American man."

"What's his name?"

"Name . . . Tolan'."

"Toland?"

"Yes."

"The man who spoke to you in Vietnamese at the police station last night?"

"Yes. He kill Thanh Chi."

I said, "Ah."

Mrs. Kiem said, "So."

I said, "How do you know he killed Thanh Chi?"

"I call on telephone. I tell."

"You called Toland?"

"Yes."

"And what did you tell him?"

"Thanh Chi baby here."

"Thanh Chi's baby was here? In this house?"

"Yes. Hung steal baby for Thanh Chi. They make plan go away, Hung and Thanh Chi. But Thanh Chi go no without baby. Make Hung steal baby from Tolan'. Yes. Hung go Tolan' house, watch all morning. Tolan' wife go in house. Xuan with baby alone. Hung take baby and tell Xuan say American man steal. Hung bring baby here. Two day. Then Thanh Chi go work shop, leave baby with me. I go Chinese store, call Tolan' come, take baby. When I am at Chinese, Tolan' come here. Thanh Chi come same time. They fight. Tolan' kill Thanh Chi. Take baby." Mrs. Kiem gestured at Detective Crack's car. "Call policeman. I tell this now."

I glanced at Oswald Crack. I couldn't see his face behind the reflections glaring off the windshield of his Olds, but I was sure he knew I was on to something, and I didn't want him to find out what, not yet anyway, not till I was satisfied of the truth. Nora Toland would lose her baby if the cops heard Mrs. Kiem's story. I looked at my watch. It was time to get to Toland's shop, but there was more I wanted to ask Mrs. Kiem. I said, "Will you come with me, ma'am?"

"Come with?"

"Yes. In my car."

Mrs. Kiem hunched her shoulders and drew in upon herself. "No. You work for Tolan'."

I shook my head. "Now I am working for the police. And they have asked me to bring you with me downtown. The policeman in the gray car will be following us. You have nothing to fear from me. Come. There's my car."

She frowned at the Volvo. "Who is in?"

"My son."

"We are go police? Tell truth about Tolan'?"

"Yes," I lied.

# 25 ◄◄◄

I introduced Eddie to Mrs. Kiem.

Eddie said hello.

Mrs. Kiem stared at Eddie. I stared at him, too, seeing him in a new light. He was wearing a maroon T-shirt that tailed out from under a grimy white sweatshirt and hung nearly to the knees of his muddy jeans. His high-top canvas sneakers were mud-caked, too. He had a canary-yellow Converse All Star on his left foot, a blood-red one on his right, but both shoes were so dirty they were almost the same color. Mrs. Kiem looked up from Eddie's footwear to his face once again, frowning a second time at the lock of hair that curled down the nape of his slender neck. The tail looked particularly precocious on Eddie's head, which had been "buzzed" about as close as the pits of Joyce's arms.

I left off with the introductions and had Eddie climb into the backseat. Then I got Mrs. Kiem into the car and helped her with her seat belt. Not glancing at Detective Crack, I went around to the driver's side of the car, started up, and pulled away from the curb, watching in my mirror as Crack began tailing me. I couldn't be certain, but it looked like he might be on his radio. I turned off my radio and told Eddie to read his *Mad*.

Eddie said, "Can't I listen to rock?"

"No."

"Why not?"

"I want to talk to Mrs. Kiem."

"Can't you do that and listen to rock, too?"

I said, "I got my limitations." I glanced at Mrs. Kiem. She wasn't paying any more attention to Eddie and me than if we were voices on the radio. I tapped the rolled cuff of her coat and said, "Why have you only just now decided to tell the police about calling Toland?"

Mrs. Kiem, still looking straight ahead, said, "I am fear."

"Of Toland?"

"Yes."

"A minute ago you said your son was your life. And yet you've let the police charge him with murder when you believed he was innocent."

"At police Tolan' say Hung go free, but we must tell nothing. If we speak truth, Hung die. But I do not trust Tolan'. So I have decide tell truth."

"You could keep the volume really low, couldn't you, Dad?"

"Eddie—"

"It's not fair."

"Read your *Mad.*"

"I already did."

"Then play with your Legos."

"I don't want to."

"And I don't want to hear another word out of you."

"Geez."

I stopped at a light and said to Mrs. Kiem, "Explain to me why you called Toland to come to Hung's house to get the baby."

"I think is dangerous Hung steal baby. I say, Hung, there is much trouble from this man, Tolan'. Give baby back. Hung was listen, but Thanh Chi not let baby go. She cry when I speak to Hung. Hung say he will tell wife of Tolan' that Tolan' make love Thanh Chi in Vietnam long ago. Make Xuan. Hung say Tolan' will do nothing. But I know this man. He will hurt Hung. So.

245

When Thanh Chi go get money from Tolan' work job, I call Tolan'. Tolan' answer. I say street and number of Hung house. I say hurry. I say door open to back. No one can see. Baby alone. Hurry. Tolan' is listen on telephone. I put up telephone. I wait at Chinese, long time. Then I go Hung house. I see Thanh Chi body dead. Hung come, too. Hung see Thanh Chi dead. Hung look baby. Baby gone. Hung understand Tolan' kill Thanh Chi, take baby. Hung say he kill Tolan', too. I say no. I am not want Hung go Tolan' house, kill. Hung is crazy. I am plead with Hung. Hung is shout he will kill all *tui mui lo.*"

"*Tui mui lo?*"

Mrs. Kiem waved away my question. "Nothing."

I said, "All right. But let me get this straight. Hung and Thanh Chi have been separated for most of their stay in this country, yet he was still very angry to find her dead? Is that correct?"

Mrs. Kiem said nothing.

"Hung must have loved Thanh Chi very much," I said.

Mrs. Kiem turned her face away so sharply someone watching us from the street might have thought I'd slapped her.

"Mrs. Kiem?"

Still looking out the window, she said, "Because of whore, Thanh Chi, my son eleven year in reeducation camp. Eleven."

I could feel hatred coming off Mrs. Kiem in waves, palpable surges of loathing. "I was told Hung did a noble thing for Thanh Chi, saved her from the Communists by telling them Xuan was his daughter and not the child of an American."

Mrs. Kiem said, "*Hung* mean 'hero.'"

"How did you feel about Thanh Chi, Mrs. Kiem?"

"Feel?"

"What did you think of her?"

"I never think of her. Thanh Chi American soldier whore."

Eddie was listening intently in the backseat. I'd been expecting him to ask me what a whore was, but he kept silent, probably because he already knew, and was waiting to see if I did, too.

I said, "Mrs. Kiem, there's a problem with what you've just told me."

"Problem?"

"Yes. You see, when the police searched Hung's house, they found no evidence that a baby had ever been there, no clothes, no bottles, no diapers. Nothing."

"Yes."

Mrs. Kiem's tone was so matter-of-fact I wasn't sure she understood me. I said, "If the baby had been there, the police would have found something."

"I take all baby thing."

"You?"

"Yes. I see Thanh Chi dead. I search house, put all baby thing in sack. Then Hung come. Then police. I run back door, throw baby thing away. All gone. Truck take all thing. This morning."

"And after you ran out the back door and got rid of the baby's things, you came up to the house from the front and told the police later that you'd just returned from the Chinese market?"

"Yes."

The light turned green. I accelerated through the intersection, glancing at my mirror. Crack was two cars back, having an easier time following me than I was having following Mrs. Kiem. I said, "But why did you throw the baby's things away?"

"Because police find baby thing, they look baby."

"You were worried that if the police found the baby's things, then they would start a search for the baby?"

"Yes."

"And you didn't want that?"

"They look baby, find Tolan'."

"You thought maybe they would look for the baby's birth certificate and find Toland listed as the father?"

"Yes. Go Tolan' house. Find baby. Then Tolan' confess kill Thanh Chi. Tell police Ba Kiem call, say come get baby. Then Hung hate me for Thanh Chi die. Same as kill Thanh Chi. So I say nothing about call Tolan'. But now I will say truth. I am want to say truth at police just now, but Nguyen Van Phuc was there and would tell Tolan', and then Tolan' would run away. So now I tell truth. Hung will hate, but hating self is worse."

I pulled into a convenience store that was just across South Pennsylvania from a low brick building with a sign out front that said MIDWEST MICROGRAPHICS. I hadn't had an opportunity to evade Crack, so he was still with me, pulling into an office supply outlet next to us. I shouldn't have brought him this far, but there was no way I could have kept Mrs. Kiem talking while managing a high-speed disappearance. I cut my engine and glanced over at Crack. He had a clear view of my car.

I sat back and looked over at Toland's shop. Despite the flow of traffic in and out of the discount appliance warehouses, tire marts, and carpet outlets, I had a clear view of the main entrance to Midwest Micrographics. I had a view of the side door that opened onto the employee parking lot, too. I dug out the Minolta pocket zoom binoculars I kept in Joyce's glove compartment, adjusted the focus ring, and zeroed in on the red Toyota Tercel parked adjacent to the side door. It was tucked into a space reserved for MR. TOLAND.

"What are you looking at, Dad?"

"A little red car."

"Is the Vietnamese woman in it?"

Mrs. Kiem said, "This is no police."

Eddie said, "Are we on stakeout?"

I said, "Not exactly. I'm just waiting for a man to come out of that building over there."

Eddie said, "That's what we were doing yesterday, right?"

"It's a different building," I said, "and we won't be waiting as long."

"But we're on stakeout, aren't we?"

"Technically, yes."

Eddie groaned and slumped down in his seat. "I don't want to be on stakeout. I hate stakeouts."

Mrs. Kiem said, "What is stakeout?"

"A stakeout," said Eddie, "is when you sit forever. It's boring!"

Mrs. Kiem glanced at Eddie, then at me. "I cannot stake-out."

Eddie was merely whining. There was something in Mrs. Kiem's tone, however, that verged on panic. I said, "Everything will be all right."

"I cannot stakeout."

"It won't be long. By the way, Mrs. Kiem, was the police lieutenant correct when he said Phuc took you to a hotel last night?"

"What'd you just say, Dad?"

"I said 'Phuc.' It's a Vietnamese man's name and it's spelled differently than the word you're thinking of." To Mrs. Kiem I said, "Was the policeman correct?"

Mrs. Kiem was frowning as if she did not like to be reminded of the trip. "Yes. Phuc take me hotel."

Eddie said, "I gotta go to the bathroom."

I said to Mrs. Kiem, "Did you mention to Phuc that you threw away the baby's things?"

"I tell nothing."

"So we can assume Toland doesn't know that you got rid of the baby's stuff?"

"I tell Phuc nothing."

"But Phuc knows something's going on?"

"Going on?"

"Do you think he knows Toland killed Thanh Chi to get the baby?"

"Assassin have no secret."

"Assassin?"

"Tolan' and Phuc assassinate my husband in Vietnam."

"They did *what*?"

"They believe my husband Vietcong cadre in our village. Nguyen Van Phuc call my husband to district meet. It was challenge to him. I was argue for my husband not go, but Phuc was rival and Kiem say must go. They find Kiem next morning. Skull crush. On trail."

"Dad, what's *assassinate* mean?"

"Just a minute, Eddie. In what way was Phuc your husband's rival?"

"For power in district. For land. For me." Mrs. Kiem said this with bitter pride. "And Tolan' kill Kiem for Phuc."

"How do you know this?"

"Tolan' was command of Marine who take our plantation, make us live peasant hut by garden."

"But how do you know he killed your husband?"

"Tolan' go out gate at dusk with men, three, four. They hide in wait for Vietcong along village path. Every night. Their amusement was boast next day of ambush. Tolan' kill with hitting head. Very silent."

"Hitting head?"

"He crush Vietcong skull with bludgeon."

Eddie said, "What's a bloodjin?"

"Always it was swing from Tolan' belt, heavy with death."

I said, "He would ambush Vietcong with a blackjack?"

"Yes. And all who defying Nguyen Van Phuc. Phuc and Tolan' gangster."

I was feeling quasi again, and not just because Detective Crack was watching me, thinking of ways to write a report that would give Fortner and the state cops an excuse to deprive me of my license. And not because of the story Mrs. Kiem had just told me about Toland, either. After the news of My Lai there wasn't anything about the war in Vietnam that had the power to nauseate me. If I was bothered, it was because Eddie—on top what he'd seen last night at Hung's house—had been listening to Mrs. Kiem's tale of midnight murder. I glanced at him. His jaw was slack, as if he were watching TV. Mrs. Kiem was staring out the windshield, expressionless.

I reached out and patted her hand. Mrs. Kiem snatched her hand away and said, "It is too late, *tui mui lo.*"

"What does that mean, *tui mui lo?*"

She looked at me and said, " 'Long nose.' All American call 'long nose' by Vietnamese. Long nose like elephant."

"Elephant?"

"Yes. In Vietnam you trample grave of ancestor. Like elephant."

Eddie said sharply, "My father wasn't ever in Vietnam."

I glanced into the backseat. His jaw wasn't slack anymore. It was clenched. He sounded offended and looked it, too. But there was more than indignation in his expression. He was flushed with pride that I'd never been to Vietnam. Given Tory Zukovich's endless boasting of his father's exploits, it made me want to hug the kid. I said, "Be quiet, Eddie."

Mrs. Kiem said, "I must use WC."

"Pardon?"

"*Pissoir,*" said Mrs. Kiem modestly.

"I gotta go to the pisser, too, Dad. My tonsils are turning lemon-color."

I looked around for a gas station. I didn't see one. I glanced across the street at Midwest Micrographics and didn't see Toland's little red Tercel, either.

"Where are you going, Dad?"

I jumped out of the car, climbed onto the hood of Joyce's Volvo, and swept South Pennsylvania with the binoculars, scanning north toward Lansing. I found the Toyota a quarter mile up the road, stopped at a light.

I could hear Crack asking me what I was up to as I jumped down off the hood, started the Volvo, and vectored it into the northbound flow of traffic, wishing I had my Chrysler. People gave way for the Chrysler.

# 26 ◄◄◄

I almost lost Toland at the old railroad underpass just south of
I-496, the one the truckers call the Eye of the Needle. There's a
photograph of it posted at the local Ryder Truck rental office.
Hanging next to it is a snapshot of a new twenty-four-foot Ryder
straight truck with its roof ripped off and a caption explaining
—in terms of liabilities—the significance of the juxtaposition.

They were working on the underpass again today, repairing the
battered masonry above the roadway, which meant all traffic
northbound had to detour through one of the southbound lanes,
not a bad bottleneck, but I was a half dozen cars back of Toland
and it was enough of a delay that I almost missed him when he
turned west onto I-496 toward downtown Lansing. He was
already heading up the access ramp when I spotted him. I also
spotted an oncoming UPS van, swung left in front of it, and
accelerated toward the ramp, pedal to the metal, slamming into
fourth. Behind us someone slammed into the UPS van.

"Geez, Dad, Mr. Crack just got in a accident!"

"Is he all right?"

"He's giving you the finger again."

"Buckle up."

Toland was almost a quarter mile ahead of me now, and even

though 496 was wide and the traffic thin, it was too much of a lead. I narrowed it substantially, much to Eddie's delight.

I was four cars back when Toland took the down ramp at the Grand Avenue–State Capitol exit and turned north onto Grand. I could see the new Radisson Hotel up on the left and the power company's stacks across from it.

Eddie leaned between the seats. "I bet we could've hit a hundred, Dad."

"Why aren't you buckled up?"

"Because if I buckle up I can't see the speedometer."

"Buckle up."

"Geez."

I took a quick look at Mrs. Kiem. She seemed unaware of all the fun we were having.

"He's turning, Dad!"

Toland had his left turn signal on, but Kalamazoo was one-way east, so he kept on straight and cornered west onto Washtenaw, cruised past Washington, circled the block behind the square, and made a left onto Kalamazoo, heading east.

Eddie said, "He's turning again!"

Left into the gated parking area in the heart of Washington Square, a yup-scale segment of old Washington Street down by the capitol. It's gated at both ends, landscaped with trees and shrubs, and paved with bricks. If you're downtown to shop or to eat or maybe just to complain to your state representative, you can park in Washington Square for a not-so-nominal sum and imagine, if your imagination is vivid enough, that you've arrived at Quincy Market, or Old Town, Alexandria, or the Baltimore waterfront.

Toland snatched a ticket from a machine, parked just down from the tollgate, and got out of his car, not locking it. I was idling on Kalamazoo at the curb, watching him across two lanes of traffic. I took a couple toots from people behind me and waved them around, watching Toland walk briskly across the brick-paved parking area. He ducked under one of the young trees that lined the square, weaved through the shoe racks and potted palms and rubber plants that a shoe-store proprietor and a florist had set up outside on the sidewalk just down from the Aux Delices, which billed itself as a "French & Vietnamese Café Restaurant." I had assumed Toland was going to meet Phuc out at Phuc's place across from the university. But they'd evidently decided to conduct their business in first-class surroundings, which was, in a word—two words—Aux Delices. According to Joyce, who lunched there regularly, it was one of the finest restaurants in town.

"Where'd he park?" Eddie's breath was hot on my neck.

"Over there."

"Where'd he go?"

"He went into a restaurant."

"What restaurant?"

"That one there with the weird windows." My guess was that the place had once been a jewelry store. They'd reworked the black tile façade so it looked more like a Left Bank art gallery than a restaurant, a deception that had been accomplished by the application of stucco over the display windows, leaving here and there several free-form openings through which you could peer.

"I didn't see him go in," said Eddie.

I looked over at Mrs. Kiem. She was staring straight ahead, which was understandable. This wasn't Rockefeller Center. But her disinterest had a trancelike quality. It was probably some kind of survival mechanism, a way of not losing your mind when a foreign world is smearing past the windows of a foreigner's car at ninety miles an hour. A trance like that might be useful, too, when soldiers overrun your village and pump bullets into anything that tries to run away.

I got a honk from behind. This wasn't LA, either, so I wasn't worried about taking a round in the head for tying up traffic, but I decided to park anyway, turning right onto Washington Avenue. You could park south of Kalamazoo on Washington without having to pass through a tollgate, and I slanted into a metered space that afforded me a view of the lot where Toland had left his car. I couldn't see the entrance to the restaurant from where we were, but the only way out of the parking lot was through the tollbooth, so all I had to do was watch the booth and I'd make Toland when he paid the attendant.

Eddie said, "Are we on stakeout again?"

"Why don't you eat one of your granola bars?" I said. "Maybe it'll take your mind off things."

"I don't want a granola bar."

I didn't blame him. I hated granola bars.

Mrs. Kiem said, "I cannot stakeout."

"Do you know who we've been following?" I asked her, hoping to take her mind off her bladder.

"No."

"I don't either, Dad. What's he look like?"

"He's tall," I said, "and he looks a little like me."

"Are you sure he's in the restaurant?"

"Yes, I'm sure."

"Did you actually see him go in?"

I paused, watching a white Dodge Diplomat stop at the gate of the Washington Square lot. The driver, his porcine pinky erect, plucked a ticket from the machine and angled into a slot next to Toland's Tercel. The driver's door opened and Detective Lieutenant Norman "Fats" Fortner rolled out of the unmarked cruiser. Zukovich got out on the passenger side and followed Fortner across the brick pavement toward Aux Delices. They went inside. My best guess was that Zook had found Toland's name on baby Mai's birth certificate and had called Toland's shop and had been told by Toland's secretary that he was meeting someone at Aux Delices. Maybe they were just looking for another translator, but I sat there fully expecting Fortner and Zook to emerge at any moment, pushing Toland ahead of them toward the cruiser.

Eddie said, "Maybe I should go check if he's in there? You know, like I did at that other restaurant yesterday?"

"You just sit tight."

255

"But Dad, I gotta go to the bathroom!"

"That's why I want you to sit tight. That's what sitting tight means. You understand?"

Mrs. Kiem looked at me as if I were as hard as the blackjack that had killed her husband.

"But what if he sneaks out the back way like that Vietnamese man did at the other place?" Eddie said.

"He's not going to sneak out the back way. His car's parked out front. Now just sit tight."

"Geez."

A moment later I saw them, not Fortner and Zook, but Toland and Nora, the two of them hurrying out of the alley that ran behind Aux Delices, hustling up Kalamazoo, pausing at the corner to take a peek around it. Toland noticed the white cruiser parked next to his Tercel, said something to Nora, who said something in return and nodded in our direction as if to suggest to her husband that he ask us for a lift. They turned toward us.

I slid down in my seat, veiled my face with my hand, and glanced at Mrs. Kiem. The old woman had slipped back into her trance, the Vietnamese version of sitting tight. Eddie, having resigned himself to a full bladder and another stakeout, was lying on his stomach on the backseat. He was rolling matchbox vehicles around on the floor of the Volvo, little engine noises sputtering from his lips, his legs bent at the knees, his ankles crossed, the soles of his tattered high-tops only twelve inches from my face. I could smell the wad of Trident that was flattened between the treads of his sneakers. I could hear Nora Toland's high heels clicking frantically nearer, passing from right to left behind us, the sound receding as I turned to watch her and Toland cross the street and climb into a Honda Accord, silver-gray. Nora's car. She'd driven here to meet Toland. They'd seen Fortner and Zook enter the restaurant and had slipped out the back . . . just as Eddie had cautioned.

I let out my breath as Toland let out the Accord's clutch. He backed into the street and accelerated down Washington Avenue, his tires humming on the bricks.

I started the car.

Eddie jumped up. "Did he come out? His car's still there. It's okay, Dad, I can hold it."

"You're doing a great job, too. And you may have to hold it a while longer because I'm tailing our man again. If we were in my Chrysler you could use the pee bottle, remember? But Mom doesn't like me to keep one in her car."

"He's turning, Dad."

Onto East Main three blocks south of Washington Square. He picked up I-496 again and cruised along at a sedate fifty-five, breaking no speed laws, which meant he was intent on minding his p's and q's, and was no doubt minding his rearview mirror as well, watching for the cops. I stayed back, my heart hopping all over my lungs.

"I don't see any red car, Dad."

"He changed cars. He had another one in the parking lot and he switched."

"Really?" Eddie craned over the seat. "Where is he? What color is it?"

"He's way up there. In fact he's turning off now, that silver-gray car, see it?"

"Yeah."

"He's taking 127 North."

"Where's he going, Dad?"

"I think I know. Look, he's getting off at Frandor. You all right, Mrs. Kiem?"

"I must use WC."

"Dad, the light's red!"

"Lost him."

"There he is. See him?"

"No, Eddie. Show me, quick."

"There, he went over there, see him?"

Toland was veering off Grand River and heading out Saginaw, picking up speed.

"Dad, you went through another red light."

"I know."

"He's turning that way."

"Which way?"

"That way."

"Right or left?"

"Uh . . ."

"Never mind, I see him."

"Dad, the light's red. Hurry! Stop! Oh, geez!"

"We're okay, buddy. We got him. I know where he's going. We got him, Eddie!"

"Why are you bouncing up and down, Dad?"

"Eddie?"

"Yes?"

"Are you okay?"

"Yes."

"You won't tell Mom about me driving like this, will you?"

"No."

"Thanks, buddy. I'll make it up to you."

"Are *you* okay, Dad?"

"I'm fine."

"Are you calm now?"

"Perfectly calm." And perfectly positioned to watch the Tolands. They'd pulled into the lot in front of Sam Agnew's office building and I'd ducked into the Shell station across Abbott Road, coming to a stop near a dumpster. I couldn't get near the side of the station because my Chrysler was in the way.

I grabbed the binoculars and saw the tinted glass doors in Agnew's building slide open to admit the Tolands. Without taking my eyes off the door, I told Eddie we'd probably have about five minutes here, and suggested he help Mrs. Kiem to the women's room in the gas station. It took a little coaxing, but he did it, guiding her with patience and care, standing guard outside the rest-room door so no one would disturb her. When she came out he helped her back into the car and ran into the men's room. I continued to watch Agnew's building, standing in the open door of the car. I had to go to the bathroom, too.

When the Tolands emerged from the building I called to Eddie and he charged out of the men's room just as Dirk Toland squirted the Accord into traffic. I fed Eddie into the backseat of the Volvo and pulled out into traffic, too, maintaining a three-car cushion as the Tolands hustled south down Abbott and over to Harrison. They were driving well above the speed limit now, hurrying the whole length of the MSU campus, braking hard to turn onto Trowbridge Road, then cornering sharply into a parking lot used jointly by a Big Boy diner, the local cable-TV station, a restaurant named Chadwick's, and a motel called the University Inn.

Toland headed straight for the north wing of the motel and parked outside a corner room. I pulled up behind a cable-TV van and watched Toland and Nora climb out of the Honda. Toland opened the trunk and stood by, nervously scanning the lot while Nora pulled out an infant's carry-all, the same little plastic suitcase I'd packed for her this morning at her home in East Lansing.

Mrs. Kiem was squinting at Toland.

I said, "Do you recognize that man, Mrs. Kiem?"

She shot me a look of alarm. "Tolan'?"

"Yes. That's who we've been following. He's picking up the baby. Thanh Chi's baby."

"You call police?"

"No. Not yet. I want to follow him to Xuan."

"But police find Tolan' with baby, they can prove he kill Thanh Chi, take baby from Hung house."

"That's no proof, Mrs. Kiem."

"Yes, proof."

"No. When you threw the baby's things away you destroyed any evidence that the baby had been at Hung's house, and

259

Toland has an entirely different explanation for where the baby's been all this time."

Eddie said, "Dad?"

"Wait. Do you understand what I'm saying, Mrs. Kiem? Even if I catch him with the baby, he can refute your testimony in court."

"I am with baby two day. I see. I touch."

"It's your word against Toland's."

"I know baby. It was at Hung house."

"Toland will say it was here."

"I know baby," insisted Mrs. Kiem.

"But, Dad."

"Shush. What can you tell me about the baby, Mrs. Kiem? That it's a Vietnamese baby? Everybody knows that. What else is there to say about it? Unless it had a mark of some kind, something that would prove you'd seen it. Did it have a mark?"

"No. Beautiful baby."

"It isn't enough to say it was beautiful, or that it was wearing diapers, Mrs. Kiem. Diapers are diapers. All babies wear diapers."

"Wear chemise, too."

"What?"

"Chemise."

"You mean a gown?"

Mrs. Kiem nodded.

"Was there something special about it?"

"Yes. Word." Mrs. Kiem turned toward me. "Three word."

"What did the words have to do with the chemise?"

"Word *on* chemise."

That qualmish, sinking feeling came over me again, a cross between seasickness and what a shipboard marine would probably feel if he heard a call to abandon ship and suddenly felt the vessel list. I swallowed and said, "There were words—three words—on the chemise?"

"Yes."

"What were they?"

Mrs. Kiem thought for a moment, then said, " 'Duty. Honor. Country.' And more. Strange word. I do not know."

"You mean you can't remember, or you don't know the meaning?"

"Not know meaning."

"Can you pronounce the word?"

"Two word."

"Say them."

Mrs. Kiem's gaze fell to her lap. She frowned, then said, "Simper feedailees."

"*Semper fidelis?*"

"Yes."

"You have a remarkable memory, Mrs. Kiem."

"Yes."

"Dad?"

"Will you wait just a minute, Eddie?" With a heavy hand I reached into my jacket pocket and pulled out my notebook. "Mrs. Kiem, do you remember the number you called from the Chinese grocery?"

"Number?"

"Toland's telephone number. Was it this number, or this one?"

Mrs. Kiem studied the two numbers, one Toland's home number, the other his work number. She said, "This."

His home number. "Do you remember exactly what he said when you talked to him?"

Mrs. Kiem thought. "He say this is Tolan', what is message."

"I see. Have you ever heard of something called an answering machine, Mrs. Kiem?"

"Answering machine?"

"Yes, a tape-recorded voice answers the telephone and tells you to leave a message, and you talk, and the machine records your words."

Mrs. Kiem looked at me blankly.

I said, "When you called Toland, did he say anything to you after he answered the phone?"

"No. He listen. No speak."

"Dad?"

"What?"

"I know that man." Eddie's eyes were bright with excitement. He was pointing at Toland, who was holding open the door to the motel room for Nora. Standing just inside the door was Xuan.

"Dad?"

"*What?*"

"I said, I know that man."

"What do you mean you *know* him?"

"I saw him yesterday."

"You've never seen him before."

"Have too. He's the man I sold a fortune to. Remember? At that Vietnamese restaurant? He gave me a dollar for it. And then he put the fortune in his wallet."

Nora had gone inside the room and Toland was taking a last look around the parking lot.

"Are you sure?"

"Yeah. He was sitting at a table with a Vietnamese man, kinda old."

I said, "Did he have gray hair, glasses, wearing a silver-colored suit with a vest?"

"Yeah. And the scary guy with the scar was at the table, too. And that lady I just saw over there in that room."

"The one who just went into the room?"

"No, the one who was inside the room, the goo—"

"The what?"

"I was going to say 'gook,' but I'm not supposed to."

I glanced back at the motel. Toland had gone inside. The door was closed. So was the case. I glanced around the parking lot. Detective Crack wasn't watching me, nor were Zukovich and Fortner. Where were the cops when you needed them? I sighed, opened the door, and got out of the car.

"Where are you going, Dad?"

I leaned down. "I won't be long."

"Can I come with you?"

"No. I want you to stay here with Mrs. Kiem."

"But—"

"No buts. You stay right here with Mrs. Kiem in case she needs you like she did at the gas station. There's a bathroom in that Big Boy over there. I'll be out in a few minutes."

"You going inside?"

"Yes."

"But then those people will know you're after them."

"It's time they did."

I eased the door shut, trotted across the lot, and tiptoed up to the motel room and listened. I heard a baby crying inside. I heard Xuan and Toland speaking Vietnamese. A TV or a radio was on, too. Rock music.

I took a deep breath and hammered on the door.

# 27 ◄◄◄

Behind the door Toland said, "Who is it?"

"The cops are looking for you, Dirk."

"Bodine? Get out of here."

"The cops are looking for me, too. We've got to talk."

I waited. It wasn't as much fun as waiting for Jack Benny to decide between his money and his life.

Finally Toland opened the door an inch. Over the security chain I got a look at his deep brown eye and a swatch of his high-boned cheek. He still hadn't shaved. He said, "What do you want?"

"I want to come in."

Toland's mouth turned down so sharply it looked as if it were sliding off his face. "How'd you know I was here?"

"I've got an informant at the desk of every motel in town. Thing is, the cops have got informants, too." I made a show of glancing around the parking lot as if maybe the LPD had someone watching us from the Big Boy. "Let me in."

Toland hesitated.

I said, "I know Nora's in there with the baby. I know Xuan's in there, too. I can save myself a lot of grief by telling the cops all the things I know. So choose."

264

He chose to open the door. I pushed inside and gave the room a look. It was a typical setup: a mirrored dressing alcove just off the bathroom and two double beds in the main room with a nightstand between them. Opposite the beds, on a long, low chest of drawers, sat a television.

Xuan, wearing fashionably faded jeans and a baggy teal-blue crewneck sweater, was lying on her stomach on the far bed, chin propped on her hands. She was watching the tube, a rock video. Guys with spiked hair were stalking through a plastic jungle teeming with durable goods. They had chains for guitar straps and were using their rifle-shaped Yamahas to shoot up refrigerators and bedroom sets. Xuan never looked at me.

Nora glanced up and smiled. She was sitting on the near bed, changing a baby as plump as a little Buddha. Nora said, "We got Mai, Jack. We finally got her." Nora's voice was choked with love. Little Mai Toland was chewing on a fist no bigger than the wad of gum I'd seen stuck to Alfred E. Neuman's nose. She'd stopped crying and was watching me with interest.

I said, "She's a cute kid."

"She's the cutest of them all." There were tears in Nora's eyes. Mine were dry as gunpowder. The chemise Mrs. Kiem had described in such accurate detail was lying on the bed beside the baby.

Toland said nervously, "We're all square with Agnew. We just came from his place. He wanted us to give him the money before he told us where Mai was, but I didn't trust him. I told him we wanted Mai first, then we'd pay. But he didn't like that. So we agreed he'd have the baby brought here to Xuan's motel. As soon as the baby was delivered, Xuan called us. I gave Agnew the money, and Nora and I drove right over. I was just about to take Xuan to the airport."

I said to Xuan, "How about killing the Mozart?"

The girl didn't hear me, or didn't understand that I was speaking to her.

Toland said, "Turn that down, Xuan."

But Xuan wasn't paying any attention to us. She was glued to the tube, watching intently as the punk warriors entered a village where half a hundred silver-haired, blue-suited executives were squatting in submission, hands on their heads.

Toland stepped over to the TV and turned it down. As he did I took a quick look in the wastebasket next to the bureau. It contained a couple of discarded diapers wrapped in clear plastic bags, half a dozen empty cans of Prosobee, and as many bottle liners. Also plenty of used Handi-Wipes.

When Toland turned back to me I said, "The police think Xuan killed her mother." I watched the girl as I spoke, but she still wasn't listening.

Toland scowled at me as if I were wasting his time. "I already told you that."

"You told me she knocked her mother down just before Hung entered the house."

"Yes."

"Is that what Xuan told you?"

"Yes."

"Well, it so happens the medical examiner has determined that Thanh Chi sustained the injury that killed her an hour before Hung entered the house. Which means Xuan couldn't have done it."

Toland frowned. "Maybe Xuan was confused about when it happened. Or maybe I misunderstood her. As a matter of fact—"

"As a matter of fact Xuan was with you and Mr. Phuc at his restaurant at the time Thanh Chi was attacked. Hung was at the table, too."

"You're crazy."

"I got an eyewitness who puts the four of you at the restaurant at the time in question."

"Who?"

"The little guy who sold you the fortune you tucked away in your wallet. Is it still there, by the way?"

Toland reached for his back pocket, but didn't come out with the wallet. He was frozen, thinking. He said, "All right. I was at Phuc's restaurant with Xuan. She called me at the shop complaining about having to work at Phuc's restaurant, the whole setup. I met her at Phuc's place to see if I could straighten things out, but Hung got nasty and Phuc fired him."

"Why didn't you tell me about that in Agnew's office?"

"Because I made a deal with Phuc that if he loaned me the money to pay off Agnew as well as Nora's father, I'd fix it so someone besides Hung's mother would take the blame for what happened to Thanh Chi."

"Hung's mother?"

"Sure. She's the one who got into the argument with Thanh Chi. When she found out Thanh Chi was running away with her sonny boy she went into a rage and knocked Thanh Chi down. She killed her."

"Who told you that?"

"Phuc. He got it from Hung at the police station. Hung said when he came home he found the old woman in the house standing over Thanh Chi's body. She's who you heard arguing with Hung."

I said, "What's the old woman to Phuc?"

"Phuc's had his eye on her ever since he first saw her years ago in Vietnam. He figures if he covers for her now, she'll think he's her hero."

I said, "You're right about one thing, Dirk. The old woman was in the house when Hung came home, but the rest of it's all wrong, and you know it. She was at a Chinese grocery when Thanh Chi was attacked. The House of Chin." I pointed down at the wastebasket. "Agnew never had the baby. She's been at Hung's house. Then last night you brought her here to Xuan."

Toland made one of his marine moves and I nailed him on the jaw before he could finish it. His head snapped back and I gave him a fist in the gut. Toland doubled over and I grabbed him—one hand on his collar and the other on his belt—and slammed him into the bureau. He bounced off it and sagged to the floor. As he went down his hand brushed the TV's volume control and the punkers' shrieks filled the room. There were shrieks from Xuan, too. She jumped up off the bed and stood with her back to the wall, shouting something in Vietnamese. Nora was up, as well, the baby howling in her arms. "What have you done?" she screamed at me.

"More or less what you did to Thanh Chi."

"What are you talking about?"

"You and Joyce were at Clara's at five thirty the day Thanh Chi was killed," I said. "You called Dirk to meet him for dinner, but he wasn't home, so you checked to see if he left a message for you on your machine. What you heard was Mrs. Kiem telling Dirk to come get the baby at 101 Clifford Street."

"No!"

"Clifford's about a three-minute drive from Clara's. You went in the back way and ran into Thanh Chi. She knew who you were and what you'd come for."

"No, Jack."

"Yes, Nora. Agnew never had Mai. The baby was there in that house with her Vietnamese mother, wearing the gown you just dressed her in. The old woman described it to a tee."

"That's not possible."

"When you got the baby home you washed the gown. I saw it the next morning in a laundry basket at your place when I helped you pack the baby's things." I was shouting over the rock music and the baby's cries, edging closer to Nora. She kept backing away from me, her eyes wild. I said, "Give me the baby."

"No. Jack, please."

I peeled one of Nora's arms off the kid. Nora was surprisingly strong, but I loosened her grip on the baby and shoved my free hand underneath, pushing up between the baby and Nora's chest. I pulled, but Nora wouldn't release the baby, so I slapped her. She let go then and I backed away, Nora crying, her nose running, arms reaching out for the baby.

I stepped over Dirk Toland, still curled up on the carpet, and made Xuan take the baby. On the way back I hit the power button on the tube and the music died, but there was still plenty of noise, what with the baby bawling and Nora sobbing. Nora had slid down onto her knees and was reaching across the bed toward Xuan and the baby on the far side of the room.

I sat on the bed beside Nora. I said, "You'll get Mai back when you tell me what happened."

"I can't."

"You two women fought for the baby, and you pushed her and she fell and hit her head? Is that right?"

"It was an accident."

"If it was, I will help you, Nora. I will do everything I can to help you. If it was an accident."

"I . . . she fell. She was stunned, and I didn't want to be there when she came to, so I picked up Mai and ran out the back door. I took her home and bathed her and threw the gown in the laundry. The gown was filthy. They were filthy people. They were using a drawer for a crib."

"And when Dirk came home and discovered you with the baby he told you it couldn't stay? Is that right?"

"Yes."

"He figured if the police found evidence of a baby at the woman's house, and if they found out she was listed as a surrogate mother for you and Dirk, they'd come to your place. And if they caught you with Mai there'd be some tough questions to answer. Is that how it was?"

Nora, hiccupping, nodded.

I said, "So Dirk set up Xuan here and had her take care of Mai while he waited to see what the police would turn up. Only he didn't tell you where Mai was, did he?"

Nora shook her head, sniffling. "He was afraid I'd try to get her back again."

"Which is why, when I came to your house the next day and told you Dirk intended to return the baby to Agnew, you believed me."

"Yes."

"And the payment to Agnew today, that's to secure his support in case the police interrogate him about the surrogate deal?"

"Yes."

I rubbed my eyes, thinking.

Nora said, "What are you going to do?" She'd pulled a tissue from her purse and was wiping her eyes and dabbing at her nose.

I said, "It seems to me if it was an accident, you won't have a serious problem with a jury, although you should have spoken up after you found out Thanh Chi was dead. And there's the cover-up and the fake surrogate deal, but I don't think they'll put you away."

Nora got to her feet and sat down on the chair across from me, her purse on her lap, her chest heaving with emotion. "What about Mai?" she said.

"I think you and Dirk have a very good chance of keeping her. Joyce and I will stand up for you. We'll do everything we can. What happened was an accident. As for the rest of it, when the judge sees how much you love the baby, I think you'll be all right."

"But there's a chance we may lose her?"

"That's something you'll have to risk."

"But—"

"The whole thing was a risk from the beginning, wasn't it? Right now we've got to call the police and tell them what happened before they track you down. I'll talk to a cop I trust. You'll be all right with him."

I got up and went over to the phone on the bureau next to the TV. The receiver had been knocked off the hook and was dangling by its cord. I picked it up. As I dialed for an outside line I turned to look back at Nora, intending to give her a smile of encouragement. But she was right behind me, reaching back as if to slap me . . . but not with her hand. Her hand was closed around the shank of a black leather sap and she was swinging it at my head. I brought my arm up and took the blow on the elbow, a numbing hit that felled my arm as if it had been severed with an ax. She swung at my head again and I stepped back and took the blow on the collarbone. The sound of the impact brought a cry of shock and disbelief from Xuan. And from me, too, but Nora Toland wasn't taking any prisoners. She came at me again, and I rolled away from her, the pain in my collarbone shooting down the right side of my body as I stepped back, ducking as Nora swung the blackjack and left a dent a half inch deep in the steel fire door, then raised the sap again as I stumbled and went to my knees, Nora leaning over me, standing on her toes to get every ounce of body weight behind the blow. She was vulnerable then and I reached out with my good arm and jabbed her below the breastbone, hard enough that I knocked the wind out of her lungs and the sap out of her hand. The sap glanced off my shoulder and thudded to the floor as Nora doubled over, clutching her midriff and stumbling backward against the bed. She sat down, holding her ribs, gasping for air.

On my knees, cradling my arm, I hobbled over to the sap and picked it up. It was heavy, hard, and smooth. The leather thong dangled from the base of the grip. I tried to slip the sap into a pocket of my sport coat, but the pocket was sewn shut. I got to my feet, my right side sagging, and slid the sap into my pants pocket. Dirk Toland was still out cold, but Xuan was chattering in Vietnamese and the baby was doing all it could to keep up its end of the conversation. I said to Nora, "You all right?"

She was sitting on the corner of the bed, bent over, one hand hard against her belly, the other hand veiling her eyes. "No."

"I'm not feeling so hot myself." The phone was hanging off the edge of the bureau again, swinging by its cord. I reached for it.

"Jack?"

"What?"

"I'll die if they take Mai away from me."

I remembered Nora's disease, and what Joyce had said about the baby, how it had been Nora's "wonder drug." I had the phone in my hand. "You murdered her mother."

Nora said slowly, "If someone gives you a baby, Jack, and you come to love it, then it's yours. No one has the right to take it back. Not the state. Not anyone. Not even its mother." Nora looked up at me, her cheeks glistening with tears. She said, "You've got a child, Jack. What if someone took him away from you, and you knew you'd never see him again? What would you do?"

I tried to think about her question, but all that came to mind was the promise I'd made to Eddie to explain everything to him when I figured out who had killed the Vietnamese lady, so he'd understand why it had happened.

Nora said, "You understand, don't you, Jack?"

I understood. I knew, too, that it was going to be a lot easier to explain it all to Zukovich than to Eddie.

# 28 ◄◄◄

Almost five months later, the week before the start of fall classes at MSU, Eddie and I drove over to East Lansing. I wanted to have a word with Celia Gore. Eddie brought along his skateboard and said he'd be okay doing one-eighties in the driveway. I went around the back of Mrs. Gore's place and found her readying one of her student rentals. Yeah, she remembered me from the spring, she said, and no, it didn't make her no mind if I talked to her, did I want some coffee?

She invited me into her kitchen. Everything was the same except for the clutch of wilting chrysanthemums in the vase on the green kitchen table. As before, the coffee was instant, and the talk was made from scratch.

"So, you been keeping busy, Bodine?"

"Sure. How about yourself? Did you get to Texas to see those Vietnamese shrimpers?"

"Yeah," she said, "but nothing happened the way I hoped." She dug a crooked Pall Mall out of the pocket of her sweater and lit it with a Zippo, squinting against the smoke. "I got a merce coming over tomorrow for an interview, though. Hope he's got a crew cut. That's important in a merce. And tattoos. Sure wish I coulda got one of them Viet shrimpers. Boy, did they have tattoos." Mrs. Gore fixed me with her right eye. Her left eye kept track of the wall behind me. "So, what you want, Bodine?"

My gaze slid away from hers, and I shifted in my seat. It was the movement of a man who'd got himself into a tight spot and was squirming with second thoughts. I said, "Well, I guess I wanted to ask you how you'd feel if you didn't have to deal with mercenaries ever again?"

Mrs. Gore lowered her head and took a drag on her Pall Mall, looking up at me. "What you talking about?"

"What if he's dead, your son Tommy?"

"He ain't."

"But what if he is and you could put him to rest? Wouldn't that be a relief?"

"Hell, no."

"Have you ever thought about it?"

"Hell, no."

"I'd like you to think about it."

She was breathing hard, her smoky lungs rough with phlegm. She appeared to be thinking hard, too. "You know something, don't you?"

"Yes."

Mrs. Gore took a drag on the Pall Mall as if she were sucking strength from the tobacco. "What?"

"I had a talk with a neighbor a while back, an old friend of your son's. He served with Tommy in Vietnam. He said he was quite sure Tommy's dead."

"Who is it, this friend of yours?"

"A neighbor. A reliable man. He's a police officer. He said he talked to you about this."

Mrs. Gore's eyes narrowed, but not against the smoke curling quietly off the glowing tip of her Pall Mall. "Mickey Zukovich? He told you Tommy stood up in a firefight and got shot by accident, didn't he?"

I nodded, rubbing my collarbone. Or maybe I was shielding it.

"Why was he talking about Tommy with you?" Mrs. Gore asked.

"It came up in connection with a case I was on. As I say, this was last spring. But since then—"

Celia Gore leaned toward me. "Listen, Bodine. Mickey Zukovich is crazy. He just feels guilty he come back and Tommy didn't."

"He seemed very sure of what happened."

"He seems sure now, Mickey Zukovich does, but when he come back from Vietnam he was a whimpering mess, had amnesia and told me he couldn't remember nothing about what happened to Tommy, not even what happened to hisself. He was loony for a long time. Army said Tommy was MIA and Mickey Zukovich, he said he didn't know, could be, he couldn't remember. Then he comes over one day and says Tommy's dead, says he shot him. Tommy's supposed to've stood up in a firefight not fifty yards in front of Mickey. Mickey said he wanted me to know so I'd quit worrying about Tommy, 'cause he was dead. Well, I didn't believe him 'cause they never found Tommy's body. I told Mickey he just thought he shot Tommy, or maybe he just wounded him. No, he said, it all come back to him in a dream he had and he's sure Tommy's dead. Well, I told him it was all right if he wanted to believe a damn dream, but I wasn't going to give up on my boy 'cause Mickey Zukovich had a dream. You understand what I'm saying?" Mrs. Gore said this in the same way she blew smoke at me, as if her speech or the smoke might wise me up.

In a voice that sounded small even in my own ears, I said, "Zook never told me he got it from a dream."

Mrs. Gore's gaze softened. "Course not. He probably forgot. He's got some kinda repression complex."

"Dad?"

It was Eddie. He had his nose to the screen door, one hand cupping his eyes against the light, the other holding his knee. I said, "What's the matter?"

"I fell off my skateboard."

I could tell he'd been crying. I started to get up, but Mrs. Gore, having stubbed out her cigarette, went over to the screen and opened it. "This your boy?" she said, looking at me.

"Yes."

Eddie stepped stiff-legged over the threshold and hobbled to the table, holding out his hands. He had ugly pavement burns on his palms. He was wearing shorts and his kneecaps, both of them, looked like glistening knobs of raw meat.

Eddie said, "I tried a three-sixty off a curb."

I got down on my knees and inspected the damage. Mrs. Gore, rummaging around in a half-bath off the breakfast nook, leaned out and said, "Come here, son."

Eddie went over to her. She had a spray can of Bactine in one hand and a clutch of oversized bandages in the other. She set to work on Eddie, spraying his scrapes and talking to him over his cringing gasps, telling him they hadn't invented skateboards when her boy, Tommy, was Eddie's age and she was glad of it, seeing what happened to kids when they crashed, though there wasn't any doubt in her mind that her boy would have been the best skateboarder on the block . . . or his kids would've been if he'd've had any . . . didn't have any though, because the Cong got him. Gooks.

Eddie protested, but she went on.

"Well, maybe your dad don't like that word, but he might feel different if you was in one of their cages. I bet he'd do anything to get you free, too, don't you? I bet even if everyone else in the world thought he was crazy, he'd still try. You believe he would? Sure you do," said Celia Gore, sending Eddie out the door, his wounds bandaged.

"Because you know what?" Celia Gore said to me. "Giving up Tommy for dead, knowing he's out there somewhere with them Cong, I'd wanna die. It'd be worse than death not doing nothing to get him home. I'd kill myself. So instead of that, I keep trying,

and someday I'll get him. Someday." Celia Gore lit another Pall
Mall and blew smoke at the future.

Eddie was outside doing one-eighties on his skateboard,
waiting for me to finish with Tommy Gore's mom . . . who
looked finished with me. Thing to do, I told myself, was to call it
quits and leave well enough alone, for if Tommy Gore had died
in one dream, he was alive in another, and I could live with that.
But I said, "Do you remember a man named Toland?"

Thinking, Mrs. Gore's eyes—one of them—left mine for a
moment. She said, "Yeah, he used to pay rent for the Viets lived
in the attic apartment. Could speak Viet like a gook, too. Heard
him talking to them from time to time. You ever find that Viet
girl you was looking for?"

"I found her. I guess that's the real reason why I'm here."

"Yeah?"

"You see, Toland got her out of Vietnam thinking she was his
daughter from a relationship he had with a Vietnamese woman
when he was in the marines over there. But it turned out the girl
wasn't his daughter after all. The woman had lost touch with her
real daughter, so she got another Amerasian girl to pose as her
daughter. Then she pretended the girl wouldn't leave Vietnam
unless several other Vietnamese could emigrate, too, the woman
herself, and a Vietnamese man and his elderly mother."

"Why you telling me all this?"

"Because this spring the woman was killed, and the man and
his mother have decided to go back to Vietnam. An infant the
man fathered here is going back with them, too. And so is Mr.
Toland. He . . . lost his wife recently, and is selling his house."

"What do you mean 'lost' her? She dead?"

"She's in prison. For a long time, too."

Mrs. Gore didn't bat an eye. "And?"

"Toland's determined to find his true Vietnamese daughter.
Toland and I are on pretty poor terms, but one thing we agreed
on was you. He's a vet, as I said, and he's very sympathetic to

your concern for your son. He told me he's willing to let you accompany him to Vietnam. He's going over with a group of ex-marines who have volunteered to help the Vietnamese unearth minefields that were laid down twenty years ago. The marines will be busy once they get there, but Mr. Toland says he'll help you in any way he can. They're leaving next month. Between now and then he said he thought you should have leaflets made up in Vietnamese offering a reward for information. He doesn't think there'll be too much of a problem with you getting a tourist visa as long as you keep your real reasons for going over there to yourself. If you're interested, you can make travel arrangements through Linblad Travel in Hong Kong."

Mrs. Gore said she was interested, but she looked more amazed than anything, as if a dream had come true. I jotted my information down, including Toland's phone number and the address of the apartment he'd taken in Carriage Hills. Mrs. Gore accepted the sheet of notepaper and folded it carefully. She didn't say anything more, and I didn't either. I didn't think she had a chance in hell of finding her son, but she probably would have told me she wasn't going to hell, she was just going to Vietnam.